Prologue

Saturday January 4, 1992
San Diego, California

"Son, please sit down on ng important to discuss."

"Sure, mom."

The sixteen-year-old b naged to get through the most r lives. One week before Christmas, they were notified that her husband, his father, was one of the early casualties in Afghanistan. A career Army officer, he was killed by a roadside improvised explosive device.

The youth sat patiently in the small apartment as he watched his mother take deep breaths.

"There's no easy way to say this. We're going to have to move in with my parents. I know this is going to be difficult for you."

"But, mom, this is my junior year of high school. I'm in the starting pitching rotation on the baseball team. And what about Julie?"

"Julie is a sweet girl. You've been lucky to have her as your first serious girlfriend. But, honey, we simply don't have enough money to keep living here on our own. I married your father right out of high school and never attended college. I can't possibly earn enough by myself to pay for the cost of living here."

"Didn't dad have life insurance?"

"Just a small policy. Not enough for us to be able to continue paying rent in San Diego."

"What if I get a part-time job?"

"That's kind of you to consider, but we'd still be well short of the money we need."

"But grandpa and grandma live in West Texas. We've never liked visiting that area. There's no ocean, and the people are so different from what we're used to."

"I'm not saying I prefer West Texas. But my parents have two empty rooms upstairs in their house, and there are a lot of waitress jobs in El Paso."

"You've often said that grandpa drinks too much."

"We'll just need to find a way to deal with that. Please understand, moving is not something I want to do. However, we simply don't have any other alternative."

The boy rose abruptly from the couch, walked into his bedroom, and slammed the door. He felt that his life was ruined. He contemplated how difficult it would be to join a new high school class two-thirds of the way through his junior year. He and Julie made a great couple. Just three weeks ago, he had considered telling her that he loved her over Christmas break. He broke into tears, spending an hour on his bed sobbing. After he was finally emotionally spent, he allowed his intellect to move to the forefront. He analyzed his situation at length, concluding that there was nothing he could do to change his immediate future. He could, however, promise himself that he would never again let someone else control his life. To fulfill that promise, he would do everything he could to become rich.

Financial Retribution

Chester Vittorio Franklin

This is a work of fiction. All of the names, characters, places, organizations, incidents, and events in this book are either products of the author's imagination or are used fictitiously, and are not to be construed as real. Any resemblance to actual events, locales, organizations, or persons, living or dead, is entirely coincidental.

chestervittoriofranklin@yahoo.com

FIRST EDITION

ISBN 978-1-7376014-5-6

With thanks to Juliet, Joseph, Jack, Dick, Anne, and Michael

Other Books by Chester Vittorio Franklin

Financial Execution

Financial Initiation

Chapter 1

Friday January 5, 2018
San Francisco, California

The sun was setting as the driver of the Mercedes Benz S Class delivered Steven Shaw to his mansion in Pacific Heights, one of the premier neighborhoods in San Francisco. The mansion, comprising about 10,000 square feet, was originally constructed in the late 1800's by a scion of one of the pioneer families who brought large-scale business to the then-new state. As he walked to the front door, Steven watched the last rays of sun glint under the Golden Gate Bridge. His wife, Veronica Hopkins Shaw, was waiting for him in the entryway. She was dressed in an indigo velvet skirt with a matching long-waisted jacket, offset in color by a French blue blouse. She was an attractive woman, two years younger than Steven.

"Welcome home, darling. Did everything proceed as planned?" asked Veronica.

"Exactly as planned, in fact, from signing to funds transfer. A press release will be hitting the wire services within the hour," replied Steven.

"I'm very happy for you, Steven. You worked so hard to turn around Opticore Products Corporation."

Veronica gave Steven a warm hug, followed by a long kiss on his lips. Although they had been married for ten years, Veronica remained warm and passionate.

"Let's sit and have a toast, savoring this moment," said Veronica.

They took a seat on the ornate French brocade divan in the parlor. The room was filled with expensive antique furnishings, primarily sourced from Western Europe. Original artwork hung on the walls. Frederick, the butler, entered the room.

"Might I bring you something, Mr. and Mrs. Shaw?"

"A bottle of the Dom Perignon 2010 Brut," responded Steven.

"An excellent selection. Right away, sir."

Once Frederick departed the parlor to walk down to wine cellar, Steven turned to Veronica and continued their conversation.

"The sale generated about an $10 billion profit for the private equity fund. Our personal share, including the overrides on the second-party capital, is close to $3 billion. Since we were successful in delaying the close until 2018, the new *Tax Cuts and Jobs Act* will apply. We will net almost $2 billion after federal and state taxes."

"My love, I'm so proud of you. I can't imagine that anyone else could have turned around the corporation so quickly. Our investors will be extremely pleased."

"And highly likely to roll funds into our next investment vehicle. Nothing attracts money like success."

"Speaking of success, does this transaction take you over your goal?"

"It does. We've discussed how I wanted us to surpass $5 billion in net worth by age forty. It took me two years longer than I had hoped."

"Oh, dear, don't trivialize such an accomplishment. With the profit and liquidity from today's events, we can make an even greater contribution to the world. The charities we support will be blessed with more resources, and I can finally fulfill my dream of implementing a network of charter schools in urban, low-income neighborhoods. Poor children deserve to have the opportunity for a quality education, and a chance to improve their lives. You remember my favorite quote, don't you?"

Steven replied:

> *"Education is the most powerful weapon which you can use to change the world.*
>
> *Nelson Mandela"*

Veronica smiled broadly. Steven smiled back and shook his head gently.

"You're such a dreamer. Local school boards, the teachers' union, and politicians at various levels will fight you every step of the way," predicted Steven.

"I acknowledge the challenges. However, I've developed quite a network of like-minded individuals. With strong funding, I know we can start making progress, if only one school at a time," said Veronica with a dream in her eye.

"Dear, I know you will. Your commitment is inspiring. I get so frustrated watching the insanity of the government spending untold sums of money on welfare, food stamps, and other programs to treat the symptoms of inadequate education, but then not allocate funding and pursue true reform at the source of the problem."

"Our group plans to make that irony one of the themes we push out through social media," responded Veronica.

Frederick entered the room, carrying the bottle of champagne, two Waterford crystal glasses, and a sterling silver ice bucket. He presented the bottle to Steven.

"That will be fine. Thank you, Frederick."

Frederick opened the bottle, poured two glasses, and placed the bottle in the ice bucket. He left the couple alone in the parlor.

"A toast to your recent success, and to our future," said Veronica.

They clinked their glasses and sipped the fine beverage.

Veronica continued, "Steven, we just spoke about my dreams. What about yours? Do you want to commence working less, taking more time for travel and philanthropy?"

"You're much more adept at philanthropy than I'll ever be," replied Steven. "I defer that activity to your good care. I know how happy it makes you."

Veronica smiled broadly.

"It does. I particularly enjoy seeing each project by our charities come to fruition. It's a wonderful sense of accomplishment, giving people the opportunity to enhance the lives of their children."

"I'm still not much of travel afficionado. However, I would like visit Rome and better appreciate the advancements of that ancient civilization, from law to architecture to engineering. Two thousand years later, and we're still using foundational aspects of the Roman Empire," shared Steven.

"That would be a wonderful trip! Some of the most beautiful art ever created is viewable within five square miles. My friends have said that the sculptures displayed in the Villa Borghese are so lifelike that you expect them to speak to you. Not to mention all of the contents of the Vatican Museum."

They both drank some more of the Dom Perignon.

"So, Steven, you really haven't answered my question. What are you dreaming of, now that you no longer need to devote all those hours to the turnaround and eventual sale of Opticore?"

"With $5 billion, we can buy any item we desire. We can purchase any experience we can imagine. We can also almost control time, using our Gulfstream jet to take us anywhere we wish to be on a moment's notice. However, I want more than that."

"What more could you possibly desire?"

Steven paused and thought for a few moments before deciding to be direct.

"To shape the future of humanity."

Veronica finished the last of her champagne, carefully contemplating her husband's statement. It was obvious that his already large ego had been supercharged by the success of the Opticore transaction. She decided to pursue a course of open-ended questions.

"Well, that's certainly ambitious! Can you be a bit more specific?"

"With sufficient monetary resources, one can directly influence the evolution of society. That can be accomplished through various avenues. Examples might be funding breakthrough technologies, globally distributing medical advancements, and influencing or even directing the political process. Let me give you two disparate examples. What if Ronald Reagan had never been President and the Soviet Empire had not collapsed? What would our world be like today? Or, as another example, what if Apple had not invented the iPhone, allowing the development of countless free or low-cost applications that benefit peoples' lives in so many ways?"

What Steven did not vocalize was his ardent desire for

power and control. The genesis of that yearning dated all of the way back to his forced relocation to West Texas at age sixteen.

"I see what you're talking about. However, in an era of trillion-dollar company valuations and U.S. deficit spending of around a trillion dollars annually, just how much in monetary resources do you have in mind?" inquired Veronica.

"I've been thinking about this over the past month, as the Opticore deal was coming together. My goal is to leverage our $5 billion today into $50 billion by the time I'm fifty years old. I'll then spend the rest of my life seeking to deploy some of that that capital to influence the direction of the United States, if not also more of the world. U.S. Senate races can now cost $100 million or more. Meaningful political power in this country is very expensive."

"You're saying that you want to increase our net worth by a factor of 10 in just eight years? Wouldn't that require an insanely high rate of growth?"

"Not quite insane, but admittedly high at a consistent 33%. And that would be the after-tax return."

"You're the financial wizard, but that sounds quite lofty to me. That level of success would need to be enjoyed each and every year, despite whatever the economic situation was. Wouldn't a recession or two make that almost impossible to produce?"

"Difficult, yes. Challenging, certainly. But impossible, no. I have a plan."

Chapter 2

Saturday January 20, 2018
Berkeley, California

It was a warmer than usual afternoon for the time of the year. By 2:00 PM, twelve individuals had arrived at the sand volleyball court located on the north side of the University of California at Berkeley campus. Teams of men and women were quickly arranged, as most of the participants were veterans of the pickup volleyball games held around campus. The players on one of the teams included Joseph Giordano and Bruce Chu. Although the two men had never met before, they instinctively teamed to score about half their side's points. At about 3:00 PM, the game broke up, with some of the individuals returning to campus to continue homework and studying, while others walked over to the nearby pizzeria for a slice and a beer. Joseph and Bruce were included in the latter group.

"That last game was close. You positioned a great set for our winning point," said Bruce. "I saw the other team leaning toward the center, so I just punched the ball down the line."

"A toast to our victory," replied Joseph.

Glasses were raised around the table.

The two men clinked their glass mugs of cheap lager and took large gulps. Bruce was 6'4" tall and gangly. Joseph was about 5'8" in height and well-muscled.

"I don't believe we've met before; not just in regards to volleyball," opined Bruce.

"Agreed. I'm Joseph Giordano, a second year MBA student

here at Berkeley, concentrating in finance."

"My name is Bruce Chu. I'm in the final stages of completing my PhD in chemical engineering."

Both men were in their mid-twenties. After the pizza arrived and the volleyball players had all poured a second glass of beer from the pitcher, Joseph and Bruce spoke at greater length.

"I assume you're looking for a job starting this summer, if you haven't already landed one," asked Bruce.

"I'm still networking and interviewing. I'd like to land a principal financial analyst position with one of the mid-level investment banking firms or with one of the larger private capital firms. However, the competition for those jobs is intense. How about you?"

"I've been doing some primary research for a professor while awaiting my dissertation defense in the spring. I have to admit that I haven't focused as much as I should have on career opportunities. The research has been so interesting."

"Oh, tell me more."

"We're aiming to develop technologies and processes that can more quickly and thoroughly clean up oil spills in the ocean. In fact, we're working towards being able to render the recaptured crude suitable for future refining, while also producing potable water for human consumption."

"That sounds incredible. I don't know much about oil spills. Aren't they usually addressed via placing a boom around the spill and more or less vacuuming up the oil?"

"That's one historical approach, often limited in effectiveness by the size or area of a large spill, plus a limited capacity to address oil that is below the surface. Another typical approach is spraying chemical dispersants designed to break down the oil. However, the chemical dispersants and the oil itself are toxic to a wide variety of marine life."

"So, in a nutshell, the historical remediation of oil spills has been better than nothing, but hardly categorized as successful."

"Exactly."

The two men finished their pizza and quaffed the last of the beer.

As they were saying goodbye to the other volleyball players at the table, Joseph turned to Bruce and asked, "How about exchanging contact information? Perhaps we can play volleyball together again in the future."

"That might be unfair to our competition, but sounds good," said Bruce.

At the time, neither Joseph nor Bruce had any inkling regarding what this afternoon's meeting would portend for their future.

Chapter 3

Sunday March 19, 2000
San Francisco, California

Eighteen years earlier, it was one of those days when the fog never completely clears from the San Francisco Peninsula.

By 10:00 AM, the extended Hopkins family was gathered at the home of Blake and Sandra Hopkins (Veronica's parents) in the Russian Hill neighborhood of San Francisco. While the house comprised over 6,000 square feet spread across three floors, it seemed small due to the combination of extensive furnishings and over forty individuals in attendance, including family members, a minister, a registered nurse, and the household servants. Blake, age 59, had been diagnosed with pancreatic cancer six months earlier, just before the start of the new millennium. Absent any effective treatment, the disease had quickly ravaged the formerly stout body of the investment banker. His devoted wife, Sandra, had recently put the word out to the family that Blake didn't have much time left. Arrangements were made for the family members to visit and say their goodbyes this weekend. Blake had asked to be allowed to die at home, without any heroic attempts to prolong his life (and suffering). The nurse was there to make him as comfortable as possible through intravenous administration of a narcotic. The Episcopal minister was present primarily to provide solace to the family members. Throughout his life, Blake maintained a strong faith in his opportunity to share in the resurrection of Jesus Christ and go to heaven. This faith provided Blake with a sense of calm and of clarity as he faced his death.

"Honey, are you ready to receive the family members?" asked Sandra.

"Yes, but no more than three at one time. My energy level is limited. Did I tell you how blessed I have been to be married to such an empathetic individual and great partner?"

"Only every other day for the past month!" smiled Sandra, giving him a soft kiss on his cheek. "I'll start with my side of the family, concluding with just us and our children."

"You've thought everything through, as usual," replied Blake.

Sandra smoothly managed the procession through the bedroom that had been outfitted with enough equipment to stock a hospital room. The nurse checked in every thirty minutes, reviewing Blake's vital signs and adjusting the medication drip. The minister positioned himself to be available to the relatives as they exited the bedroom, offering a hug, a shoulder to cry on, or soothing words, as he judged each individual's needs.

By 3:00 PM, all of the family members had shared some time with Blake, plus been nourished by the catered buffet set up in the atrium. As Sandra walked the final relative to the front door, she suddenly realized how draining the day had been for her. The nurse noticed this and gently touched Sandra's arm, leading her to sit in one of the ornate wingback chairs in the grand salon. Twenty-two- year-old Veronica, the younger child, pulled up a chair next to her mother.

"Mother, you appear flushed," expressed Veronica with concern in her voice. "Is there anything I can do for you?"

"I just remembered that I haven't had a bite since dinner last night. Might you be so kind as to bring me a plate of food and a cup of tea?'

"Of course. I'll be right back."

The seat next to Sandra was quickly filled by her other daughter, Maureen, three years older than Veronica.

"Mother, how are you holding up? Is there anything you need?"

"I'm trying to do the best I can. This is a hard day following many difficult days..."

Maureen reached over and hugged Sandra.

As Sandra sat back upright in the chair, she said, "Veronica is bringing me something to eat and drink. As soon as she returns, let's discuss our upcoming meeting with your father."

Once Veronica returned and Sandra ate a few mouthfuls and sipped about half the cup of tea, she looked intently into the eyes of her two children.

"Thank you both so much for your support this weekend. It was important to your father to be able to say his good-byes and share his final thoughts with our extended family. Blake always has been one to bring things to a clear conclusion."

"We know, mother. How can we ever forget the conversations at the dinner table, with dad asking questions and debating us until the topic had been fully vetted and a conclusion reached," said Maureen.

Sandra smiled, thinking back to all of the Sunday dinners shared by their family, a ritual as scheduled as their attendance at Sunday morning church services.

"Your father wishes to meet with us now, perhaps our final time all together. I know he has contemplated at length his parting words to us. Let's go in and listen."

Veronica and Maureen both hugged their mother, each holding one arm and shoulder as they approached the bedroom.

Blake looked up and smiled as best he could.

"Please come in and sit. The nurse has just adjusted my medication, so we should have some time now without interruption."

His voice was weak and his breathing strained.

With his wife and children seated around him, Blake continued, "First, the practical matters. Veronica and Maureen, do you have any questions about our meeting two weeks ago with the estate planning attorney and the CPA?"

Veronica replayed in her mind the key details of that meeting. The Blake Family Trust was a typical A | B trust accompanied by a tax qualified life insurance trust. Half of $200 million in the Trust would remain in trust for her mother's benefit. The other half of the Trust would be divided into two new, equal trusts, one for each child. The life insurance trust would cover the required federal estate taxes.

"No, father, that meeting was quite thorough. All three of us have the contact information for the attorney and the CPA if we develop any questions," replied Veronica.

Maureen added, "As usual, you selected highly competent professionals. They assured us several times during the meeting that they have everything necessary to timely process the estate. That's not something you need to worry about, especially today."

Sandra nodded her concurrence.

Blake continued, "Veronica and Maureen, I ask that you each wait a year after my death before accessing the assets in your trusts. While you both are well educated and each are on a path to impressive careers, I recognize that the availability of such wealth can be disruptive. It's prudent to take some time to contemplate your options."

Veronica replied, "We will, father."

Maureen echoed, "You've always known what's best for us, father. We will wait."

"Now to the important matters. Veronica and Maureen, I ask that you each take care of your mother. Spend time with her, helping her through the upcoming transition. Nothing can compare to the value of family. While I have provided for her financially, only you can furnish her with the love of a child."

Maureen squeezed Sandra's hand. "Of course, father."

"My life gained immeasurable worth the day I married Sandra. I pray that both of you find a similarly good spouse."

"You've always said that a good spouse is priceless," replied Maureen.

Blake began to wheeze. Sandra increased the oxygen flow that was being piped into his nostrils. After a few moments, Blake's breathing improved enough to allow him to continue.

"I've left funeral instructions with the minister. Nothing too elaborate. I'd like those in attendance to simply remember the joys shared with me, recognizing that I'm now happily living in God's house."

"I've spoken with the minister. Everything is arranged," said Sandra.

"Veronica and Maureen, I have one final word of advice. This cancer came on so suddenly. I didn't have the opportunity to make the positive difference in the world that I wanted, that I had planned to commence working on upon retirement next year. Recognize that none of us knows how much time he has left. Ensure that you allocate time along the way to achieve what is really important to you."

Both children nodded affirmatively.

"Be strong in your knowledge of three key things. First, that you have always been loved by your parents, from the very moment of conception. Second, know also that your God has similarly loved you. Third, never forget that you have each other."

Veronica and Maureen each grabbed one of Blake's hands and squeezed, tears filling their eyes. They kissed him together, one on each cheek.

"We love you too, father," said Maureen.

"Now, let me have a moment alone with your mother."

Veronica and Maureen each again kissed their father. They walked out of the bedroom with their arms around each other.

Once in back in the atrium, Maureen looked at Veronica and said, "Our parents have enjoyed a marriage that must be one in a million. Always loyal to each other. Unquestionably faithful to each other. Focused on making decisions based upon what was best for their relationship and the family, rather than concentrating on the needs of either individual. Mother is really going to miss him."

"We'll be there for her," responded Veronica. "While we can never replace him, there is much of him inside each of us."

The sisters waited for their mother to exit the bedroom, reaching out to her once Sandra had left Blake alone to get some rest.

The nightshift nurse awakened Sandra, Maureen, and Veronica at 2:15 AM. Blake had passed.

Chapter 4

Monday January 29, 2018
San Francisco, California

It was a rainy day, with dark clouds suspended low in the sky over the entire San Francisco Peninsula. The chauffer pulled the Mercedes over as close as possible to the main entrance to the Bank of America building. Steven Shaw sprinted from the back seat to the entrance to the skyscraper, one of the pre-eminent addresses in the city. Stepping out of the elevator onto the 45th floor, Steven walked through the ornately carved mahogany doors into the suite that housed the Shaw family office.

The receptionist stood up immediately.

"Good morning, Mr. Shaw. Is there anything I can bring you?"

"A cappuccino would be great. Also, please ask Mr. Winters to join me in the main conference room."

"Right away, sir."

In the three weeks that had passed since the closing of the Opticore Products Corporation transaction, Steven had taken several days to fly with Veronica to Vail, Colorado on their private jet for some skiing and relaxation. That trip was quickly followed by Steven's gearing up for the next stage of his career. Today's meeting with Charles Winters would launch the first step in Steven's master plan to achieve his over-arching objectives. Charles was the Chief Investment Officer to the family office, with an MBA in finance from the University of Chicago and an undergraduate degree in economics from the University of Illinois.

"Good morning, Steven," said Charles as he walked into the large, wood-paneled conference room. "I was a bit surprised to receive your meeting request so soon after the closing of your recent M & A deal."

"As a wise and wealthy man once said, *time is money*," replied Steven.

"I certainly can't disagree with that."

Charles sat directly across the table from Steven. He was a large individual, 6'2" in height and weighing about 275 pounds. He had a weakness for fine cuisine. His fifty-sixth birthday was just a month away.

Steven then commenced presenting the next stage of his plan.

"I'd like you and one of our in-house attorneys, Jennifer Franklin, to establish a new, paired management company and private equity fund."

"Standard legal structures?" asked Charles. "The fund will execute a services agreement with the management company?"

"Yes. I will front the start-up money for the management company, and our family office plans to invest $4 billion in the fund. We'll team to identify suitable investors for another $16 billion of investment, bringing the total equity funding to $20 billion. We'll leverage that with Wall Street debt financing of at least $10 billion more."

"You must have some large potential targets at that level of funding."

"Charles, I believe I've identified the next wave in the capital markets. Something akin to the personal computer and networking wave of the mid-1980's, or the dot com wave of the late 1990's."

"You've certainly piqued my interest."

The men quickly fell silent as the receptionist arrived with Steven's cappuccino, plus a café macchiato for Charles accompanied by a croissant filled with Bronte pistachio cream. Once the conference room door was again closed, the men continued their conversation.

"Charles, have you heard about the ESG movement, one primarily prevalent in northern Europe at this time?"

"Yes, a bit. It's an evolving investing concept based upon 're-sponsibility'; focused on improving Environment, Social, and Governance, or ESG for short, aspects of the planet. I believe it's an outgrowth of the 'sustainability' movement that arose in the early 2000's."

"Well said. I've performed extensive research augmented by anecdotal conversations. I believe ESG investments will be the next big wave through the global capital markets."

"Steven, not to disagree with your research, which I am sure is well grounded, but I would like to present two key issues."

"I would expect nothing less from you, Charles."

"Investing for the good of humanity and the planet does not exactly integrate with the perspective of President Trump."

"You're on point with that comment. However, Trump won't be President forever. In fact, I predict he'll be in office just a single term. The man simply can't keep his mouth shut."

"I'm an investment guy and hardly a political savant, so I won't belabor that point. My second issue is more concrete. If we're investing to benefit the Earth, aren't we by definition for-feiting the opportunity to maximize our profits?"

"Viewed linearly, yes, your point is valid. However, I don't plan to operate the fund on just one plane."

"I like where this is heading. Tell me more."

"We'll name our new vehicle something like Blue Planet Investment Fund. I predict there will be increasing interest by at least some investors to allocate a portion of their capital to advancing ESG concepts. These are people who allow their conscience to guide at least some of their financial activity."

"Okay, I can see that."

"Next, we increase our annual management fee from the usual 0.50% of assets to 0.75% of assets; for two reasons. First, we explain that more intensive work will be needed to identify and vet ESG investments than ordinary investments. Second, we communicate that monitoring ESG investments for effectiveness is more intensive than the typical financial analyses."

"That sounds like something we could potentially justify and market."

"Second, because our fund participants will be investing, in at least part, for social reasons rather than solely financial ones, we increase our over-ride on their portion of the profits from the usual 20.00% to 25.00%. I believe the growing social and political pressure to achieve ESG goals will facilitate our obtaining these financial terms. In addition, since there are not yet many ESG targeted investment vehicles, we shouldn't have much competition and therefore can charge more."

"I'm with you so far. Everything you've shared makes sense to me. You shouldn't have difficulty attracting investors after the rate of return you provided on the Opticore Products Corporation transaction."

At this point, Charles paused and looked up at the ceiling.

Steven recognized this behavior and patiently waited, eventually stating, "Charles, we've known each other for years. No need to hold anything back with me. Please share what's on your mind."

Visibly relieved, Charles continued, "Steven, there's the crucial issue of actually identifying, purchasing, operating, and then selling ESG related companies for an adequate profit within our typical fund 5-year timeframe. There aren't that many well-defined targets. In addition, it's questionable whether the current potential targets will be able to produce an adequate rate of return. I'm also concerned about the possibility of there being limited expertise available to effectively manage these types of companies, many of which are focused on technologies that are still in the early development stage."

At these comments, Steven smiled broadly, pausing to sip some of his cappuccino. Charles recognized the gleam in Steven's eyes.

Steven elaborated, "Since ESG is not that well defined; in fact, there are multiple organizations currently working to define the concept, each with different approaches and metrics; we can create our own definition as we proceed. How many opportunities does one have to play a game with the capacity to alter the rules in one's favor at any point in time?"

Charles bit into the croissant, followed by a sip of his caffe macchiato. He then nodded for Steven to continue.

"In addition, I believe we can market a seven-year investment cycle for all of the reasons previously mentioned. That will give us more time to achieve our financial objectives, if we need it, not to mention the 0.75% annual fee on the $16 billion of external capital."

Steven then paused and looked into Charles' eyes.

"To quote late night television, *but there's more!*" exclaimed Charles.

"Yes. As with every investing wave in history, the early entrants acquire assets at what are likely to later be perceived as bargain prices. As more capital flows onto the wave, prices inevitably rise, caused by the at least implied scarcity of the subject assets. Whether tulip bulbs in the early 1600's, conglomerates in the 1960's, or companies operating over the Internet in the 1990's, the later entrants provide a profit opportunity and exit strategy for the early investors."

"That might be referred to as an application of the *greater fool theory*."

"There's some truth to that. However, with the increase in global warming, more destructive weather events, rising sea levels, and periodic droughts, I don't think we'll need to rely on foolish investors. Rather, these events plus political parties and governments responding to climate change will facilitate a steady inflow of investors and capital into the ESG space."

Steven leaned back in his chair and stretched his back and neck. His joints often tensed when he was fervently addressing some aspect of his work.

He added, "With the reputation already we have, augmented by the 'blue planet' image we will create, plus the financial resources at our disposal, I'm confident that we'll be able to attract whatever technical and managerial talent we'll need."

Steven paused and again intently peered directly into Charles' eyes.

"Steven, you've convinced me. I'm ready to join the project. Whom do you want on the core team in addition to Jennifer Franklin as an attorney?"

"Since Jennifer is only a year out of law school, we should

also arrange for the services of our current lead partner from the law firm of Greene, Robinson, and Sanders. If I remember correctly, his name is Trent Hawthorne. We'll pay him some billable hours at his outrageous rate for some of the legal work, nominally to support Jennifer, but with the true objective of having him become a conduit for attracting investors into the fund."

"While I don't think any attorney is worth $2,500 per hour for his legal expertise, I do recognize the potential ancillary benefits of having Trent involved with this project."

"Good. We'll also need an ESG enthusiast, a true believer, for marketing, preferably a well-educated, but also highly attractive woman in her late twenties to early thirties. It wouldn't hurt if she presented certain informalities associated with her sexual behavior."

"I understand where you're headed with that comment. Note taken."

"We'll supplement the individuals we've discussed with the usual set of paralegals, financial analysts, and accountants."

"When do you want to get started?"

"Did you already forget my earlier quote?"

"*Time is money.* I'm on it," replied Charles.

Chapter 5

Monday October 19, 1987
Chicago, Illinois

About thirty-one years earlier, twenty-five-year-old Charles Winters arrived at his desk on the thirty-seventh floor of the Sears Tower at his usual time of 7:30 AM. This allowed him to have an hour to prepare for the opening of the stock market at 9:30 PM Eastern Time. He felt fortunate to land a financial analyst position with the prestigious money management firm of Sutcliffe & Swayne upon completing his MBA degree last May. He found the capital markets to be both intellectually challenging and exciting, with a bit of adrenaline rush following each profitable transaction. Sutcliffe & Swayne managed about $1 billion of primarily 'old money' sourced from families resident in the Chicago area for generations. Many of the accounts could trace their wealth back to the railroads, cattlemen, and manufacturers who had made Chicago a vital link in the expansion of the United States in the 1800's.

Charles sipped a cup of coffee and ate a large chocolate muffin as he turned on his personal computer and his trading terminal. Last week had been brutal. The Dow Jones Industrial Average declined each of Wednesday, Thursday, and Friday. The aggregate drop totaled about ten percent. This resulted in a flood of client calls into the firm. Some clients wanted to understand what was happening, while others were panicked and demanded that Sutcliffe & Swayne move some or all of their accounts into cash, U.S. Treasuries, or similar investments viewed as safe. Charles worked long hours each day and even came into the office over the weekend. It was challenging to decide which investments to sell in this environment.

The markets weren't behaving as expected based upon traditional financial metrics.

At the 8:30 AM Central Time opening of the stock market, there was a huge imbalance between the volume of buy and sell orders. Stock prices resumed the decline from last week. The growing wave of sell orders soon overwhelmed the computer systems and other financial plumbing used by the stock exchanges, banks, and even the Federal Reserve. Trading in many stocks opened late, while trading in other equities, particularly those listed on NASDAQ, was suspended for various and sometimes lengthy periods of time. Charles was instructed by his boss to shift from deciding what to sell based upon financial analysis to determining what to sell based upon liquidity and the ability to get the transactions executed in the choppy environment. By the end of the day, the Dow Jones Industrial Average fell almost twenty-three percent. October 19, 1987 would forever be remembered as 'Black Monday'.

Charles collapsed into the bed in his apartment once he finally got home at 7:00 PM. Everyone in the firm had stayed late to update client accounts and try to respond to the deluge of incoming phone calls. Just before falling asleep, Charles set his alarm for 5:00 AM. He knew that tomorrow was also going to be a difficult day at the office, so he wanted to arrive early to prepare as best he could.

At 3:15 PM Central Time on Tuesday, October 20, just after the close of the stock market, Charles' boss, Alan Baker, called him into his office.

"Have a seat, Charles."

"Yes, Mr. Baker. The past week has sure been intense."

"I've read that many individuals never forgot where they were, the weather, what they ate, etc. on October 28, 1929."

"The day of the stock market crash that ushered in the Great

Depression," noted Charles. "We studied that in my MBA program."

"I'm afraid today is a day that you'll not forget. Our firm's revenue base is down over a third with the decline in asset values. We have no choice other than to lay off an equivalent percentage of our staff, including you. It's not related in any way to your performance, Charles. You're just a relatively new employee without much experience, and therefore relatively expendable. I am sorry, as I've enjoyed working with you."

Charles sat in silence, trying to digest what had just occurred.

"Here's an envelope with all of the information and documents associated with your separation from the firm. There's a phone number for the Human Resources Department if you have any questions. I'll have to ask you to now collect your personal items from your desk and leave the office. Again, I'm sorry about this."

Charles took the envelope and didn't say anything. His mind was racing. He hadn't been working long enough after graduate school to save much money. He had student loans outstanding from the MBA program. The rent in Chicago was not cheap. He didn't want to be a burden on his lower-middle class parents. They had already devoted a large percentage of their meager net worth to paying for his undergraduate degree from the University of Illinois and his sister's recent graduation from Northwestern.

Upon arriving at his apartment, Charles began to update his resume on his IBM PC. He also drafted template cover letters for a variety of industries that might hire an MBA in finance. He fell asleep at the PC at 8:00 PM, exhausted following a very long and trying day.

....

Despite Charles' best efforts, three months passed without a single job offer. Black Monday had led to the layoff of tens of thousands of workers from the investment and commercial banking industries. As someone with limited experience, Charles was at a disadvantage in landing any of the relatively few positions that were available. He had cut his personal budget to the bare bones, including for food. He was now down to just 180 pounds on his 6'2" frame, always hungry, and on the verge of having to ask his parents to allow him to move back home.

Over the past month, Charles had reached out to substantially everyone he knew, hoping for at least some lead that might result in even part-time work. Just as he was again contemplating calling his parents, his phone rang. It was a colleague from MBA school. He was working for a high-net-worth family in San Francisco. Their family office had just decided to hire another investment analyst. The associate could get him an interview. Charles thanked his colleague and scheduled the interview for two weeks from then.

After he hung up, Charles brainstormed. How was he going to get to San Francisco for the interview? He determined that the only way to accomplish that would be to move out of his apartment, place his few possessions in a storage unit, sell his car, and buy a roundtrip bus ticket. Airfare would have consumed too much of his remaining cash. Ten days later, Charles boarded a Greyhound bus with one suitcase containing his best business attire and a backpack filled with a water bottle and enough food to barely sustain him for the three-day trip.

Chapter 6

Friday February 12, 1988
San Francisco, California

Charles Winters rode the MUNI bus from his cheap hotel on the outskirts of the San Francisco Financial District to the Bank of America building. He was wearing his best suit and had polished his black wingtip shoes until they shined. The suit hung on him like a curtain following his losing almost fifty pounds. The brown skyscraper was as impressive as the Sears Tower in Chicago. Taking the elevator up to the 45th floor, he greeted the receptionist.

"Good morning. I'm Charles Winters. I have an appointment scheduled with Mr. Hopkins."

"Yes, I see that on his calendar. Please have a seat. I'll let you know when Mr. Hopkins is ready."

"Thank you,"

After about ten minutes, Charles was greeted by an affable fellow, apparently in his late forties.

"Hello. I'm Blake Hopkins. A pleasure to meet you."

Blake extended a warm handshake, again smiling.

"Mr. Hopkins, thank you for the opportunity to interview," said Charles. "I'm most interested in the open position."

Charles followed Blake in to his office. It was professionally appointed, but not overdone.

"Please have a seat. I've reviewed your cover letter and resume. Let me tell you a bit about the open position and our family office."

The interview proceeded favorably. The investment analyst job fit in well with Charles' education and work experience at Sutcliffe & Swayne. By half-way through the meeting, Charles decided that he would accept the position regardless of the salary. He liked Mr. Hopkins' down to earth, calm, and direct style. While he knew that he would be reporting several levels lower in the organization, the profile of the leader would undoubtedly influence the overall environment. In addition, thought Charles, he didn't exactly have any other options.

Towards the end of the interview, Blake excused himself, nominally to get a glass of water. He wanted a few moments to finish sizing up the candidate. Charles was clearly well educated, sufficiently intelligent, and would likely perform well. Dozens of other candidates also fit that profile. What differentiated Charles was his personality. This young man was without question highly motivated, in fact likely hungry given the looseness of his suit. Blake perceived that Charles would be loyal to the family office, most appreciative of the opportunity to join the enterprise. Just to be sure, he quickly developed a line of questioning.

"Charles, what would you say most differentiates you from other candidates for this position?"

Charles thought for a moment before responding.

"Based upon what I know of the current job market, you could hire any number of similarly educated and experienced financial professionals, so those factors would not be a differentiator."

"Please continue."

"I'd therefore answer that I am more determined to perform well than other candidates."

"How so?"

"To be completely open, Mr. Hopkins, if I don't get this job, I'll have no choice but to move back home with my parents. While I love them dearly, I don't want to be a financial burden on them. They're both blue collar workers. They spent almost everything they had to put me and my sister through college. I shudder at asking them to sacrifice any more for me."

"Thank you for your honesty in that answer. You know, I feel similarly about my family. I have two daughters. I want to take the best care of them that I can, ensuring that they have the brightest future that I might possibly provide. I seek an analogous profile of commitment and loyalty in the employees here at our family office. What do you think about that, Charles?"

"I remember reading about loyalty in a philosophy class I took as an undergraduate. The quote I remember is something to the effect of *blood makes you related, loyalty makes you family.*"

"I couldn't have said that better myself."

Charles was hired for the job and began a long-term employment with the Hopkins family office. He fulfilled his promise in being loyal to Blake and the Hopkins family. That relationship continued with the passing of Blake, Veronica's marriage to Steven Shaw, and Steven's eventual rise to lead the family office.

Chapter 7

Friday February 16, 2018
Berkeley, California

At 5:00 PM, Joseph Giordano and Bruce Chu were sharing a pitcher of cheap beer and a pizza following another victory in pick-up volleyball. They had now played together three times, becoming more coordinated and effective each time. Joseph was highly skilled in setting the ball, while Bruce's height plus leaping ability resulted in many kill shots.

"Another great set of games; and a toast to our teamwork and success," said Joseph.

The men clinked their beer mugs and each swallowed a substantial quaff.

"Joseph, that reminds me. There's something I wanted to discuss with you," said Bruce.

"I'm all ears."

"What would you think about possibly going into business together?"

"Well, that's not what I was expecting to discuss over pizza and beer this afternoon, but I *am* curious. Tell me more."

"Well, the professor with whom I've been conducting primary research has been funding the science from his own pocket. We've enjoyed favorable initial results. The professor approached me last week and shared that, at seventy years old, he doesn't have the health or stamina to take the project to the next level. He also explained that he doesn't have the financial resources to scale the science to outside of the current laboratory environment. He offered to assign the intellectual property to me and continue to serve as a technical advisor if I was interested in taking the lead on advancing the project."

"I'm a finance guy and hardly a chemical engineer like yourself. We've generically discussed your work before, but can you help me understand it at a deeper level?"

"Do you have some time now? I think showing you in the lab would be more productive than my verbalizing the science."

"I was thinking about what bar to hit this evening in search of some female companionship, but I'll willingly postpone that. Your work has always sounded interesting to me."

The men finished their beer and pizza, and then walked across the University of California campus to the lab housed in the basement of the environmental sciences building.

Once in the lab, Bruce showed Joseph what he thought was the oddest-looking contraption he had ever seen. There were tubes and tanks and wires spread out over about twelve feet in length, six feet in width, and eight feet in height.

Bruce explained the machine to Joseph as he prepared a sample experiment.

"I'm filling this first tank with five gallons of salt water. The salt water is a proxy for the ocean."

"Okay."

"The density of a liquid is measured by dividing its mass by its volume. I'm now adding a pint of motor oil to the tank of salt water. While this is lighter than crude oil, which generally has a density of 700 to 950 kilograms per cubic meter, it will suffice for testing. Salt water has a density of a bit over 1000 kilograms per cubic meter, which is why oil generally floats on water."

Joseph observed the motor oil floating at the top of the tank of salt water, saying, "I'm with you so far."

"I'll now add our unique material to the tank of salt water and motor oil. The primary components of the material are powdered iron and a bonding agent. The composition of crude oil is generally 83% to 87% carbon, 10% to 14% hydrogen, plus varying amounts of nitrogen, oxygen, and sulfur. The bonding agent is needed to get the finely powered iron to adhere to the carbon molecules in the oil."

Joseph nodded.

Bruce then flipped some switches. The large machine came to life, with a deep humming sound.

"I'm now activating a pump which will suck the liquid from the initial tank into the chamber labeled 'A'. The wiring, tubes, and other components placed along the upper half of this chamber are carefully placed at constant intervals of spatial degrees. This creates a more or less uniform electromagnetic field."

Joseph watched the liquid flow into the translucent chamber, which, with the exterior ribbing, reminded him of a beer keg.

Bruce continued, "The oil that is now infused with the powdered iron is attracted to and held by the electromagnetic field. I'll next open a valve at the bottom of chamber 'A' to allow the salt water to drain into the chamber labeled 'B'.

Joseph watched the liquid flow into the lower chamber.

"I'll now close the valve between chambers 'A' and 'B', and open the valve between chambers 'B' and 'C', activating a pump that will force the salt water in chamber 'B' through a reverse osmosis process."

"You're now losing me. What's reverse osmosis?" asked Joseph.

"It's a well-established process by which water containing various contaminants is forced under pressure through a series of special membranes that filter out any residual oil and iron powder, plus the salt and any minerals present in the fluid. The process is a component of the desalinization process of sea water utilized by some arid countries in the Middle East."

"Now that you mention it, I've read about desalinization as a way to address drought conditions, such as we've experienced in recent years here in California."

"Exactly. Now, I'll next open valves and activate pumps to transfer the water from chamber 'C' to chamber 'D'. This final chamber in this part of the machine adds a proportional amount of chlorine to the water to kill any bacteria."

"Sort of like a swimming pool, but on a more measured scale," said Joseph.

"That's a good analogy. Now, let's return to chamber 'B', which contains the magnetically suspended oil. I'll reverse the magnetic field, which, along with gravity, will force the oil to the bottom of the chamber."

Joseph watched the thick substance fall to the bottom of the chamber.

"I'll next deactivate the electromagnetic field, open the valve from chamber 'B' to chamber 'E', and turn on a pump. This next chamber is a centrifuge. I'll add a new chemical reagent to the oil which facilitates the breakdown of the bond between the carbon molecules and the iron molecules, reversing the effect of the bonding agent we added in chamber 'A'. By spinning the fluid at a high rate of speed, we take advantage of the differing relative densities between carbon and iron."

"I'm glad you decided to show this to me in person. I don't think I ever could have followed this in a verbal conversation," replied Joseph.

"The next step is to activate another pump and open another valve. The oil is pumped into chamber 'F', while the iron powder and other chemicals remain in chamber 'E'".

"I can see that," responded Joseph.

"The oil is now recovered and is actually suitable for use in refining, just as if the spill into the salt water had never occurred."

"That's impressive."

"What is even more impressive is the last step." Bruce handed Joseph a glass.

"What do we do with this?"

"Open the spigot on the side of chamber 'D', and have a drink."

"Really?" asked Joseph.

"Absolutely," replied Bruce.

After Joseph drank about half a glass of the water, he looked at Bruce.

"Tastes fine, just like the bottled water I buy at the supermarket, maybe even better."

"Chemically speaking, it *is* better. It's purer, and therefore healthier."

The two men sat down at one of the nearby tables in the lab. Bruce silently waited for Joseph to process everything he had witnessed.

"So, this technology cleans up oil spills, actually recovers the oil for future use, and generates potable water for drinking, while also being far more environmentally friendly than the dispersants and other chemicals historically utilized to try to ameliorate oil spills."

"Yes, and forecast with a greater recovery rate for the oil than historic remediation methods."

Joseph thought some more, and then added, "The recovered oil and the purified water can be sold to at least partially offset the cost of the cleanup, therefore representing a more financially attractive approach than anything existing today."

"That's my hope, although the professor and I haven't performed any financial analyses. In addition, we're not exactly certain how this technology would scale and operate in a real-world environment outside of a laboratory. The ocean contains molecules other than solely water and salt, plus is subject to tides, currents, and waves. Similarly, crude oil from various regions varies in chemical and physical properties, as do refined products such as gasoline and jet fuel."

"I understand most of what you're saying. Tell you what, if you have some more time, let's go down to one of the bars on Shattuck Avenue and have a drink. I need some time to digest everything I've seen and heard. I want to think through whether there is a business opportunity here. Who would the customers be? What could be charged? What is the profit potential? How much capital would need to be invested? Could we market and sell the intellectual property rather than actually operate a remediation company? Are there likely to be competitors with similar or better technology? What is the likelihood of being able to perfect intellectual property rights in the U.S. and abroad, and how long would that take?"

"I was hoping you'd respond like that. I'm skilled at chemical equations and certain aspects of physics, but I have little background in financial matters. I must admit to having no idea whether there is a true business opportunity here. I thought you'd be the right person to ask as someone about to graduate from one of the nation's premier MBA programs."

"Thanks for the faith and compliment. I have no doubt we'd make as good a professional team as a volleyball team. Now, let's get that drink. Maybe we can hit a trifecta today and also team to meet a couple of interesting women before the end of the evening."

Chapter 8

Tuesday February 12, 2018
Berkeley, California

At 2:00 PM, Bruce's iPhone rang and indicated an incoming call from Joseph.

"Hello, Joseph, what's up?"

"Bruce, what would you think about my texting the two roommates we met at the bar last Friday night and seeing if they might be interested in joining us for a dinner out sometime this coming weekend?"

"I could think of many worse ways to spend an evening! However, before you contact them, perhaps we should have a discussion."

"That sounds serious."

"I don't mean to be dramatic. I was thinking about which of the women we would each prefer to focus upon. I'd like to avoid any awkwardness in that regard."

"Always thinking the experiment through! No wonder you're a scientist. Well, we barely got to know them at the bar. It was loud and crowded. I felt fortunate to get their phone numbers."

"I remember that they each are employed in the technology field, although it sounded like in quite divergent areas. They're both currently working in Emeryville, but for different companies. Kathi Chan seemed like a real live-wire, a first generation American whose parents emigrated from the Shanghai area. Sofia DeMarco struck me as a sort of Renaissance woman, but it's difficult to know for sure if I'm right about that. At this point, I don't know which individual I'd be most interested in."

"I'm in the same place you are," replied Joseph. "I feel like we've just scratched the surface regarding those two. All I can tell for sure is that they're both bright, well-educated, and modern women."

"We could be stereotypical and pair me with Kathi and you with Sofia, based solely on similar ethnic backgrounds."

"I think we'd both readily agree that our generation has evolved beyond such simple considerations in relationships. That approach would be no more valid than pairing me with Kathi because she is the shorter of the two. In fact, if I were to dance with Sofia, there is the distinct possibility of my resting my head on her breasts. How tall do you think she is?"

"Well, I'm 6'4" tall, so I'd estimate Sofia at about 6'2" in height, maybe a tad more. I don't remember that she was wearing heels at the bar, so your dance floor scenario appears quite valid."

Joseph laughed. Although he and Bruce had not known each other for long, it was apparent that their personalities were compatible.

After thinking for a bit, he replied, "Bruce, tell you what. We'll signal each other part way through the dinner. A finger pointed up indicates a preference for Sofia, and vice-versa for Kathi. In the event of a tie, I'll defer to you. It's the least I could do in return for your introducing me to our potential business opportunity."

"An effective solution to a problem achieved through negotiation. Just like a finance guy... I'll keep Friday and Saturday evenings open pending news from you."

The men hung up and continued with their days, each focused on completing the requirements for their advanced degrees.

Chapter 9

Friday October 17, 1997
San Diego, California

Over twenty years prior to the highly profitable sale of Opticore Products Corporation, the U.S. was entering the Internet age. New online content was being added at an increasingly rapid pace. Each generation of modem provided faster connectivity. A sea change of innovation was working its way through the global economy. This was an exciting time for Steven Shaw to be in college, learning about the forthcoming era that would integrate commerce and technology as never before.

It was another perfect afternoon in San Diego. Seventy-five degrees Fahrenheit, without a cloud in the sky. Twenty-one-year-old Steven, a junior at San Diego State University, returned to his dorm room at 3:30 PM after completing the last of his mid-term examinations. The academic rigor of SDSU was much more advanced than the community college Steven attended in El Paso, Texas, over the prior three years. During that time, he succeeded in earning his Associate of Arts degree while working twenty hours per week as a bank teller to supplement his mother's limited income from her job as a waitress. Six months ago, he received the good news of his acceptance into SDSU as a finance major and also that his scholarship application had been approved. The prior August, he eagerly drove west from El Paso back to the area he remembered fondly, from when his father was still alive before being killed in Afghanistan.

On the one hand, Steven would miss seeing his mother. On

the other hand, he had never assimilated into the west Texas culture. That was simply incompatible with his growing up as a California youth. With the passing of his grandparents about a year ago, his mother received title to the house in El Paso and a modest inheritance, enough for her to get by. This relieved Steven of any guilt associated with his moving back to San Diego.

After settling in to the University, Steven tried to track down Julie, his high school sweetheart. However, her family had relocated out of the area a number of years ago. With a last name of Smith, it was impossible to find her despite Steven's spending multiple hours online through his AOL account.

Upon opening the door to his dorm room, Steven saw that his roommate, Vince, had just returned from exercising in the recreation center.

"Whew! I could smell you down the hall," said Steven.

"The proof of a quality workout," smiled Vince. "How'd your last mid-term go?"

"I think I did pretty well. Some of the questions regarding the differences in various types of debt financing were tricky, but I studied that topic last night."

"Good to hear. You up for some fun tonight?" asked Vince.

"I could use a break. I don't have a work shift until Sunday."

Steven had taken a part-time on-campus job in the financial aid office to provide cash for expenses not covered by his scholarship.

"A guy in my marketing class told me about a party tonight. There's supposed to be a live band at one of the large houses just off campus."

"Sounds good," replied Steven.

Vince and Steven arrived at the location of the party at 8:30 PM. It was still seventy degrees outside, so college students were gathered in groups throughout the spacious back yard. A beer keg was centrally located in the garden, with a make-shift bar under the porch at the rear of the house. The band was warming up in the basement, with most of that space organized as a dance floor. While waiting in line for a cup of beer, Vince recognized several fellow students from his business administration classes, peeling off with a couple of them to instead get some hard liquor from the bar.

Once Steven was almost at the beer keg, he heard a woman's voice from behind him say, "Can you pour for me while you're there? I've got my hands full."

Steven turned around. Standing behind him was a tall, thin co-ed with waist-length, straight blonde hair. She was holding a plate of food.

"Sure."

Steven filled two of the red plastic cups with beer, the typical inexpensive PBR. He walked over to one of the tables in the backyard and put down the cups. The woman with the flowing hair was right behind him.

"Thanks. My name is Kari."

"I'm Steven."

"Want to have a seat?"

"Okay."

Kari provided Steven with the typical college social profile. She was a music major, played the piano, and was from Los Angeles. She was a senior, with plans to attend one of the prestigious graduate programs in music if accepted. She lived off campus. Steven reciprocated with a summary about himself.

Kari consumed the plate of food while he spoke, eating with vigor. Steven noticed this, but was not surprised given how thin Kari was. By then, the band was playing *Macarena* by Los Del Rio.

"How about a dance?" asked Kari.

"Yeh, that'd be great."

Thus began Steven's long evening with Kari. They danced many songs together, at one point taking a break to cool down outside and each do two shots of tequila. At 11:00 PM, Kari recognized a friend of hers from her freshman dorm. She pulled Steven over to say hello.

"Kim, what've you been up to?" inquired Kari.

Steven listened as the attractive woman with wavy brown hair responded, "I'm finishing up this semester and have a job lined up in the Bay Area starting in January."

"Good for you, girl!" exclaimed Kari.

"Now that I'm through mid-terms, I just have a few papers to write and then finals. I'll be working south of Market Street, great neighborhood. I'll probably rent an apartment or condo there as well."

"Sounds exciting," commented Steven. "I read that they're planning a new baseball stadium for the Giants in that area."

"Oh, really? I'm not much of a baseball fan," said Kim. "Say, you two up for some coke?"

Before Steven could reply, Kari responded with, "Yes! Glad I bumped into you."

Kari took Steven by the hand and followed Kim away from the dance floor and to a relatively secluded part of the garden. Kim opened her small pursue and produced a mirror, a razor blade, a small bag of cocaine, and a straw. She arranged three lines of the drug on the mirror, helping herself first. Kari took the straw and inhaled deeply through her nose, tilting her head back as the cocaine rushed into her system.

"Quality stuff," said Kari.

"Got a good supplier. I'm going to miss him when I move up north."

The two women turned their attention to Steven.

Noticing this, he commented, "I've never done coke before. Don't know if I want to."

"Nothing wrong with this, as you can see from us," advised Kari. "You'll feel so very fine. Trust me."

She leaned in and gave Steven a deep kiss. Kim held out the straw and the mirror with the last line of cocaine. With a good-looking woman sitting on each side of him, encouraging him, Steven took the hit. The rush of positive energy surprised Steven. His sense of well-being soared. At the same time, he felt more at peace than he had in months. The stress of managing his classes and work hours melted away.

"Wow. I can see why coke's so popular," commented Steven.

Kim smiled.

Kari leaned in and whispered into his ear, "How about going to my place?"

Steven whispered back simply, "Okay."

Kari bid good-bye to Kim and placed her hand in Steven's, leading him away. Once they had walked about fifty yards, she placed her arm around Steven's waist, drawing him closer. Her apartment was just a block off campus in one of the relatively newer buildings. Once they were in the front door, Kari kissed Steven intently, placing her tongue in his mouth. She followed this by quickly pulling off his shirt, unbuckling his belt, and pulling down his pants. Once she had him naked, she grabbed his left butt cheek and guided him onto a queen-sized bed. Although Steven was hardly a virgin, he had never experienced such a sexually aggressive and assertive woman.

Steven watched intently as Kari removed her clothes. Consistent with his earlier observation, she was very thin, with no figure to speak of. Perhaps self-consciously, Kari pulled her long hair in front of her, and then laid down next to Steven. After several more passionate kisses, she guided him by touch and whispers to provide the specific stimulation she desired. It didn't take long for Kari to shudder violently and vocalize a series of deep moans.

After catching her breath, Kari said gently and with a bit of mischievousness, "Relax, and let me return the favor. Turn over."

She commenced giving Steven a deep back massage, using her long, strong fingers honed by years of playing piano. After ten minutes, Steven was completely relaxed, a feeling augmented by the lateness of the evening and his cumulative alcohol consumption. Sensing this, Kari nudged him to turn over and then used the same highly coordinated fingers to stimulate him to a rock-hard erection, while being careful not to bring him to orgasm. Steven felt as if every nerve in his body was on fire. Kari climbed on top of him, facing away from him, and lowered herself onto his penis. She began moving up and down, and to a lesser extent forward and backwards. She listened to his breathing and felt his hip muscles to repeatedly bring him to the point of orgasm and then stopped.

Finally, Steven called out, "Please! Please!".

Kari re-initiated her motion, gradually accelerating in speed, until Steven cried out in a loud scream and ejaculated. He quickly fell asleep afterwards.

Around 9:30 AM the next morning, Steven gradually stirred awake, opening just one eye at first. He saw that he was alone in the bed. The smell of freshly brewed coffee filled his sinuses. Kari was already dressed and approached him with a standard fast-food 'to go' paper cup. It was warm from the coffee.

"I added one sugar and a splash of cream. I hope that's okay," said Kari.

"That's fine," replied Steven.

Kari glanced over at Steven's clothes, which were neatly placed on a chair next to the bed.

Before he could speak, she said, "Last night was great, but you're really not my type. I usually date musicians, writers, and other artists. I thought it would be fun to try a business guy for a change of pace."

Steven suddenly pictured himself as a free food sample located on one of the demonstration tables set up in the big box stores. Not knowing what to say at this point, he quickly got dressed, took the cup of coffee, received a brief hug good-bye from Kari, and walked back to his dorm room.

"Look who finally showed up! What happened to you last night?" asked Vince as soon as Steven walked in the door.

"Quite an experience," responded Steven. "One I doubt that I'll ever forget."

Chapter 10

Friday February 15, 2018
Albany, California

The hostess at Gino's restaurant sat Joseph, Bruce, Sofia, and Kathi at a relatively secluded booth towards the rear of the establishment. Gino's was a local favorite, resident for over ten years in the same simple brick building in the town just to the north of Berkeley. The men sat on the same side of the booth, facing the two women in order to facilitate conversation.

"We were pleased to receive your text that you could join us for dinner tonight. It was difficult to talk much at the bar last week," opened Joseph.

"I've heard of Gino's over the years, but never had the opportunity to eat here. Have you?" asked Kathi of Sofia.

"Just once, perhaps five years ago. I can't remember anything specifically, but I do have a general, favorable memory of the meal," replied Sofia. Looking at the two men, she added, "I was pleased to hear of your suggestion to meet here."

The waitress approached the booth.

"Good evening. My name is Maria. I am Gino's wife. We're short-handed today, so I'm helping out with tables."

Maria's English had a moderate level of Italian accent.

Picking up on this, Sofia responded with, "*Che consiglia per noi stasera?*"

Maria did not pause in responding, "*Abbiamo preso il vitello per un osso buco delizioso. Lo consiglio.*"

Bruce, Kathi, and Joseph were each surprised and stared at Sofia.

She quickly recognized this and said, "They have a special tonight of veal shank cooked northern Italian style. I've had the dish before. It's delicious."

The other three individuals seated at the booth nodded their agreement.

Joseph quickly added, "Perhaps you might also select the appetizer course for us. It sounds as if you have quite a background in Italian cuisine."

"My grandmother and I spent many summers in my youth preparing family meals. I've found cooking to be a pleasant distraction from all of the computer work."

"*Maria, ho visto gli sformati sulla lista. Sono consigliati?*"

"*Si, mi piacciono molto.*"

"*Va bene. Due piatti di condividere tra noi.*"

"*Certo. Cosa di bevere?*"

"*Forse una bottiglia di Dolcetto, da Piemonte?*"

"*Si, l'abbiamo. Torno subito.*"

The other three seated individuals again focused on Sofia.

"I didn't mean to monopolize the ordering. I hope I didn't upset any of you."

Bruce replied, "Not at all. Can you tell us what we're having, in addition to the veal shank?"

"The appetizer course is an array of seasoned, blended, cooked, and formed vegetables. It's one of the more difficult Italian dishes to cook well. I assure you that they are tasty. Maria shared that they are among her favorites here."

"And, most importantly, what are we drinking?" inquired Kathi.

"I selected a red wine from northern Italy that pairs well with the *osso buco*."

"Oh, so your culinary skills extend also to wines?" asked Joseph.

"I'm by no means an expert. However, part of preparing good food involves matching each dish with a suitable beverage. Enough about my hobby! Please tell us more about you two guys. How did you meet?"

The conversation flowed smoothly throughout the dinner. The men learned that Kathi had a PhD in computer science from the University of Washington. Sofia had a master degree in network security and cryptology from MIT on top of an undergraduate degree in computer science from California Polytechnic State University. Both were working for tech start-ups funded by venture capitalists from the nearby Silicon Valley area.

The women excused themselves prior to the arrival of the dessert course, a sorbet made from imported lemons from the Amalfi Coast of Italy, infused with *limoncello* liquor imported from the adjacent foothills of Mount Vesuvius.

Bruce and Joseph used this opportunity to supersede their previously established plan of finger signals.

"Joseph, what do you think?" asked Bruce.

"I could go either way. Sofia shares my ethnic background, although she is much more Italian than I am. I'm a sixth generation Italian-American. On the other hand, I find Kathi's approach to her profession quite interesting. Her line of work is something I would have considered for myself if I had not decided to pursue finance. What about you?"

49

"I really like Kathi's playful spirit and sense of humor. However, I worry about being at least a foot taller than she is. I don't know if that significant a height and size discrepancy might not be attractive to her. I'll admit that I could eat at Sofia's house for the rest of my life and die a happy, and certainly well-fed, man."

The men saw the women approaching the table and quickly fell silent.

"We're ready for dessert," said Kathi. "The description sounded marvelous."

"Bruce, would you mind changing places with me for the dessert course?" inquired Sofia.

"Of course."

Bruce stood up and slid into the booth across from Joseph. Kathi then joined Bruce on the one side, with Sofia seating herself next to Joseph.

As they relished in the sorbet, which was served inside hollowed out, large lemons, Joseph thought to himself. I've learned a valuable lesson tonight. While planning ahead is a good thing, it's even more important to identify who will be in charge of the negotiations...

Chapter 11

Monday February 6, 2012
San Francisco, California

About six years before Steven's efforts to launch the Blue Planet entities, the country was buzzing this morning about Super Bowl XLVI. Yesterday, the New York Giants, led by quarterback Eli Manning, defeated the New England Patriots and their superstar quarterback, Tom Brady, 21 to 17. Television viewership for the game set a new record.

In the over four years that Steven and Veronica had now been married, Steven gradually assumed more indirect financial control over Veronica's wealth. While the trustees of Veronica's trust technically made all investment decisions, in practice quite a bit of the money was invested into entities with which Steven was involved. Steven performed admirably through the Great Recession, astutely selecting a range of investments which multiplied the value of Veronica's trust many times over. With the financial crisis now history and the S&P 500 Index starting the new year by rising over four percent in January, Steven was eager to make his next score. He had arranged to have dinner with Charles this evening at a steakhouse in the Financial District.

Once they were both seated at the table, the men each made comments about the recent Super Bowl. Following that topic, Steven launched into the discussion he had planned for this evening.

"Charles, do you remember the potential investment opportunity I spoke about last week, the e-commerce S corporation?"

"Yes, the one with the advanced technology for instantly suggesting cross-sell opportunities. I believe the example you gave me was someone ordering a flat-screen television would be encouraged to purchase a compatible sound bar, with a limited time discount offer presented as soon as the television was placed in the shopping cart."

"That's the one. The entrepreneurs have developed an amazing database of complementary items, with the on-screen presentation quite compelling, including short product videos and online testimonials. Even more than that, they continuously monitor their purchase patterns to update and prioritize the recommended supplementary purchases. Their software even has an algorithm that incorporates the gross margin on each product in determining the precedence of recommendations."

"I can see how that would be quite lucrative," said Charles.

"I believe that one of the huge e-commerce sites is going to identify and then purchase this company for their technology. Applied on a greater scale, the financial value of the software is in the hundreds of millions of dollars," opined Steven.

"That makes sense," replied Charles. "Are you interested in purchasing the entire company, and is it for sale?"

"I've had a private detective perform background research on the principal shareholders. Most of them appear totally committed to growing and managing the company on their own, at least for now. However, there is one fifteen percent owner with a wife who has Lou Gehrig's disease. Most earlier stage companies don't provide great health benefits, so there might be significant medical bills to pay. My guess is that this particular owner would be receptive to selling his shares; particularly if confronted with photos of the affair he is conducting with his secretary."

Charles paused to digest everything Steven had said. He picked up his menu to buy some time in thinking through his response. He had been loyal to the Hopkins family for many years now. First to Blake, then to Veronica, and now to Steven. Up to this point, he had always conducted himself professionally. He decided to try to lead Steven in a somewhat circuitous conversation.

"I've heard that the dry aged porterhouse steak is particularly good," said Charles, pointing to the item on the menu. "The sides look tasty, especially the sauteed mushrooms."

"That sounds right. I've never eaten here before, but the online reviews said that this is one of the best places to have beef in the city," noted Steven.

The waiter arrived at their table. Steven ordered the ten-ounce porterhouse with a side of the mushrooms. Charles ordered the sixteen-ounce cut along with both the mushrooms and a baked potato. Steven also requested a bottle of Duckhorn Merlot.

Once they had ordered, Charles looked at Steven and said, "I'm curious. What prompted you to hire the private detective?"

"I thought it unlikely that we could purchase the entire company. Therefore, I decided to investigate if there might be an avenue for acquiring at least some of the shares. Since the shares are owned by a relatively limited number of individuals, it made sense to review their backgrounds and profiles."

"It's of course not unusual to research counterparties to potential negotiations. However, the detail you provided about the wife's health and the husband's behavior was a bit more that I've typically seen," expressed Charles.

"There's nothing illegal in gaining knowledge about an individual through public records, observation, and communication," pointed out Steven.

"Agreed, but the implication of potentially using that information to perhaps coerce a business transaction..."

Steven interrupted Charles.

"There's no harm in making him an offer for his shares. If he needs the money for his wife's medical treatments, we've actually done him a favor. If we happen to comment on his affair, that's just part of a conversation, no quid pro quo presented. There's plenty of room in the grey area for nuance without stepping over the legal line."

Charles took a deep breath to consider the conversation to this point. Steven was technically correct. There were always some grey areas in business transactions. That was just the nature of commerce. As long as certain tripwires were not hit, there shouldn't be any criminal issue or undue litigation exposure. There was nothing unethical about making an offer to purchase shares. Charles decided to give Steven the benefit of the doubt.

"I understand where you're coming from. I'll generate some proforma valuations for the shares to help us be well prepared for the price negotiation. I'll defer to you for the other aspects, if any."

"I knew I could count on you, Charles. This deal is a potential five to ten bagger. Too good to miss. At some point, one of the e-commerce giants is going to make the owners an offer they can't refuse. We'll be in position to share in that ride."

The waiter arrived with their food. The men discussed various other topics throughout the meal. They had developed a good friendship following Steven's introduction into the Hopkins world. As Charles swallowed the last of the excellent red wine, he had no way of knowing that he had just taken the first step down a long and slippery slope.

Chapter 12

Monday March 19, 2018
San Francisco, California

It was fortuitous that 10,000 square feet of office space on the 44th floor of the Bank of America building became available in early February. After some limited remodeling, today was the grand opening of the offices of Blue Planet Investment Management and Blue Planet Investment Fund. Jennifer Franklin and the law firm of Greene, Robinson, and Sanders had filed all of the necessary documents to form the new entities. A CPA firm had been hired by Charles Winters to help establish the initial technology infrastructure and implement various software systems, including those for client and corporate accounting, and payroll. Steven Shaw was named as the management company President, with Charles serving as Chief Investment Officer. Steven furnished $2 million of funding to pay for setting up all aspects of the new businesses, plus to provide initial liquidity for the management company. A temporary employee was hired to respond to incoming calls and emails while Steven and Charles commenced interviews for permanent staff.

Charles' primary focus this morning was on interviews with three candidates for the position of Chief Marketing Officer. This would be the individual who would orchestrate the marketing of the new Fund to potential investors, leveraging the relationships of Steven, Charles, and Trent Hawthorne, the lead partner at the law firm. All three candidates were women, selected from over fifty applicants. Charles and Steven recognized the importance of not having an all-male executive suite in the year 2018. They also knew of several potentially large clients who would respond more favorably to a woman than to themselves, particularly to a woman presenting a specific profile.

The temporary receptionist brought the first candidate to Charles' office at 9:00 AM. Charles walked from behind the desk to greet the short, somewhat plump woman who was well attired in a dark blue skirt and jacket, with matching pearl earrings and necklace.

"Good morning, Ms. Morris. It's a pleasure to meet you."

Charles extended his hand and made direct eye contact.

"Thank you for providing me with this opportunity to interview. I must say that Mr. Shaw has a most impressive track record."

"Yes, he does. We're eager to continue that success, plus perform some notable social good, with our new entity, Blue Planet Investment Fund, or the 'Fund' for short. Might I get you a glass of water, or anything else?"

"No, thank you."

"Please take a seat. I've reviewed your resume and cover letter. A most impressive education and professional history. An undergraduate degree in environmental engineering from Northwestern and an MBA with a specialization in marketing from the University of Santa Clara. You've spent the past five years working for a global non-profit organization whose mission is to reverse climate change."

"Yes. We've worked diligently to first identify and then categorize production sources of carbon dioxide, methane, and other greenhouse gasses, using that information to inform and lobby both the generators and the applicable regulators and politicians to implement changes to the businesses in order to reduce their environmental footprint."

"I see. Please tell me about how you assisted the generators with developing or adopting new technologies or operating practices that lessened their aggregate environmental impact."

"The non-profit's focus is primarily on highlighting large contributors to climate change, such as cement and steel producers, and then approaching those entities to encourage them to change. Absent achieving concurrence from the generators, we would then approach and educate the regulatory bodies and politicians with the greatest potential impact upon the polluters."

"So, your work has been primarily oriented toward enforcement and politics, as distinguished from a focus on finding creative solutions, new technologies, or best practices that might form the basis of proactive resolution to the production of greenhouse gasses."

"Excuse me, Mr. Winters, but, by your last comment, I perceive that you might not value the great achievements accomplished through our process. As but one example, our non-profit was instrumental in the closure of five coal-fired power plants."

"And how did you propose to replace the lost generating capacity?"

"Through higher and tiered pricing for electricity. That approach encourages conservation."

"I certainly won't argue that increasing prices reduces demand; but too often with the unintended consequences of distorting efficient capital allocation and adversely impacting the poorer members of society."

"I'm sorry you feel that way. However, you must agree that any solution to climate change will inevitably have some negative repercussions. Those unfavorable aspects must be endured for the greater overall good."

"Ms. Morris, call me an unbridled and foolish optimist, but I believe this country is blessed with sufficient human intelligence, drive, and capital to achieve our environmental objectives while also improving the human condition. What I like to call the 'win-win' scenario."

"Mr. Winters, I must admit that I'm more of pragmatist and much less of a dreamer. If your win-win scenario is the basis for the Fund, I'm afraid that's a foundational aspect that I can't see myself committing to, solely on practical grounds."

"I'm disappointed to hear that, but understand your position and thank you for your time and interest this morning."

Ms. Morris then rose, shook Charles, hand, and exited the office. As the office door closed behind her, Charles thought to himself. I'm new to this ESG environment, and therefore slower to perceive things. These interviews are going to be good on-the-job training for me. We never even got to the marketing aspect of her professional profile. However, in my experience, individuals with a background in enforcement hardly ever transition effectively to sales and service. It's simply a completely different mindset.

Since the first interview ended earlier than planned, Charles used the time to catch up on his emails. At 10:00 AM, the receptionist brought the second candidate, Ms. Kehoe, to his office. After exchanging introductions, the candidate sat across the desk from Charles, similar in position to that of Ms. Morris. That was where the physical similarities between the women began and ended. Ms. Kehoe could only be described as stunning. She was about 5'10" tall, with long, thick blond hair, an attractive face with what Charles guessed must be a nose made as perfect as possible through rhinoplasty, and a taught, athletic body. The latter aspect was accentuated by the tight fit of her linen suit, worn over a white blouse with a hint of plunging neckline that was further highlighted by a long, dangling amethyst necklace. Charles was able to quickly compose himself and commenced the targeted interview.

"Ms. Kehoe, I see that you have an undergraduate degree from Chico State University in environmental planning, followed by eight years of work experience marketing solar panels and related battery systems for both residential and commercial applications."

"Yes, that's correct. I've successfully marketed installations ranging from one single family residence to large apartment complexes and congregate living facilities to rooftop industrial applications. A number of the buildings in the Financial District are topped with our solar panels, often connected to our battery storage system."

"What motivated you to pursue this line of work?"

"I've been environmentally conscious since my teenage years. That led to my degree from Chico State and seeking work in the solar industry. I believe that solar power will be the solution to climate change, as we replace coal, nuclear, and natural gas electricity generation with clean energy."

"Well said. I'm also a proponent of solar panels and related technologies. What do you think the prospects are for distributed versus centralized solar panel installations?"

"A different division in our company sells products to solar farms, so I'm not familiar with marketing to that type of client."

"But have you thought through the issues of land utilization and transmission line cost, not to mention the loss of electricity associated with transmitting energy from remote locations to large cities where demand is concentrated?"

"While I've heard of those issues, I'm afraid I'm not sufficiently informed to provide you with a good answer to your question."

"Thank you for your honesty. It's refreshing. Let me change the focus to potential upcoming changes in the clean energy industry. What do you think about the prospects for new generations of solar panels, such as those that capture energy on both sides and / or that use different materials to capture a broader spectrum of light?"

"I'm not plugged in to the product development side of my company, so I can't answer your question. I know that our solar panels have significantly increased their energy conversion ratio over my time with the company. In fact, so much so that I've even been able to sell a new generation of installations to customers who bought from us, say, six to eight years ago. That's been a great source of repeat business."

"I acknowledge that. Your answer leads me into my next question. What has been your greatest professional accomplishment?"

"That's an easy question for me. Being the top salesperson for my division for three consecutive years. I really enjoy the satisfaction that follows closing a sale."

"That *is* impressive. How have you overcome concerns or objections from potential customers about such things as technological obsolescence, economic risk stemming from changes to utility pricing structure, or possible political actions resulting in revised tax benefits?"

"My company provides us with a fact sheet, talking points, and summary product information for use in marketing. Salespeople can call in a technical specialist to respond to detailed product questions or other complex matters as described in your question. In my experience, the technical specialist is only needed in ten to fifteen percent of the sales calls. Most of the new customers are satisfied with the summary information, as they are often motivated to do something good for the planet. Just like your new Fund, if I understand such correctly."

Ms. Kehoe then paused, leaned back, crossed her legs in the other direction, brushed her long hair slowly from her face, and looked into Charles' eyes with just a hint of a smile on her thick lips. Charles had no doubt that Ms. Kehoe could sell snow to an Eskimo, to quote the familiar phrase. However, he doubted that she could parlay with well-educated individuals thinking about investing tens to hundreds of millions of dollars into the Fund. The Fund's target market was simply too different from that historically served by Ms. Kehoe.

"I see that our time is up. Let me return the honesty you shared earlier. While you are a most impressive individual, I don't think you're the right fit for our enterprise. Our target investments are by nature often quite complex. In addition, our client base is sophisticated, but in need of guidance on certain aspects of our Fund. This profile will require our Chief Marketing Officer to respond with detailed and often technical information on the fly."

"Mr. Winters, I now understand that. Let me again express that I have appreciated your time and the opportunity to speak with you."

Ms. Kehoe then rose, shook Charles' hand, and exited the office. As he watched the door shut behind her, he thought about her poise in being turned down on the spot. That was a skill infrequently understood by Millennials, in his experience. It's a small world. Salvaging a losing situation with class can often lead to future opportunities. As he finished this thought, he glanced at his iPhone and realized he had just five minutes until the next scheduled interview. Just enough time for what his nephews referred to as a 'biological break'.

Right on time at 11:00 AM, the receptionist walked the third candidate into Charles' office.

"Good morning, Ms. Moore. It's a pleasure to meet you. One of our in-house attorneys, Jennifer Franklin, spoke very highly of you in recommending you as a candidate for our Chief Marketing Officer position."

"Thank you for the opportunity to interview. I hope that I don't disappoint relative to Jennifer's recommendation."

Charles noted the gentle self-deprecation in Ms. Moore's comment. Yet another skill too often absent from the upcoming generation. Charles also noticed Ms. Moore's personal presentation. She was also an attractive woman, although not quite in Ms. Kehoe's league. She was relatively tall, likely about 5'11". Her auburn hair fell just below her shoulders. The medium gray suit was well tailored, if perhaps a bit tight around what appeared to be an ample bust. The sapphire earrings were the only jewelry worn. Her smile presented perfectly arranged, brilliantly white teeth.

"I've reviewed your resume and cover letter. You graduated from UCLA with a degree in environmental sciences. Since then, you've worked for about four years in the consulting industry, most recently for one of the global firms specializing in ESG related projects."

"That's correct. I would like to note that I've undertaken continuing education in all three aspects of ESG, including evolving technologies for improving environmental results, the latest trends in firms being ranked as employers of choice in their industry, and best practices in corporate governance under both the European and American systems."

"Thank you for sharing that. Quite impressive. Please tell me what motivated you to pursue your particular career."

"I view climate change as one of the largest challenges facing mankind. Some of my colleagues define climate change as the single most important issue on the planet. I'm of an opinion that I'm not qualified to make that type of judgement. Endemic poverty, limited access to sufficient volumes of clean water, various health considerations including horrible viruses such as Ebola, and racial injustice are also enormous problems. I identified climate change as the topic I was most interested in and felt that I could best make a contribution to."

"Well said. Our new Fund is similarly oriented toward improving the quality of life on the planet across all three ESG components. That said, I believe we'll likely be able to have the greatest impact upon the environmental component. Our capital investment and management expertise are better suited to identifying and investing in new technologies, many of which present the prospect of effective environmental remediation."

"I thought that might be the case, based upon the limited information thus far available on the Fund. Please share with me, are you thinking about opportunities as far out as nuclear fusion, or do you plan to stay more focused on short to medium term opportunities such as increased efficiency in wind turbines and chemistry associated with carbon capture from the air?"

"The Fund will have a target maturity of seven years, at which time we plan on returning the capital, plus profits, to our investors. We'll therefore need to focus on environmental solutions that are practical over the nearer to medium term. God bless the scientists devoting their lives to nuclear fusion. That energy solution has been forecast as available thirty years in the future since the 1950's."

"Mr. Winters, please tell me more about your target market, in terms of investors."

"We'll be marketing the fund only to institutions and accredited investors. The business entities we've listed as potential clients likely have some overlap with your current client list. We'll be marketing globally, seeking to attract a total of about $16 billion in investment. Now that I'm explaining this, sovereign wealth funds and high-net-worth family offices will also be solicited. The Shaw family office will provide a substantial lead investment, visibly committing Mr. Shaw to the success of the Fund."

"Mr. Shaw's commitment will be an effective marketing tool from a financial perspective. Each hurricane and wildfire will similarly support the marketing of the Fund for social reasons. With the right team and sales material, I have no doubt that the Fund will be achieve its goal for capital raising," opined Ms. Moore.

"Your confidence is appreciated. We're embarking on no small task with this project."

"Mr. Winters, please tell me about the plans for investment and management once the Fund is fully capitalized."

"We plan to hire some of the best and brightest minds in the ESG space to identify emerging technologies and other trends that might support the Fund's objectives. The Fund will provide seed capital to newly formed ventures, convertible preferred stock or debentures to later stage entities, and deeper financing to companies ready to commence marketing their product or service. The Fund will also purchase various operating companies with the objective of accelerating their growth and pace of technological development. We plan to retain much of the human capital from any acquired entities as a means of further enhancing our intellectual resources. Finally, we envision synergies from our ecosystem. For example, a technology to capture carbon from the air might also be applied directly into the manufacturing process for carbon intensive industries."

"That's what I would have designed, particularly with regards to your ecosystem comment. It's often amazing how a new technology can be deployed in a completely different venue with great efficacy."

Ms. Moore paused to drink from her glass of water.

She then continued, "Mr. Winters, one final question. How do you plan to close the deal, so to speak, on attracting such large investments? In my experience, it's not easy to pry tens of millions of dollars loose from the hands of individuals, even if they are solely acting in a corporate or fiduciary capacity."

"That is another superb question. First, we believe we have a compelling story and mission. Second, we intend to leverage the reputation of Mr. Shaw and other early investors. Third, we plan on developing first-class marketing materials, to be supplemented by the sales efforts of the Chief Marketing Officer, Mr. Shaw, myself, and other key individuals. Fourth, we plan to pre-identify various investments. That will provide confidence to our investors and also bolster the projected returns of the fund through timely investment. Fifth, we intend to retain an experienced Chief Financial Officer who will both expertly invest excess liquidity awaiting allocation and obtain up to perhaps $10 billion in leverage to magnify the Fund's return."

"That's a great official answer. However, we've both operated in the world of high finance. Are you willing to go the extra mile to ensure the Fund's success, if necessary?"

Ms. Moore casually brushed her hand across her breasts as she concluded the last sentence.

"While we don't envision needing to take extraordinary measures, let me assure you that Mr. Shaw and I are completely committed to the success of this new venture."

Ms. Moore then stood up and extended her hand.

As Charles similarly and extended his, Ms. Moore stated, "I'm very interested in this position. Thank you for considering me. I look forward to communicating with you further."

Ms. Moore exited the office. As the door closed, Charles sunk into his chair and leaned back. What had just happened? In fact, *he* had just been interviewed for the last hour. Ms. Moore accomplished such in a natural flow of conversation, while also being technically astute across a range of subjects. As he contemplated the past hour a bit further, he realized that in his career to date, he had never met anyone quite like Ms. Moore. While he would of course need to speak with Steven, the Chief Marketing Officer position was hers if she wanted it.

Chapter 13

Friday April 2, 2010
Hemet, California

About eight years before Charles' interviews with candidates for the Chief Marketing Officer position, the U.S. economy was finally coming out of the Great Recession. The first quarter of 2010 generated positive growth in GDP and most economists predicted steady GDP expansion throughout the year. The S&P 500 Index rallied during the first three months of 2010. After several difficult years for most types of businesses, U.S. consumers were finally again buying goods and services in greater volumes, from automobiles to travel.

The thermometer passed 100 degrees at 3:00 PM. That was not unusual for this time of year in Hemet, a small town located in the 'inland empire' portion of southern California. It wasn't a rich town by any means, although some of the local business owners were relatively well off, including Bud Simmons. Bud owned the town's Chevrolet dealership, selling mostly pickup trucks to tradesmen, ranchers, and outdoor enthusiasts who enjoyed the nearby San Jacinto mountains.

Bud's foster-child, seventeen-year-old Samantha Moore, arrived home from high school at 5:00 PM following softball practice. She noticed a letter addressed to her on the small table in the foyer of their four-bedroom, three bath ranch-style house. It was from UCLA! Samantha tore open the envelope, reading of her acceptance into the University. She was overjoyed. After being taken from her junkie mother at seven years old and living in five different foster homes over the ensuing ten years, she would finally be able to start living life on her own terms. Her mother had never identified her father, un-sure of which of the many men she slept with while high on meth donated the sperm that helped form Samantha.

Samantha shared the letter with her foster mother, Gayle.

"Honey, I'm really happy for you, but you'll need to discuss that with Bud."

"What are you talking about?"

"As your foster parents, we're only obligated to take care of you to age eighteen."

"Meaning?"

"We don't have to pay for you to attend college. Honey, you know that I'd write a check for you in a minute. You're a hard-working and bright girl. However, Bud controls the money in this household. I've always just been a foster mother. That hasn't been a big source of income. The car dealership is our meal ticket, and Bud controls the car dealership."

"I get it. I'll talk with Bud when he gets home from work."

Samantha left Gayle and went into her room, closing the door behind her. She collapsed onto her bed, crying. She had only been with Bud and Gayle for about 12 months following the divorce of her predecessor foster parents. While she and Gayle had developed a strong bond, Bud was always somewhat distant, and never played the role of a loving father. It was as if Samantha was Gayle's pet, or Gayle's community project.

Samantha knew that, while she was bright, she was unlikely to win enough scholarships and other aid to cover tuition, room, board, and books at UCLA. She also recognized that she had no employment experience at this point, something that never worked out with her being transferred between foster homes. The best part-time job she could get would probably be in fast food or some similar work. That would never generate enough income. She resolved to ask Bud as nicely as she could. If he could at least pay for her freshman year, that would give her some time to apply for more scholarships, financial aid, and student loans; plus earn some money from a part-time job.

Bud didn't arrive home until 6:00 PM. He was accompanied by Jake, the sales manager from the car dealership. They were both covered in sweat, a consequence of selling metal cars parked on asphalt on a bright, sunny day with a temperature in the triple digits.

"Gayle, baby, bring us some cold beers. We're hitting the pool," yelled Bud as he walked through the house.

The backyard featured a pool with a waterfall and a hot tub. As Bud and Jake cooled off under the waterfall, Gayle brought them a cooler filled with iced Millers.

"Great, baby. How about some snacks? Jake, you up for some pigs in a blanket?"

"Sounds good to me," replied Jake.

Gayle popped the frozen food into the oven for warming up. She also prepared a frozen pizza. She knew that the men would be hungry after walking the car lot all day. When the food was ready, she called out to Samantha.

"Samantha, can you help me carry the food out?"

"Sure, Gayle."

Gayle set up the tray of pigs in a blanket next to the shallow end of the pool where the men were now relaxing. Samantha followed her after slicing up the pizza. As Samantha turned to go back inside, Jake spoke.

"Samantha, why don't you put on a swimsuit and join us? It's been a long, hot day. I'd like to hear what you've been up to lately."

"Okay."

Samantha went to her room and put on her white bikini from last swim season. It was a little snug. Samantha had been underfed by the divorced foster parents as a means of increasing their profit from her sponsorship.

By the time she returned to the pool, Jake had lit up a joint.

"Dive in, the water's cool," said Jake.

Samantha dove into the deep end, swimming over to sit on the ledge in the shallow end of the pool.

"Would you like a hit?" asked Jake, extending the joint toward Samantha.

"No thanks."

"I'll take one," said Bud.

He inhaled deeply, followed by a large gulp of beer.

"So, Samantha, what's new?" asked Jake.

"I'll be graduating in about two months. Our softball team has a good chance at making the playoffs."

"Good to hear. You didn't mention a boyfriend."

Samantha looked down at the water, splashing some on her face.

"Not really. It's been tough enrolling in a small high school as an upper classman, especially with a group of kids who've known each other since kindergarten."

"I get that. Makes sense," said Jake. "Anything else going on with you?"

"I was going to mention this later, but since you asked, I got accepted into UCLA today."

"Congratulations," responded Jake.

He looked at Bud, who was simply staring up at the evening sky.

"Bud, what do you think of that?"

"I knew Samantha was sharp, but…"

Samantha stared at Bud, expecting what was about to come next.

"You know we're only committed to supporting you to when you turn 18 in a month. That's when the state money stops and we complete our agreed upon service."

"I understand," said Samantha. "If you could please just help me get started, I'd work hard to get financial aid and work part-time. I'll do everything I can to minimize the burden on you, plus agree to pay you back after I graduate and get a real job. This is a great opportunity for me."

"I appreciate that, but you have to understand that any cash I spend on you is money I won't have available to buy inventory for the new and used car lots – just as demand is rising. Plus, you've only been with us for about a year…"

Samantha's eyes began to well up with tears. While this is how she expected the conversation might proceed, its reality was still painful.

"Don't cry now," said Jake, sliding over to put his arm around her.

On the one hand, Samantha appreciated the comfort. On the other hand, she recognized that Jake had positioned himself tightly against her, from hip to shoulder.

"Maybe there's another solution," said Jake.

Samantha simply turned toward him and listened.

"You'll be eighteen soon. You're an attractive girl. I and a few fellows I know might be willing to pay good money for some attention from you, if you know what I mean."

Samantha leaned forward and looked at Bud, expecting him to say something. He again looked up at the sky, followed by gulping another half-bottle of beer.

Finally, he turned to her and said, "Your decision, darling. You're not getting the money from me."

Chapter 14

Friday March 30, 2018
Emeryville, California

Joseph and Bruce talked nervously on the brief drive from Berkeley to Emeryville. They had an appointment at 4:00 PM with Ken White. Joseph had met Mr. White when he was a guest lecturer in his entrepreneurship class earlier this semester as part of the MBA program. Mr. White was a retired venture capitalist who now filled part of his days with leading a local angel investor group, Soaring Eagle Capital. That entity provided initial funding for conceptual and very early-stage technology companies. Successful investments were typically later passed on to the larger venture capital firms located on the renowned Sand Hill Road in Silicon Valley.

The men pulled their car up to the given address, a relatively non-descript concrete tilt-up building located in an industrial park.

"Joseph, you're the finance guy, so no offense if you take the lead in the conversation."

"I'll do that, so long as you jump in as soon as we are asked about molecular bonding and chemical processes."

"Agreed."

Joseph and Bruce introduced themselves to the receptionist and were led into a conference room. One wall was a large digital whiteboard, a cool new technology that was just beginning to be introduced in the UC Berkeley academic buildings. One other wall contained a large projector screen, with the remaining two walls lined with traditional physical whiteboards.

They were seated for just a few minutes when a man entered, apparently in his mid-60s, with his long hair tied back in a pony tail.

"Good afternoon. I'm Ken White."

"Hello, Mr. White. I'm Joseph Giordano. We met when you recently lectured at UC Berkeley."

"Oh, yes, I remember now."

"My name is Bruce Chu. Thank you for agreeing to meet with us today."

"My pleasure. Please have a seat."

The men positioned themselves around the conference room table, facing the digital whiteboard. Ken took a laptop from the counter and plugged it into the room's network.

"I've reviewed the files you emailed me, including your resumes and the technical schematics. With the proviso that I'm a capitalist, and certainly not a scientist, I'd like to first discuss the summary process illustration."

A diagram of the prototype machine housed in the basement of the University environmental sciences building appeared on the wall.

"My initial observation is that your process contains three key pieces of intellectual property. The first is the agent that facilitates the bonding of the carbon and iron molecules, occurring here at the start of the remediation progression."

The initial tanks of the machine were highlighted on the digital whiteboard.

"Yes, that's correct," replied Bruce.

"But why iron? Why not use magnetite, Fe_3O_4? Magnetite is more magnetically responsive than typical iron oxide.

Wouldn't that improve the efficiency of your process?"

"We considered that. However, magnetite is toxic to the human brain. Therefore, we elected to proceed with a slightly less efficient, but also far less noxious, approach," responded Bruce.

"I wasn't aware of that property of magnetite. Thanks for clarifying that for me," said Ken.

"The second key piece of intellectual property appears to be the particular filters or membranes utilized in the reverse osmosis process between chambers 'B' and 'C'."

The subject portion of the machine was again highlighted on the digital whiteboard.

Ken continued, "If I understand correctly, those membranes must need to be customized to be particularly effective in addressing any contaminants remaining after the magnetic separation of the oil from the water. Off-the-shelf membranes utilized in typical desalinization plants would likely not be adequately effective."

"You're correct, Mr. White," replied Bruce. "The professor spent years of trial-and-error process to develop customized and effective membranes for that segment of the process."

"The third key piece of intellectual property is the reagent added in chamber 'E', along with the determination of the optimal speed for the centrifuges."

"Yes, with the recognition that the amount of centrifugal force can be dynamically adjusted in light of the specific density of the petroleum product being processed."

"That makes sense to me," said Ken.

He then clicked some keys on the laptop, replacing the machine schematic on the whiteboard with an Excel spreadsheet.

"While the final decision in this regard is up to the Soaring Eagle Capital investment committee, this is what I envision from a financial planning perspective. As you can see on the digital whiteboard, the first step of advancing your laboratory testing toward real-world implementation would be to form an S corporation. The second step would be to transfer ownership of the intellectual property to the corporation, including obtaining a release from the professor with whom Bruce has been working. The third step would be to apply for and eventually obtain patent protection for both the individual and the integrated intellectual property components. While those first three steps are being accomplished, you can parallel track by continuing to perform primary research on your remediation process, investigating if the system might be further improved. These first steps, shaded in yellow on the spreadsheet, will likely take three to six months. At the end of that period, you'll still be awaiting patent issuance, but will be ready to commence the second set of steps, highlighted on pale blue on the spreadsheet. Are you following me so far?"

"Yes, we do, Mr. White," replied Joseph. "Everything you've described thus far from a financial planning perspective parallels what I've been taught in the entrepreneurship class."

"Good to hear. I've always been impressed with the UC Berkeley MBA program. Let me now address the pale blue shaded steps. The fourth step is to build a prototype machine at some reasonable scale that can be utilized in real-world testing. The fifth step is to obtain approvals for testing in the open ocean. The sixth step is to actually conduct that testing, carefully measuring and documenting the results."

"That's similar to what I've been thinking," said Joseph. "My primary concern in that regard is obtaining the necessary governmental and regulatory approvals to conduct a test in the ocean by creating a small oil spill."

"I agree with your concern. Fortunately, the members of Soaring Eagle Capital are well-connected at various levels of government. They can facilitate your obtaining the necessary approvals, with that process eased by the vision of the world's having access to effective oil spill remediation in the future."

"I don't want to get too far ahead, but I'll briefly address the subsequent potential steps, highlighted on the spreadsheet in pale green. If the first six steps are all successful and patent protection is obtained, at least in the U.S., but also hopefully in the European Union, you would then proceed to evolve the corporation from a small testing company to a full operating entity. As a full operating company, the corporation could either conduct business by building and selling oil spill remediation machines, simply licensing its intellectual property to larger corporations, and / or producing and marketing the bonding agent, membranes, and reagent we discussed earlier. A comprehensive business plan would of course need to be developed prior to entering into the green shaded steps. Experienced executives would be brought in to manage the operating entity."

"I understand everything you've presented," said Joseph. "If Soaring Eagle Capital is interested in teaming with us, how would we proceed?"

"Typically, we'd initially provide seed capital for the first steps. That capital would be a form of debenture or preferred stock convertible into common stock of the S corporation. In essence, you would be exchanging an ownership interest in the corporation for the combination of the capital plus managerial support from Soaring Eagle Capital. At each subsequent major stage of the development process we discussed, Soaring Eagle Capital would inject more funds into the S corporation in exchange for an increased ownership percentage. If you are successful, the implied valuation of the corporation at each funding stage would increase."

"Mr. White, I'm a bit light in my financial education. Might you be willing to provide me with an example of what you just said?" asked Bruce.

"Certainly. Let me give you a hypothetical example using the spreadsheet. Let's look at the digital whiteboard."

Ken quickly typed various entries into a new Excel spreadsheet.

"As you can see, the first round of funding provides $100,000 in capital in exchange for a ten percent potential ownership interest in the corporation. The implied value of the corporation as a whole is therefore $1.0 million."

Bruce and Joseph nodded their heads.

"Continuing with the hypothetical example, the second round of funding furnishes an additional $100,000, but this time in exchange for just a five percent potential ownership interest in the corporation. The implied value of the corporation as a whole is therefore $2.0 million, equivalent to $100,000 divided by five percent."

"We're following you," said Joseph.

"Just to finish our example, a third round of funding injects a further $200,000, again in exchange for five percent potential ownership interest in the corporation. The implied value of the corporation as a whole is therefore now $4 million. I should note that it is the general policy of Soaring Eagle Capital to not own more than twenty percent of any of our entities selected for investment. We want the principals to be motivated by a strong ownership interest. In addition, while we provide technical, legal, accounting, and managerial support to firms selected for investment, we are by nature investors and not operators of businesses."

"Mr. White, if Bruce and I wish to proceed, what would be the next steps?"

"When do you each complete your degrees?"

"We'll both be wrapped up with our classes, examinations, and other academic requirements, including my thesis defense, by the end of May," replied Bruce.

"The first and most important step is for the two of you to decide whether you want to devote the next, say, two years of your life to this endeavor. You're both well-educated and have many career opportunities. While Soaring Eagle Capital provides some salary to our entrepreneurs, the compensation would be a fraction of what you could each earn working for established companies. In short, is pursuing this remediation technology and forming your own corporation what you most want to do with your lives?"

"We understand what you're saying," said Joseph. "Starting a new venture is an enormous amount of work and is by nature risky. If we're not one hundred percent committed, the probability of success likely declines rapidly."

"That's our experience," responded Ken. "If you two do decide to commit to this endeavor, let me know and I'll assist you in preparing a comprehensive proposal package to our investment committee. If your proposal is approved by that committee, we can inject funding and start the steps we discussed almost immediately. The members of Soaring Eagle Capital have done this many times before, and benefit from an extensive network of attorneys, accountants, and other professionals which can be drawn upon."

Bruce and Joseph then stood, shook Mr. White's hand, and thanked him again for his time and support. Bruce and Joseph talked non-stop on the short drive back to Berkeley, thinking through all of the pros and cons of committing themselves to this undertaking. They agreed to take a couple of weeks to thoroughly contemplate their options, also recognizing that they had a wave of academic work to accomplish in order to complete their degrees.

Chapter 15

Friday April 10, 2009
San Francisco, California

Steven and Veronica had been married for over a year. They moved into their Pacific Heights mansion just months after their wedding and over recent months had settled into somewhat of a routine. This weekend was the first significant break from that pattern. Veronica had flown out this morning with her sister to investigate a potential residential program in Colorado that might benefit Maureen's teenage son. Steven had just closed a significant transaction, selling an Internet security company for four times his purchase price. Steven was particularly proud of himself in this regard. U.S. GDP contracted over four percent in the first quarter of 2009, and the U.S. economy had been suffering through the Great Recession for the past couple of years. Despite this, Steven had been able to earn significant profits through his intense research and dedicated follow-through. He was in the mood to celebrate.

Steven called his college roommate, Vince.

"Hello."

"Hey, buddy, this is Steven. How you doing?"

"Can't complain."

"Say, there's a Black Eyed Peas concert in town tomorrow afternoon. I can score some front row tickets through a source of mine. You interested?"

"I was going to hit one of the local bars that evening, but that's a far better offer. Count me in."

"I'll pick you up at noon. My driver will take us, so we won't have to hassle with parking. We can grab some lunch nearby and then walk over to the venue."

"Sounds great," replied Vince.

....

While Steven and Vince had stayed in touch since their days at San Diego State University, they hadn't spent as much time together once Steven had married. They caught up over lunch, which included several glasses of beer each. The concert was wild, with the screaming fans erupting once the group started playing their hit song *Boom Boom Pow*. The front row seating put Steven and Vince just a few feet from the band members.

About half-way through the concert, the young woman seated next to Vince yelled into his ear over the sound of the music, "You want to share a snort with me?"

Vince nodded affirmatively. A vial of cocaine was passed to Vince, who inhaled, and then passed the vial to Steven. Steven paused for just a moment. He thought, what the hell! We're celebrating today. Steven breathed in a fingerful through his nose and passed the vial back to Vince, who returned it to the young woman.

Following the loud crescendo of the closing set, Vince turned to Steven and suggested, "How about a shot for the road?"

Vince led Steven to a nearby strip club, where they each consumed two shots of a high-end tequila while ogling the dancers. Now approaching his mid-thirties, Steven didn't have the stamina he enjoyed in college. Feeling tired, Steven called his driver to pick them up. Vince was returned to his place, with the men fist-bumping each other over a day well spent. It was 7:00 PM when Steven stumbled into the mansion, completely relaxed, but also feeling randy from the visual stimulation at the strip club.

The evening maid had been hired just a few weeks ago. She had recently legally emigrated from Poland, was in her early twenties, and quite attractive. She was upstairs placing freshly washed and ironed sheets made of Egyptian cotton on each of the beds when Steven saw her. His willpower impaired by the combination of alcohol and cocaine, Steven approached her from behind and wrapped his arms around her breasts. The maid quickly turned around and landed a hard kick into Steven's groin. She then ran out of the room.

....

Veronica thought through her upcoming conversation with Steven as she was driven from the airport to the mansion on Sunday afternoon. The maid had called Veronica on her cell phone following the incident with Steven, describing what had happened, and worrying about possibly losing her job. Despite only being on site for a few weeks, the maid had soon figured out that Veronica was the head of the household. Veronica calmly approached Steven, who was sitting at a desk in the room used as his home office.

"I'm home, Steven."

"How was the trip?"

"It was great spending some time with my sister, although the facilities and the program did not live up to their brochure-ware hype. We concluded that such wasn't a good alternative for her son."

"I'm sorry to hear that."

"Well, I was sorry to hear that you sexually attacked the new maid."

Steven froze. He had no idea that the maid had called his

wife. His recollection of the event was also a bit hazy; a result of his faculties being compromised. He did, however, clearly remember the excruciating pain of receiving a square kick into his testicles. He pursued the best line of argument he could develop on the spot.

"I didn't attack her. I didn't have sex with her. Perhaps there was some misunderstanding, compounded by her limited English language skills."

"Oh, she was quite explicit about your grabbing her from behind and squeezing her breasts."

Steven quickly realized that he would need to pivot his defense.

"Vince and I had a few too many drinks after the concert. I was quite inebriated."

"That's no excuse. You're a grown man, a professional, and well educated. We made a commitment to each other, one that I take very seriously."

Steven hung his head down, not knowing what else to say.

"Let me be perfectly clear, Steven. I recognize that we're both human and will make mistakes from time to time. That said, fidelity is paramount to me. I will never be unfaithful to you. I expect the same from you."

Steven realized that he had no venue other than to throw himself upon his wife's mercy, knowing that she was by nature a kind and warm-hearted person.

"My dear, I'm so sorry. It was a momentary lapse that will never happen again. I love you, and value our marriage above all things. You can count on me."

"I believe in your intent, dear. I pray that we never have a conversation like this again."

Chapter 16

Saturday March 31, 2018
San Francisco, California

At 9:30 PM, Veronica Shaw had just begun to fall asleep, alone in the bedroom. It had been an exhausting, but rewarding, evening. The fundraiser for the new non-profit Veronica formed shortly following the close of the Opticore Products Corporation deal was wildly successful. Not just in terms of money, but also in regard to contacts and building a social network to support the entity's mission of bringing educational choice to the many racial minority and low-income youth condemned to a childhood of inadequate learning under the current public-school regime.

While Steven tried his best to be quiet, he awakened Veronica as he slid into bed just after 10:00 PM.

"Steven, you missed our first fundraiser. We could have used your presence with some of the potential donors. You're so adept at speaking their language."

"I'm sorry, dear. How did it go?"

"The introductory audio-visual presentation was a home run. The lead quote, accompanied by soaring music, set the tone for the entire evening."

"What quote was that?" asked Steven.

"You've heard me say it before:

> *The purpose of education is to give the body*
> *and to the soul all the beauty and all the*
> *perfection of which they are capable.*

Plato

It's one of my favorites."

"I wish work wasn't so demanding right now. I should've been there for you. Getting the new entities launched has been far more challenging than we envisioned."

"Why? You and Charles have formed and capitalized multiple investment entities over the years."

"It's different this time. Since the Fund is focused on Environment, Social, and Governance, or ESG for short, we need to walk the talk, so to speak. Among other criteria, that means presenting a strong diversity and inclusion profile among the management company's employees, particularly the executive team, plus on the Board of Directors."

"I can understand that."

"We've identified a superior female candidate for the Chief Marketing Officer position, although she is of northern European ancestry and apparently heterosexual, so she only checks some of the boxes. In addition, she has countered our job offer by requesting a gratis equity interest in the Fund, to be parsed from my profit-sharing override."

"So, we put up the money. She earns the return?"

"It's a bit more complicated than that; but, in essence, yes."

"Have you ever done that before?" asked Veronica.

"This would be the first time. I'm worried about setting a precedent."

"Why not hire one of the other candidates for the Chief Marketing Officer position?"

"This woman is far and away the best candidate. In fact, we worked together on a transaction about three years ago.

She was high energy and relentless in getting the deal done. I lost track of her afterwards, but she recently interviewed with Charles."

"Is she really that good?"

"After processing over fifty applications and conducting multiple interviews, no other applicant was even close. This is a quite experienced and highly motivated individual."

"Haven't you always said that deciding on the right investment is far more important than the entry price?"

"Good analogy, and leveraging my own words. I've been blessed with a smart wife."

"Thank you, dear."

"There's one other current vexing problem, somewhat similar in nature."

"I'm well awake now. Tell me about it."

"Ideally, we'd fill the Chief Financial Officer positions with a seasoned veteran, likely mid-50's in age and a licensed certified public accountant. That profile provides reassurance to certain potential investors."

"You and Charles know many such professionals."

"True, but none of them are female and African-American. We simply must have minority representation on the executive team."

"Why don't you inject more capital into the management company and use some of such to hire one of those top-drawer executive recruiting firms to locate an individual meeting all of your criteria? You could sweeten the pot by offering a similar equity interest to the CFO as we discussed for the Chief Marketing Officer. That way, the CMO arrangement would not be one-off. You might similarly use one of the elite recruiting firms to source directors for the company."

"We designed the governance structure of the management company to be quite progressive in having a large number of well-regarded and independent directors. That's a leading best practice in the private equity space. It would be even better external optics to have at least one openly gay director."

"That should hardly be difficult to find in San Francisco."

"Both gay and well-qualified. The investments we'll be considering are likely to often be complex in terms of emerging technologies and science. We'll need a well-educated and experienced Board of Directors. With a targeted $30 billion, including debt, to manage, Charles or I simply won't be able to take the lead on every investment evaluation."

"If spending some more money can solve your up-front problems, what does that really matter in the grand scheme of a multi-billion-dollar fund with a seven-year time horizon? Why not therefore provide the compensation packages needed to attract the right executives, and why not pay the white-shoe recruiting firms their admittedly outrageous fees?"

"You're right again. Thank you, dear. Let's get some sleep."

"Good-night, Steven."

"Sweet dreams, my love."

Chapter 17

Friday April 6, 2018
Berkeley, California

Joseph nervously checked the time on his phone. He did not want to be late in meeting Sofia at the bistro / enoteca located on University Avenue in Berkeley. This would be their first one on one date, without the presence of Bruce and Kathi.

Joseph ran the last five blocks, succeeding in entering the bistro exactly at 7:00 PM. Sofia was waiting for him on the bench located in front of the hostess station. He smiled and greeted her, thinking to himself that his decision to sprint was a good one. Thank goodness it was a cool evening, with the fog having rolled in over the Golden Gate bridge, settling as usual above the San Francisco Peninsula and onto the East Bay hills.

Once the hostess seated them, Joseph paused to take in Sofia. She was simply but fashionably dressed, including not wearing high heels. He was pleased that she had suggested dinner at the bistro rather than clubbing; still sensitive about her being so much taller. Sofia had braided her long, dark-blond hair on top and to the side of her head. This allowed greater visibility to the long, silver earrings dangling down about four inches. She wore a French-blue slip dress, with just a hint of cleavage on display.

"Have you eaten here before?" asked Sofia.

The question stirred Joseph from his thoughts. "No, have you?"

"Just once. It's a bit of a different culinary experience. They only serve various *antipasti*, with each one paired to a small glass of a specific wine."

"I don't think I've ever had such a meal. Sounds interesting."

"We'll just need to select, say, three of the *antipasti* from the ten available. Do you have a preference?"

Joseph looked at the list of *antipasti*. He only recognized about half of the names, all of which were in Italian.

Thinking quickly, he responded, "You have a much deeper culinary knowledge than I do. Why don't you choose and I'll simply ride along?"

Sofia smiled. When the waiter approached their table, Sofia caught his eye (not difficult since he was admiring her in the first place).

She said, "We'd like to have the *buffala* with *prosciutto*, the *bruschetta Toscana*, and the mixed *antipasti* plate, plus a bottle of mineral water."

"Excellent. Would you like the water *naturale* or *frizzante*?"

"*Frizzante*, please."

After the waiter had departed, Joseph asked, "Just how Italian are you? I'm sixth-generation, with my relatives forming part of the great emigration wave out of Sicily in the early 1900's. I must admit that I actually know very little about my ancestry and cultural background."

"My *nonna* moved to America in the mid-1950's as a young woman. Her family was from the northern part of Italy, the Veneto. I was fortunate that *nonna* lived with us through all of my childhood. She taught me to speak, cook, and gesture in Italian. In fact, she's still alive today, living in an assisted care facility. She'll be ninety years old next month."

"What a great background! I assume you never went hungry as a child, with a *nonna* in the house?"

"That's a quite accurate assumption!"

Two hours flew by as Joseph and Sofia got to know each other better. The food and wine were excellent. One of the wines, a white wine called *Gavi*, was new even to Sofia. They shared information about their jobs, with Joseph mentioning the career decision that he and Bruce had before them. Sofia explained her work in artificial intelligence and machine learning, although she lost Joseph during her discussion of the envisioned processing power of deep-ultraviolet lithography and seven nanometer semiconductors.

As Joseph was paying the check, Sofia asked, "Would you mind walking me back to the apartment? There can be some crazy people on the streets of Berkeley once the sun sets."

"Of course," replied Joseph.

The apartment was only about six blocks from the restaurant.

Upon arriving, Sofia turned to Joseph and inquired, "Would you like a *digestivo*, perhaps a glass of *Vin Santo*?"

"I'm not certain what that is, but if you recommend it, I'm game."

Sofia ushered Joseph into the apartment she shared with Kathi. It had two bedrooms, one bathroom, a living room, a dining area, and a kitchen. The location was only a couple of blocks from one of the BART train stations, allowing the women to easily travel throughout the Bay Area on public transit.

"Please have a seat on the couch. I'll bring each us a glass of *Vin Santo*, along with some *cantucci*."

Joseph was amazed at the flavor of the dessert wine. The taste was a bit like sherry, but with less alcohol and a richer essence. Sofia explained to him that the *cantucci* was a special type of cookie designed to be dipped into the *Vin Santo* and then eaten as the beverage is sipped. About half-way through the *Vin Santo*, Sofia leaned in towards Joseph and stared into his eyes. Taking the cue, he reached out and drew her into their first kiss. Ten minutes later, they unlocked their lips and paused for a breath of air and another sip of the dessert wine.

Looking again directly into Joseph's eyes, Sofia softly said, "Our generation is so focused on hooking up. Just look at all of the dating apps, most of which are actually hook-up apps."

Joseph simply nodded.

"I want to share that I'm not into hooking up, but rather into relationships. I hope that doesn't disappoint you, Joseph."

"Not at all. Sofia, you're unlike any woman I've ever dated. Well-educated, a computer technology expert, skilled in all things Italian and culinary, and my guess is that I've just scratched the surface."

"That's kind of you to say. I'm also impressed with you, Joseph. What you're contemplating with Bruce is exciting. How many individuals have such an opportunity before their thirtieth birthday?"

After mutual comments about their looking forward to seeing each other again, a final kiss, and a warm embrace, Joseph left Sofia's apartment for the walk to his flat on the north side of the Berkeley campus. He welcomed the cool, night air, as it helped moderate the heat of his body and calm the excitement in his mind.

Chapter 18

Tuesday May 1, 2018
San Francisco, California

At 9:00 AM, a large gong was struck, with the sound echoing to every corner of the 44th floor of the Bank of America building located in the San Francisco Financial District. Most of the Blue Planet Management Company employees and directors were gathered in and around the largest conference room. A few employees and directors who were not able to be present attended via video conference. Steven Shaw approached the microphone and signaled for everyone's attention.

"It gives me great pleasure to announce that today is the marketing launch for the Blue Planet Investment Fund. We received the final legal and regulatory approvals last Friday. All of the applicable documents are now posted on our intranet, accessible by all employees and directors."

A round of applause filled the conference room.

"I am so proud of the mission we have before us. We aim to set an example of prudent and successful ESG investing, benefiting our climate, our society, and our planet, while also providing an attractive rate of return to our investors. I would like to thank all of you for joining in this mission."

Another round of applause followed.

"Many of you have just recently joined the firm. You are encouraged to spend much of today getting to know each other. The better we're acquainted, the more effective we will be. In that regard, I believe our new Chief Financial Officer just arrived from the airport. I'd like to introduce Shantelle

Jones. Shantelle will manage all of the usual accounting, treasury, and tax functions, as well as contributing her substantial financial expertise to our research team. Shantelle, please step forward so everyone, including those on video conference, can see you."

An African-American woman apparently in her mid-50s approached the podium and smiled broadly to the assemblage. As she did this, Steven thought to himself that the outrageous recruiter fee he paid to land Shantelle was worth every penny, as was his giving up an equity interest out of his share as a part of her compensation package. She was a bright and experienced Chief Financial Officer with an excellent reputation among the Big Four accounting firms. She was also unabashedly bisexual, based on her social media postings, and therefore checked the maximum number of diversity boxes via her hire.

"Before we break up to allow you to start the internal networking, let me briefly recap our next steps. Shantelle will lead the internal operation of the management company. Our Chief Marketing Officer, Samantha Moore, will quarterback the solicitation of institutions and accredited investors for investments into our private equity Fund. Charles Winters, our Chief Investment Officer, will manage the research team responsible for evaluating potential investments with the Fund's capital. I will be responsible for the overall coordination of our activities, including with the management company's Board of Directors. Are there any questions at this time?"

A hand was raised toward the rear of the large conference room.

After being acknowledged by Steven, the young man asked, "Is there a minimum and a maximum investment level for the new Fund?"

Steven replied, "Not formally. However, since the Fund is

being marketed only to accredited investors and eligible institutions of various types, in general, we'd anticipate investments to start at a minimum of $1 million, up to a maximum of about $4 billion, with the latter simply to ensure that no single investor can dominate the Fund. That said, if you are fortunate enough to identify an entity interested in investing more than $4 billion, please let me know and I'll happily assist in addressing that!"

Steven then smiled broadly.

"Any other questions?"

The conference room stayed silent, with no hands raised.

"Then, let me close my remarks by thanking you all again for joining in this exciting journey. Blue Planet aims to provide you with a challenging and rewarding professional life, while at the same time visibly benefiting mankind. Let's get started!"

The loudest applause yet filled every corner of the 44th floor. As he was stepping down from the podium, Steven caught Charles' eye. Charles followed him to his office.

"Great opening, Steven. The team appears highly motivated. We should be able to generate some very favorable publicity along the way. That should further enhance employee morale."

"Thank you. Charles, critical path is finalizing the solicitation list for potential investors, and allocating each possible investor to a lead seller. Can you please email me the latest iteration for a final look? I want to ensure that we're best leveraging past relationships and personality profiles. I also want to get my money's worth out of Trent Hawthorne. He charged us a ridiculous amount for his legal review of the Fund offering documents. That's but one reason we've burned through $5 million just to get to this point."

"I understand, and will do."

"Oh, and please ensure that Herman Phillips is assigned to Samantha. He's a tough nut to crack, but his family office must control around $10 billion at this point. I'd like to get him to invest at least $50 million."

"When I think of Herman Phillips, I picture a short version of Clint Eastwood in one of those spaghetti westerns. Tough, quiet, hard as iron, and with an attitude. You're spot on in assigning Samantha to him."

"I just thought of one more thing. Let's get a lunch on the calendar with you, me, Shantelle, and the Managing Director from Huffman Brothers. I think they're the best situated investment bank to lead the syndicate for the leverage line for the Fund."

"I'll follow up with Shantelle and let you know."

"Charles, it's great to be starting another adventure with you."

"Likewise, Steven."

Chapter 19

Saturday May 5, 2018
Berkeley, California

Joseph's iPhone rang as he was walking to Sofia's apartment at just before 6:00 PM. The caller ID indicated that it was Bruce.

"Hello, Bruce."

"Good evening. I reviewed the documents from Ken White and Soaring Eagle Capital. I'm not a guru in that regard, but they looked fine to me. What's your opinion?"

"They followed exactly what I would have expected based upon our visit to Ken a while back."

"Do you think we should identify and evaluate other angel investors?" asked Bruce.

"From what I learned through the MBA program, as confirmed by several conversations with fellow MBA students with backgrounds in this regard, we're getting a straightforward and fair deal from Ken's group. Based upon the professor in my entrepreneurship class, Ken and Soaring Eagle Capital are highly regarded as among the best in the Bay Area."

"The way I'm looking at this, we have some opportunity cost in not taking much better paying positions with established companies. Soaring Eagle Capital is taking hard-dollar investment risk on two rookie entrepreneurs and a cutting-edge technology. You and I still control most of the financial upside, and we can walk at any time. Seems like a good deal to me," opined Bruce.

"I agree. So, I'll email Ken that we'd like to meet next week at his office to execute the required documents?"

"Sounds good. This may be a hell of a roller coaster ride, but at least we're doing it together. I should run now. I've got a busy evening lined up."

"I'll text you after I hear back from Ken," advised Joseph.

"Talk to you later."

"Good-bye."

Joseph arrived at Sofia's apartment just after hanging up. As Sofia opened the door, Joseph was overwhelmed by an intense aroma.

"Wow, what's that smell?"

"I'm cooking *bistecca fiorentina* along with *patate arroste*, Tuscan style."

"I have no idea what you are talking about, but, based upon the scent in this apartment, it's going to be delicious. Oh, and I brought a bottle of wine."

As Joseph presented the bottle of wine to Sofia, her face lit up.

"Why Joseph, how did you know about *Vino Nobile di Montepulciano*? In fact, that will pair perfectly with the dinner."

"I'll confess to having placed myself and my credit card at the mercy of the proprietor of a local wine shop."

"Please have a seat at the table and open the wine. Dinner will be ready in just a few minutes."

The meal was delicious. An hour of conversation flowed by without a single awkward pause. Joseph shared that he and Bruce had decided to take the plunge and pursue starting their own company to advance the technology that Bruce had been working on with the professor. Sofia told him about some of the latest developments at her firm. They also discussed their family backgrounds and shared stories of their college experiences. After the main course was eaten, Sofia motioned to the couch. Some *biscotti* and a small bottle and two glasses were positioned on the nearby coffee table.

"Have you ever had *passito*?"

"I don't believe so. What is it?"

"It's a very special Italian dessert wine, only made during years when the *sagrantino* grapes in the Italian province of Umbria display just the right characteristics. It's a bit like a port, but with less alcohol and a richer overall taste. It's one of my favorites."

The *digestivo* was heavenly. After a few sips, Sofia slid closer to Joseph. They kissed, at first slowly, and then progressively more intensely. As they paused for a moment, Sofia smiled, looked into Joseph's eyes, and slowly began to unbutton her blouse.

Observing this, Joseph's pulse rate quickened further. He took another sip of the *passito* in an effort to calm himself.

"I thought you wanted to wait."

"I think I've waited long enough."

She unclasped her bra and pulled Joseph toward her. It wasn't long before they were deep into foreplay.

Looking up for a moment, Joseph realized that he was naked in the middle of the apartment's living room.

He whispered, "What if Kathi walks in?"

"Don't worry. Based upon what I saw Kathi pack in her duffle bag this afternoon, she won't be home tonight. Bruce should be a happy man tomorrow."

Chapter 20

Friday June 1, 2018
San Francisco, California

Veronica was reading in bed at 9:45 PM when Steven arrived home. This had become a regular pattern over the past week. Her husband departed for the office no later than 7:30 in the morning and had not been returning until sometime after 9:00 PM.

"Steven, are you okay? You've been putting in a huge number of hours recently. I'm worried about you. You could develop high blood pressure, or worse."

Steven gave his wife a light kiss on the cheek.

"I appreciate your concern. The marketing of the new Fund is not proceeding well. We're a month into the solicitation, and we've only secured external investment commitments of $3 billion, far from our $16 billion goal."

"Why do you think that is? You certainly have an excellent track record with the prior closed-end funds."

"I may have been too far ahead of the curve in initiating an Environment, Social, and Governance oriented fund. Or, I may have been too greedy in setting the annual management fee and profit-sharing formulas too much in my favor. Or, both."

"Can you change any of that to facilitate the solicitation?"

"That would be difficult at this point. We have all of the offering documents approved and have already been marketing based on those. It would take some time and money to change course. However, the worst aspect of such a change would be the appearance of having made a mistake in the first place. The capital markets aren't forgiving and tend to have a long memory."

"I understand what you've said. How about that Chief Marketing Officer you hired? I believe you described her as an outstanding candidate."

"She's been actively following up on our list of potential investors, with some successes to date. Just not enough so far. Charles and I are meeting with her Monday morning to strategize."

By this point in the conversation, Steven had climbed into bed. Veronica rolled over and rested her head on his shoulder.

"Steven, not to burden you, but there's something I promised Maureen I would discuss with you."

"Okay."

"Might you be able to hire my nephew to work at the management company?"

"I thought Billy had his heart set on programming computer games."

"He did. However, he hasn't gotten past the first interview with five different companies. You know that he was never able to finish college. That, combined with his limited social skills, has prevented him from getting hired."

Both Veronica and her sister Maureen suffered from endometriosis, a genetically inherited physical condition that rendered becoming pregnant very difficult. That was why Veronica and Steven did not have children. Maureen had undertaken extensive medical treatments to be able to conceive despite the condition, with one pregnancy achieved. That pregnancy was a difficult one, with Maureen assigned to bed rest beginning in her fifth month. Despite excellent medical care, Billy was born two months prematurely, with what was later diagnosed as a form of autism.

After a pause to reflect, Steven continued, "I'm sorry to hear that. I've enjoyed Billy's visits over the years, especially once he got through early adolescence. But what work could he possibly perform at the management company?"

"Can't you create a make-believe job somewhere in the organization? Billy needs to feel valued and have a purpose. He likely wouldn't be treated well by someone who is not family. You know that he's not stupid, just interpersonally awkward, while also challenged in dealing with new situations."

"Would we have to pay him?" asked Steven.

"I think he should be paid the same as other employees with the same level of nominal responsibility. He shouldn't be singled out because of the family relationship or due to his autism," replied Veronica.

After they both pondered for a few moments, Veronica added, "Of course, this has nothing to do with money per se. In fact, the attorney for my mother's estate called today. The assets in Sandra's trust should be distributed to my and Maureen's trusts by the end of the year. The trustee evidently managed mom's trust very effectively. Even after federal estate taxes, Maureen and I should each receive over $100 million. Billy will be a beneficiary of Maureen's estate, and she is currently establishing a separate trust to ensure that there is always someone looking out for Billy's best interest. However, Billy needs to have a life."

"I'll brainstorm with Charles about this on Monday and see what we can come up with."

"Thank you, dear."

Veronica hugged Steven before rolling over to sleep.

Chapter 21

Monday June 3, 2018
San Francisco, California

Steven walked through the main entrance to Blue Planet Management Company at 7:45 AM. He immediately went to Charles' office. Upon entering, he saw Charles at his desk with two large blueberry muffins and a venti coffee in front of him.

"Good morning, Charles."

"You look particularly tense for so early in the day."

"I'm becoming increasingly concerned about the slow pace of investment commitments to the Fund. Are we still meeting with Samantha at 8:00?"

"Yes, in the small conference room. I'll meet you there in a few minutes."

As Steven turned to exit the office, Charles took a large bite of the baked good, followed by a long drink of the coffee. He knew he'd need energy for the upcoming conversation.

Samantha Moore opened the door to the small conference room right on time at 8:00 AM. Both Steven and Charles noted her appearance. She was of course dressed professionally, although her skirt was a tad short and her blouse a bit tight around the bust. She smiled at the men with her perfect and dazzling white teeth.

"Good morning, Samantha. Please have a seat," said Charles.

"Samantha, we know you're well aware of the marketing status of the new Fund. After a month of sales effort, we're still below twenty percent of the targeted external raise. We're here this morning to strategize."

"I was planning on calling a meeting with you two about this, if you hadn't done so. The company has excellent connections, an outstanding call list, and favorable external optics. However, the ESG concept is proving to be a difficult sell to the larger institutions and higher net worth individuals. To be direct, they're having difficulty committing significant capital to the pursuit of environmental and social good. They're typically signing up for small investments, likely because of the prior relationships with Steven and / or for political correctness. However, there's been a consistent pattern of their being unwilling to pledge a more significant portion of their assets. In addition, the management fee and profit-sharing structure of the Fund hasn't helped."

"I've been concerned that we're ahead of our time with the ESG concept. Also, in hindsight, we got too greedy in establishing our revenue terms," said Steven. "Where do you think we should go from here?"

"I see three alternatives," replied Samantha. "First, we can down-market the Fund to smaller institutions and more accredited individual investors who would likely be more receptive to the ESG story, on purely emotional grounds. That approach would require more time and expense to raise capital, with the aggregate funding still likely to fall below target. However, that's a viable approach to improve the situation."

"That makes good sense to me," opined Charles.

"The second alternative is to pre-identify some of what I'll call sexy prospective investments, the type of companies or technologies that would spur interest in the Fund. An example would be a company with a solution to solid-state energy storage, thereby advancing by years the electrification of the transportation industry. We'd have to be careful how we proceed in this regard to stay within the bounds of the security laws and otherwise avoid potential litigation."

"I see where you're going with that. Perhaps we could execute some conditional purchase or investment agreements with such opportunities, with the subject contracts being contingent upon the closure of the Fund," said Charles.

"I don't see any downside to that, other than we'd need to accelerate some investment decisions, perhaps making some with less than complete information," added Steven. "Samantha, what's your third alternative?"

"We all know that individuals operating in corporate or fiduciary capacities are by nature conflicted by their own personal considerations. We could take advantage of that innate situation in carefully selected marketing."

Both Steven and Charles immediately understood what Samantha was saying. They had trod that path in prior financial transactions over their many years together

After the men looked at each other for a few moments, Steven turned to Samantha and said, "Might you take a few minutes to get yourself a cup of coffee?"

Samantha exited the conference room and proceeded to pick up a cup of coffee in the lunchroom. She then sat at her desk. She recalled her difficult childhood, including the mean and selfish foster parents who meted out food to both control her and maximize their earnings from her sponsorship. Her thoughts then drifted to the trade-off she made to be able to attend UCLA. While some of the men were considerate, more than a few were aggressive, demanding, and rough. Looking out the window from her office at the city view, she was further determined to build a much better life for herself - one with wealth and the power and flexibility that accompanied it. If she was successful in this role at Blue Planet, the next stop on her career journey would be as a principal with a hedge fund or a private equity firm. Events were now teed up for her, particularly if she read Steven and Charles correctly with regard to their level of commitment to Blue Planet's success.

After Samantha departed the small conference room, Steven turned to Charles and said, "Do we need to consider reinvigorating Atlas? It worked well for us on the Newmont deal."

"I was perhaps naively hoping that we wouldn't have to go there again."

Charles paused and stared up at the ceiling.

He then continued, "However, we can't proceed with just $3 billion in external investment given the forecast cost structure, not to mention the adverse reputational impact of missing our targeted raise by so much. Atlas worked before. Samantha is sharp and aggressive. I have no doubt that she could execute. I also believe that we can trust her, for three reasons. First, she has a significant personal financial stake in our success. Second, the performance of the Fund is key to her career ambitions. Finally, and this is admittedly less grounded, my perception of her personality is that she recognizes the long-term value of being able to keep certain matters confidential."

Charles paused. The two men stayed silent for several minutes while they contemplated the recent discussion.

"I agree with what you've said, and she did bring up the topic," replied Steven, with a sigh and some lingering reluctance in his voice. "Let me call Samantha back in."

Samantha returned, sitting patiently at the conference room table, waiting to hear from the men. Steven spoke first.

"Samantha, we believe each of your three alternatives to be valid and worth pursuing. If you'll lead on the first proposal, Charles will quarterback the second. With regard to your third suggestion, we'll make an offshore entity called Atlas available to you. Atlas will be initially funded with $5 million. Of course, no mention of Atlas will occur in conjunction with the management company or the Fund. For plausible deniability, you are not to inform Charles or me of any aspect of your work with Atlas. The only future communication among us in this regard will be if Atlas needs more funding. Do you clearly understand what I am saying?"

"Absolutely, Steven. I'm hardly a virgin of the financial markets."

Steven motioned for Samantha to exit. After she had again left the room, he turned to Charles.

"I'll initiate a funds transfer from selected accounts within my family office. We'll wash the funds as before through the intermediate Azure Sky LLC maintained by the lawyer in Chicago. He'll take his usual ten percent cut and forward the funds to Atlas in the Cayman Islands. He'll also create all of the requisite synthetic documentation for both sides of the funds transfer."

"Agreed. That process worked well in the past," replied Charles.

Steven reached over to the counter, opened a bottle of water, and took several gulps to moisten his throat.

"Not to bury you, Charles, but I have one more request this morning, courtesy of my wife."

"You know that I would do anything for you and Veronica. How can I help?"

"We need to give Veronica's nephew, Billy, a make-believe job in the management company. He's autistic, with a deficit in social skills. We'd need to isolate him from the other employees to the extent possible. Any ideas?"

Charles took a deep breath, leaned back in his chair, and stared out the window for a few minutes.

"We could give him one of the empty offices on the 45th floor, and have him report directly to me. Our funds always attract an avalanche of unsolicited, and typically poor, potential investments from various outside sources. Most of these opportunities have been declined many times before by other investors, with the principals broadly distributing their PowerPoint decks in the hope of finding that one fool. We could task Billy with reviewing these voluntary submissions and writing recommendations to me. He wouldn't need to interface with anyone else in the company. We could well appoint his office and assign him secretarial support by someone aware of the overall situation."

"Charles, I'll again say that you're brilliant. I'll discuss your idea with Veronica later this week and circle back to you."

Chapter 22

Saturday June 23, 2018
Saratoga, California

Samantha Moore organized her thoughts on the drive south from San Francisco to the posh town of Saratoga, home to many of Silicon Valley's billionaires. Charles and Steven had directed her to follow up with Herman Phillips. The initial Fund investment submission by Herman was for just $25 million, a rounding error for someone whose family office managed $10 billion. While Charles and Steven provided a profile of Herman largely centered around the Clint Eastwood tough, ornery cowboy image, Samantha had spent her entire day yesterday tapping all of her sources for additional information. Herman was the only child of a family descended from one of the barons who organized and then controlled much of the commerce in the Golden State in the latter half of the 1800's. His ancestors also included a former Governor and one of the early, and successful, miners in the 1849 Gold Rush. His wife of forty years died five years ago after a long fight against breast cancer. He lived alone, except for a swath of servants, in a mansion ideally positioned on the hills above the center of the town.

Using the navigation system in her BMW, Samantha located the gated entrance to the estate. After confirming her identity through the security system, the dual ornate, wrought iron gates swung open, revealing a long driveway lined with cypress trees. She followed the driveway over a rise to the courtyard in front of the mansion. Leaving her three duffel bags in the trunk, Samantha approached the front door, which was opened upon her arrival by a suitably attired butler. It was 2:00

PM, the time of her appointment.

"Good afternoon, madam. I'll show you to the drawing room. Mr. Phillips will join you shortly. Might I bring you a beverage?"

"A glass of iced tea would be wonderful. Thank you."

As the butler left the drawing room, he commented to himself that Mr. Phillips would welcome this guest. She was pretty and dressed in form fitting skirt with a long slit up the side. The skirt and the matching short jacket were made of silk dyed a rich azure. The more lightly colored blouse was a fine fabric, drawn tightly around her bust with just a hint of cleavage at the top.

A few moments after Samantha took a seat in an ornate wing-backed chair, a man of about seventy years in age and about 5'6" tall entered the room.

"Hello, I'm Herman Phillips."

"Thank you again for taking the time to see me, Mr. Phillips."

"You were quite insistent, and I've profited handsomely from some of Steven's prior ventures. What would you like to discuss?"

"Well, Mr. Phillips, to be direct, we were a bit disappointed to see your investment indication for the new Blue Planet Investment Fund."

"Out of respect for Steven, I agreed to participate. However, I would also like to be direct in that I don't see the logic in this whole ESG concept. My family has invested for generations based upon cash flow and total rate of return. Why, at age seventy-two with no children, should I invest for racial justice or the environment? I'm not convinced of this whole global warming issue. Even if I were, I'll be long dead before it would become my problem."

The butler arrived with Samantha's glass of ice tea, along with a fresh squeezed lemonade for Mr. Phillips and a plate of assorted cookies. This gave Samantha a moment to calculate her options. It was clear that she could likely not sell Herman on any aspect of the ESG movement. It was also evident that he could not be swayed by any resources from Atlas. That left her with only one avenue of attack.

"Mr. Phillips, you know that Mr. Shaw has never failed to provide compelling returns to his investors. In fact, based upon that track record, my personal financial package is highly dependent upon the scale and success of the Fund. I'd be willing to share evidence of my high level of motivation with you this afternoon, optimized for your preferences. If you found that worthwhile, we could arrange future such occurrences, perhaps as a sort of periodic performance review for your increased investment in the Fund."

Herman cocked his head and exhibited just a hint of a wry smile.

"Ms. Moore, this is hardly the first time I've received such a proposal. Why is yours any different?"

"I work harder and do more research than my competitors, so to speak. I believe you will be highly impressed with what I have developed through my advance preparation. What harm is there in a preliminary review?"

Herman paused to consider the situation. She was quite attractive. He had been lonely in recent months, and it had been a while since he had enjoyed the pleasures of a woman. While he usually refused such enticements, she was associated with Steven, and as such was likely to conduct herself properly afterwards.

"I accept your offer. I'll have the butler show you upstairs."

Samantha asked the butler to wait while she retrieved one of the duffel bags from the trunk of her car. She was then escorted to a large bedroom with its own bathroom. The bedroom was centered around a king-sized bed with a four-post canopy carved from some evidently rare wood. The bathroom was finished with a white marble that Samantha identified as likely sourced from northern Italy. She took the duffel bag into the bathroom.

When she emerged from the bathroom, Herman was sitting on the edge of the bed. His eyes quickly opened wide. Samantha was dressed as a dominatrix. She wore black leather boots that rose to above her knees, with a matching black leather thong and long black leather gloves. A belt of similar material was around her waist. Attached to the belt were whips, handcuffs, and leather ties. The outfit was completed with a black Cat Woman-style mask and a short black leather bustier that was two sizes too small for her ample breasts.

Samantha cracked the largest whip.

"Mistress orders you to disrobe quickly. If you delay, your punishment will only increase."

At 5:00 PM on the return drive north, Samantha called Steven on the hands-free Bluetooth in her BMW.

"Hello Samantha. What's up?"

"I wanted to report that Mr. Phillips will be in for $100 million."

"That's four times his initial indication! How did you accomplish that from such a taciturn old man?"

"Let's just say that I'm very good at reading personalities. I figured out exactly how to communicate with him."

"Well done. I'll update Charles. See you Monday morning."

"Good-bye."

Chapter 23

Sunday July 15, 2018
San Francisco, California

Steven was home to share dinner with Veronica this evening. Such occurrences had recently become rare due to Steven's preoccupation with Blue Planet. As they ate in the dining room of their mansion in the tony Pacific Heights neighborhood, served by Frederick, Veronica led the conversation.

"Steven, you seem to have been in a better mood the past week or so."

"I'm sorry that I've been so focused on the marketing and upcoming formal launch of the Fund. It's been far more challenging than I anticipated. However, the pace of pledged subscriptions has picked up recently. The Chief Marketing Officer is showing results."

"I remember that you were confident in her hire."

"It's impressive how much a highly motivated individual can accomplish."

After they each ate a bit more, Veronica posed a query.

"You never really explained to me why you want us to amass so much money. You've been working terribly long hours, while at the same time my trust contains more wealth than we could ever spend. I can't imagine that many similarly positioned people would follow the path you've taken."

Steven took a long drink of the *Barolo* wine that they were having with dinner. He didn't want to admit to his wife that he wanted to be wealthy on his own, distinct from her inherited assets. That focus was an outgrowth of his painful teenage years, when he promised himself that he'd have the power to control his own destiny, no matter what. So, Steven proceeded to share his other motivation.

"Have you ever really listened to many of our members of Congress speak? In more than a few cases, their brains apparently died years ago, living on in their zombie bodies. I don't think they can put more than three sentences together in a coherent thought."

"That's a brutal representation! However, I will agree that politicians should have an expiration date and that many politicians at all levels of government appear devoid of real-world experience and common sense. It's ridiculous what my nonprofit has to do simply to grant money for the benefit of poor children."

"Exactly. It will take large sums of money, and a pool of like-minded individuals, to change the social and political direction of this country for the better."

"Are you contemplating trying to guide one political party or the other?" asked Veronica.

"Not per se. Rather, I'm thinking of an approach where we use many of the new media channels to uncover and shine a light on the idiocy of the really bad ideas, thus avoiding the most systemically damaging actions."

"Can you give me an example?" asked Veronica.

"Let's take the concept of universal basic income or UBI. That idea is currently being pushed by some California politicians. UBI deprives individuals of the pride of work and self-reliance, while moving the state toward socialism. Socialism has failed in every country where it has been tried over the past one hundred years. Just look at the shambles of Venezuela today despite their incredible oil resources. Yet, too many naïve individuals continue to promote destructive socialistic policies. I want to expose the stupidity; and bend the policy curve for the benefit of future generations."

"I think I understand what you're saying," replied Veronica. "Take the money targeted for UBI and instead use it to promote and encourage work and the development of marketable skills. Give the individuals a future other than being dependent on the government."

"Precisely."

"Steven, you know that I support your vision. In my own way, I've behaved somewhat similarly, redirecting my disappointment at not being able to conceive towards helping the children of others. I also want a better future for our country, and the world. Since we can't leave behind progeny, we can pass our values into the future via the institutions we fund and the individuals we financially support."

They paused to each eat a few bites.

"Darling, I'm glad we had this conversation," said Veronica.

"Me too," responded Steven.

Chapter 24

Friday August 31, 2018
On the California Coast Outside the Golden Gate Bridge

Bruce nervously checked every aspect of the prototype. The past three months had been a blur. He and Joseph worked seven days a week starting in late May to rapidly complete the steps outlined in their initial meeting with Ken White. The professor who began the research had also devoted countless hours to the project, wanting to secure an intellectual legacy.

The planned S corporation, Environmental Remediation, Inc., was formed, patents applied for, and the prototype constructed in marine warehouse space rented at the Berkeley Marina. The principals of Soaring Eagle Capital had been instrumental in assisting Bruce and Joseph, particularly with regards to obtaining governmental permits for today's testing. A total of $500,000 had been invested into the S corporation by the angel group in return for a twenty percent ownership interest. About thirty percent of that funding was associated with today's events. In addition to the permit fees, the men arranged to rent a large floating barge that was normally used for responding to natural disasters. If a hurricane devastated a coastal area, the barge could be floated to near the shore to provide emergency assistance. The barge contained three 2,000-kilowatt diesel generators, each the size of a semi-truck. The generators were wired to activate in phases as needed to supply the amount of required electricity. The barge also contained huge tanks for various types of liquid, including gasoline, diesel, and potable water. Each tank was connected to a high-capacity pump, with hundreds of yards of color-coded tubing strapped to one side. The prototype, about three times the size of the machine in the laboratory, was secured to a portion of the barge normally used to store emergency pallets of food, medicine, and clothing. A tugboat hired for the day pulled the barge.

Accompanying the tugboat and barge were three smaller boats. These carried the booms and dispersant historically used in the event of an oil spill, as a back-up in case the prototype testing was not successful. A professional videographer was hired to record the testing from start to finish. Ken White was positioned at the top of the tugboat, while Bruce and Joseph rode on the barge. All involved wore brightly colored vests with life jackets and LED signal lights.

The ocean swells were mild compared to those typical in the winter months – only averaging three to four feet today. Despite this, both Bruce and Joseph were nauseous as they discussed the events about to commence. The barge was rolling from side to side and also up and down. At one point in their conversation, Joseph ran to the side of the barge and vomited loudly. After he returned and rinsed his mouth out with some bottled water, he continued their discussion.

"We've been through the checklist twice. Can you think of anything we might have missed? Given the expense, we likely won't be able to afford a second chance at this."

"I've racked my brain. I can't identify anything we've missed. We'll know the answer in about an hour," opined Bruce.

Workmen on the small boats radioed to the barge. Bruce gave the okay to start. The small boats laid out the booms in a circle with a diameter of about twenty yards. The tugboat positioned the portion of the barge containing the prototype adjacent to the circle. Following a final radio confirmation, one of the small boats started pouring a standard forty-two-gallon barrel of crude oil into the circle. Once that was finished, Bruce radioed to a second of the small boats to commence dispersing the powder containing the iron and the bonding agent. Two drums of the powder were spread inside the area surrounded by the booms.

Bruce then activated the prototype. Two retired Navy seamen operated a swing boom on the side of the barge. The open end of a twelve-inch diameter, flexible plastic pipe was suspended from the boom and inserted into the oil spill. The other end of the plastic pipe was connected to the prototype. A pump quickly began filling chamber 'A' with the mixture of crude oil, seawater, iron, and the bonding agent. Once chamber 'A' was about fifty percent full, Bruce radioed to the boom operators to pause. He then flipped a switch that initiated the electromagnetic field. Just as in the laboratory, the dark fluid rose to the top half of chamber 'A', suspended by the magnetic field, while the salt water remained on the bottom. Bruce then opened the valve to chamber 'B', allowing the salt water to drain out. After closing that valve, he opened the valve and initiated the pump between chamber 'B' and chamber 'C'. This pump forced the salt water under high pressure through the specially designed membranes utilized in the reverse osmosis process. The oil mixture continued to be suspended by the electromagnetic field in chamber 'A'.

"How's it looking so far?" yelled Joseph.

It was quite loud between the operation of the prototype, the diesel generators, and assorted other machines.

"Looking good," shouted Bruce, as he brought the pump moving the salt water from chamber 'B' to chamber 'C' to maximum throughput.

Once the desalinated water filled much of chamber 'C', another pump was activated to move the fluid into chamber 'D' for chlorination.

Ken White radioed from the tugboat.

"How's it going? I'm watching the barge with binoculars, but I can't see everything clearly."

"No surprises so far," said Bruce loudly into his walkie-talkie.

Bruce continued with the planned sequence. He next turned off the electromagnetic field and activated a pump to transfer the recovered oil mixture from chamber 'A' to chamber 'E'. Opening a lid on the top of chamber 'E', he poured in a generous amount of the reagent. After that, the motors creating the centrifugal force were turned on. While the centrifuge itself had been properly balanced in advance on shore, there was a notable amount of vibration caused by the combination of the rise and fall and changing pitch of the barge on the ocean swells and the operation of the centrifuge. It was now too noisy for Bruce and Joseph to communicate, other than by yelling directly into each other's ear. After about ten minutes, Bruce opened the valve to chamber 'F' while also activating the subject pump. This transferred the oil into chamber 'F', while leaving the iron powder and the remains of the bonding agent and the reagent in chamber 'E'. A panel at the bottom of chamber 'E' was opened, allowing the contents to fall into a container.

The overall process was repeated. After the second suction of the oil spill out of the ocean, there was no visible oil remaining within the circle of booms. The prototype was turned off. The diesel generators shut down. The men on the third boat applied a small amount of traditional oil dispersant into the area, solely as an abundance of caution. The booms were then collected, and the aggregate team began the return trip to the Berkeley Marina.

As they rode the barge back under the Golden Gate Bridge, Bruce and Joseph started documenting their initial assessment of the testing into their laptops. This information would be supplemented by the recording from the videographer, and by more advanced chemical analysis of the contents of the various chambers once they returned to shore. They began by drinking a glass of water from chamber 'D'. It tasted delicious, and without a trace of saltiness, in fact still chilled because of the temperature of the ocean water that far north. After that, they inspected chamber 'F'. Based upon the markings on the side of the chamber, about 40 gallons of dark fluid were present. At this point, they could not determine the exact composition of that fluid. The follow-up chemical testing would ascertain that.

Once they were within cell phone range as they entered San Francisco Bay, Ken called Bruce. They discussed the preliminary observations. Ken expressed his enthusiasm with how smoothly the testing had proceeded.

It would be late evening before the prototype was lifted back into the marine warehouse by a shoreside crane. The truck from the chemical testing company was scheduled to arrive on Monday. Bruce and Joseph each collapsed into bed that evening, followed by sleeping much of the weekend.

Chapter 25

Steven, Charles, and Samantha stayed late at the offices of Blue Planet Investment Management. After all of the other employees had departed for the weekend, they met in the large conference room.

"What's the latest pledge tally?" asked Steven.

Samantha replied, "Just over $4 billion external, with a potential additional $3 billion in the pipeline based upon the latest sales reports."

Steven did not even try to hide his disappointment. Four months into the marketing for the Investment Fund, and they had only received commitments for twenty-five percent of the planned external capital raise. Keeping the marketing period open for much longer would present the appearance of failure, which in turn could endanger the funding commitments they had received to date. The excuse of the newness of the ESG concept could only buy them so much time with their targeted investor base.

"Is there anything else we can do?" inquired Steven. "We have to conclude the marketing period by the end of September."

"I could accelerate some of the initial investment research and negotiation of conditional purchase agreements," responded Charles. "It's a small world. Even without any publicity on our part, word will circulate about the deals we have lined up."

"I agree with that. Let's push in that direction. Anything else?"

"We could request Shantelle to twist the arms at Huffman Brothers to increase our margin ratio. The offering documents allow margin up to seventy-five percent, not that we could likely ever get that ratio given the illiquidity of some of the ESG related investments," expressed Charles.

"Good idea. I'll speak with Shantelle about that first thing on Monday," said Steven.

A look of concern filled Samantha's face.

"Won't that aggressively compound our risk profile? Some of the Fund's likely investments are in and of themselves fairly high risk, comprising cutting edge technology. By pushing the leverage over fifty-percent, aren't we essentially doubling-down on our bet?"

"That's mathematically correct. However, we need sufficient scale to pursue some of the prospective investments. Frankly, we also need enough size to enable an adequate return on the organizational costs," responded Steven.

Steven did not mention that the establishment of the entities and the operation of the management company over the past six months, including rent, recruiter fees, leasehold improvements, technology investment, personnel costs, and funding Atlas had consumed a notable percentage of what he termed *his money*. Most of his and Veronica's collective net worth was associated with Veronica's trust. That trust held title to their mansion and most of their other assets of meaningful value. *His money* was comprised of funds earned over the years from his compensation and management company income. While Veronica's trust would be the largest investor in the new Fund, it would not be available to pay for organizational and operational costs. This was the arrangement he and

Veronica had maintained for years. In fact, he had no legal authority whatsoever over Veronica's trust. That authority was reserved to the professional trustees employed by the Hopkins family for decades.

"Is there anything else we can do over the next month to bring this over the finish line?" asked Steven.

After an extended silence, Samantha spoke.

"Add $3 million to Atlas. Everyone has a price. In particular, I think we can pick up some union pension fund money by motivating the right officers."

"Steven, has there been any indication to date that Shantelle or the Board of Directors has become aware, even indirectly, of our use of the funds from Atlas?" interjected Charles.

"None that I know of. My experience is that individuals who accept bribes are highly motivated to their mouths shut."

"So, are we a go on pumping up Atlas?" again inquired Samantha.

Steven looked at Charles, who nodded affirmatively. Steven then did the same.

Chapter 26

Friday September 7, 2018
Emeryville, California

At 3:00 PM, Bruce and Joseph were driving together for a follow-up meeting with Ken White at his offices in Emeryville.

"Bruce, you'll first walk Ken through the results we just received from the testing company."

"Got it."

"I'll then bring up a discussion of potential next steps and related financial considerations, if Ken does not do that himself."

"Agreed. I don't think I've ever been this nervous and excited at the same time," said Bruce.

Once the three men were seated in the conference room with the digital whiteboard, Ken led the conversation.

"I must say that the prototype testing last week was quite an experience. The huge barge, a tugboat, and three other boats outside of the Golden Gate Bridge – that was one hell of an operation. I reviewed the preliminary file from the videographer. With some further refinement, I think it will present a compelling story."

"We agree. Perhaps we can pool our feedback to the videographer in finalizing the file. Then, we can post it to a confidential YouTube Channel for easy access," said Joseph.

"Sounds good. Did you receive the final testing results?" asked Ken.

"An email arrived with the last set of test results just this morning," said Bruce. "Let me run through all of them. The desalinated water was potable, in fact superior to that of some municipal water systems. There was a small presence of iron, at far below toxic levels. We could likely eliminate that residual presence by further refinement of the membranes, along with variation in the pressure and temperature inherent in the desalinization process. Worst case, we could pass the desalinated water through a magnetic field to capture the residual iron."

"That makes sense to me, although I'll again admit that I'm a capitalist, not a scientist," replied Ken.

"If you watch the video carefully, you'll see that Bruce and I drank a glass of the desalinated water while still on the barge. We thought it tasted pretty good," interjected Joseph.

Bruce then continued, "The recaptured oil collected after the reagent and centrifuge stage totaled 39 gallons, or 92.9% of the initial 42-gallon barrel. A chemical analysis of that oil displayed that 97.0% of the content was inherent to oil; in other words, carbon, hydrogen, nitrogen, oxygen, and sulfur molecules. The other 3.0% was an assortment of molecules from the sea water, the bonding agent, and the reagent. The testing company concluded that the recaptured crude was suitable for refining. Multiplying the aforementioned two percentages together, we successfully recaptured a bit over ninety percent of the oil."

"That's impressive. A far better environmental result than traditional approaches to oil spill remediation," noted Ken.

Ken then hooked a laptop up to the digital whiteboard.

"Let's talk about our options at this point. The first thing I thought about on the way back from last week's testing is that commercialization of your technology is going to be very capital intensive. That was certainly evident in the amount of equipment used for remediating just one barrel of oil. That makes inherent sense to me. The petroleum industry is one of the most capital-intensive on the planet. Oil spills can create significant financial liabilities for oil companies, so they might not blink when considering the application of your technology on a macro scale. I'll say right up front that Soaring Eagle Capital is not in a position to provide that volume of funding."

"We understand that, as well as your firm's already being at its designated maximum twenty percent ownership interest," replied Joseph.

"Therefore, we can help you solicit a capital source that could provide the necessary volume of financing for commercial application of your technology, whether that be a large venture capital firm or an oil company. However, in furnishing that level of capital, they would inevitably demand a majority ownership interest in the S corporation."

"We would essentially become employees of a large entity with some small level of retained ownership interest," said Joseph.

"That's likely the case. Maybe with no ownership interest whatsoever, but with some type of profit participation, incentive compensation, and / or stock options," presented Ken.

Joseph and Bruce nodded to signal their understanding.

Ken then continued, "As another alterative, you could seek to license your technology to various parties following the confirmation of your patent applications. You'd have to wait a while for the confirmations, and that process would largely be driven by attorneys with a specialization in intellectual property. You'd also need to identify a further funding source to carry you through this process, which would of course demand an equity interest, although likely a smaller one than an entity fronting the funds for full-scale commercialization. My firm could also help you in these regards."

"While that makes business sense, it doesn't sound like a great career for us over the next couple of years," opined Joseph.

"It would be primarily paperwork, although you could perhaps obtain some additional funding to further enhance your technology," replied Ken.

"I do believe the technology can be made more efficient," said Bruce. "There are multiple variables we could experiment with, both in the chemical and physics domains."

"I didn't quite understand your physics reference," said Ken.

"The physics variables include the various fluid pressures and temperatures, the strength and size of the magnetic field, and the rotational velocity of the centrifuge as a means of varying the centrifugal force, to name a few. In addition, further refinement might be possible with the thickness and pore size, shape, and pattern of the membranes," explained Bruce.

"Thank you for clarifying that. I see what you mean. I assume that to vary and test those parameters would require additional supplies and equipment, and perhaps the construction of another prototype?"

"Yes, that's true," confirmed Bruce.

"Hmmm..." Ken thought for a few moments and then continued, "Another alternative pathway at this point is to market the S corporation, using the recent testing results and video to help attract a buyer. You two and Soaring Eagle Capital would all be selling our equity interests in the company, but I'd think a decent profit might be achieved. We might be able to land consulting contracts for both of you with the buyer, giving that entity confidence in the transfer of the intellectual property and you two a period of time to decide what to do next with your careers. No commitment of any type would be made, of course, unless we collectively agreed to the deal."

Joseph asked Ken to give him and Bruce some time alone. After Ken left the conference room and returned to his office, the men debated their alternatives. They also discussed that they had been fortunate to meet two wonderful women, individuals whom they hadn't been able to devote much time to the past several months. Both Bruce and Joseph wanted to be able to spend more hours with Kathi and Sofia, respectively, plus were still worn down from the intense pace of recent months. To lighten the discussion, Joseph stated that there were likely quite a number of volleyball players in Berkeley with an overblown opinion of their skill level give their absence from the courts. After talking back and forth for a bit longer, they agreed to pursue the latter option.

After calling Ken back into the conference room, they explained that they were in complete agreement for Soaring Eagle Capital to commence marketing Environmental Remediation, Inc. for sale. Ken advised that he would keep them well informed.

Chapter 27

Saturday September 15, 2018
Albany, California

At 7:00 PM, the hostess sat Kathi, Bruce, Joseph, and Sofia at one of the booths towards the rear of Gino's restaurant. This time, there was no question regarding the seating arrangements.

"You two have been ghosts for the past month. What's up?" asked Kathi.

"It's been a whirlwind," explained Bruce. "We had to organize and then conduct validation of our prototype outside of the Golden Gate Bridge, analyze the test results, and then decide what to do with the corporation and our angel investors."

"And the answers are…," said Sofia.

"The prototype recovered ninety percent of the simulated oil spill. That's a great result," advised Bruce.

"However, commercializing or licensing our technology would be extensive processes, plus we don't exactly have a surplus of capital to deploy. Our angel investor is also tapped out in our regard," added Joseph.

"So, where do you go from here?" asked Kathi.

"We've decided to allow the angel investor firm to market the corporation for sale. The value is in the intellectual property. We're going to see if there is any interest and, if so, what that interest looks like," explained Joseph.

"What's that timeframe likely to look like? I see that Joseph has lost at least five pounds absent my cooking," smiled Sofia. "I can't allow that to continue."

"It's uncertain at this point. Our contact, Ken White, has promised to keep us well informed," said Bruce.

The waitress approached the table.

Joseph apologized for not having yet looked at the menu, and then quickly pivoted.

"I'll defer to whatever Sofia selects."

"Me too," chimed in Bruce and Kathi in unison.

Sofia ordered two appetizers to share; and a pasta course for each of them. Despite being of Sicilian heritage, Joseph did not recognize any of the dishes. Sofia also ordered a bottle of wine with a name that was unfamiliar to Joseph.

"So, tell us what you two have been up to," said Bruce.

"Both our jobs have been interesting. We're each working on truly bleeding edge technologies, if in completely different areas," replied Kathi.

"That, and being lonely waiting in the apartment for some handsome gentlemen to call," added Sofia.

"Ah, the Italian guilt! That cultural attribute I *am* familiar with," laughed Joseph.

The waitress quickly arrived with the wine. The label said *Aglianico del Vulture*. Sofia tasted the red wine and approved its pouring. It was smooth and rich, with a lingering finish.

"I could become addicted to this wine," proclaimed Kathi.

"That's another experience we could share together," grinned Bruce.

The appetizer dishes arrived. One was *fiori di zucchini ripi-*

eni, or zucchini flowers stuffed with a complex and delicious filling. The other was *caponata*, a dish with a unique flavor comprised of more than a dozen ingredients, chief among them a special species of Sicilian eggplant, onion, garlic, olives, capers, and sun-dried tomatoes.

While both couples had developed an attachment, the four friends also shared a genuine comradery.

As they awaited the pasta dishes, Kathi openly asked, "Who's getting our apartment tonight?"

Both men looked down at the table. With all of the events of the past several weeks, neither had paid much attention to cleaning and stocking their flats.

Picking up on this, and wanting to return the favor after Kathi suggested eating at Gino's, Sofia replied, "It's yours."

The pasta dish selected by Sofia was *gnocchi*, a type of small potato dumpling. Two of the dishes contained a red sauce, *sugo di pomodoro* (tomato), and two a green sauce, *pesto* (crushed basil, olive oil, and pine nuts). Both sauces were excellent.

As the meal was wrapping up, Sofia got everyone's attention and paused for effect.

"I know you two have a big decision in front of you about the corporation. If there is any way we can be of assistance, we want you both to know that we're here for you. We may not know the perfect answers, but we're good listeners and also accomplished at working through challenges."

"I second the motion," smiled Kathi.

After sharing a simple dessert of twice-baked almond biscotti, the couples split up, each traveling to the agreed upon apartment. Both couples enjoyed the night, which extended until the early afternoon on Sunday.

Chapter 28

Tuesday September 18, 2020
San Francisco, California

Charles Winters called the investment team meeting to order at 8:30 AM. Twenty individuals employed by Blue Planet Investment Management filled the large conference room on the 44th floor of the Bank of America building. Billy Hopkins Jenkins was not among them.

"Let's begin by recapping the investments we have under conditional contracts at this point. The solicitation period for the Fund will conclude soon, so we should be able to commence putting capital to work sometime next month," said Charles.

"We'll be inking the $200 million deal on the wind farm in Minnesota by the end of the week," advised Dustin Lucas, one of the senior financial analysts. "The weather studies indicate excellent wind persistency and velocity. In addition, it's relatively close to the Prairie Island Nuclear Power Plant, so the existing transmission infrastructure can be leveraged to keep costs down. The turbines are in transit from a new manufacturer in Southeast Asia, which also helps control expense. Installation will commence very soon."

"Excellent. That will be an early marquis investment for the Fund. We can trumpet the replacement of carbon-based electricity generation with clean energy," said Charles. "That reminds me, I'll see if Steven and I can get a video interview recorded with Heather Smythe of the local ABC affiliate. The favorable publicity will reassure our investors and perhaps bring us some preferred leads for future investments. Who's next up?"

"We're well into the negotiations with the company that recently developed the most efficient heat pump technology on the market," presented Julian Bingham, another senior financial analyst. "The economic opportunity to replace existing building heating that burns oil or natural gas is enormous. In addition, there is the environmental benefit of swapping carbon-based fuel consumption with green electricity."

"Sounds promising," responded Charles. "Make sure we obtain the intellectual property rights to the application of their technology to both ambient air and geothermal installations."

"Will do," said Julian.

The assembled group discussed seven other investments being pursued under conditional contracts, to be finalized once the Fund marketing period concluded. Charles then directed the conversation to investment opportunities in the process of evaluation.

"Speaking of positive media coverage, I've got an opportunity on my desk that should be a winner," said Jonathan Martin, one of the junior financial analysts.

"We're all ears," replied Charles.

"The opportunity just came in from one of our angel investor contacts. It's a small S corporation with proprietary technology for remediating oil spills much more effectively than existing methods, and with less adverse environmental impact."

"What's the investment level?" asked Charles.

"Open to bid, but I think we could buy the corporation, including all of the patents and intellectual property, for around $8 to $10 million."

"The halo image to the Fund would almost be worth that alone. Jonathan, give Jennifer Franklin a call and pursue the opportunity together. It's a small deal, so let's save some expense and just utilize in-house legal counsel."

"Will do."

The analyst team spent another hour discussing potential investments for the Fund. The meeting wrapped up at 10:15 AM, concluding with Charles thanking everyone for their hard work.

After getting a cup of coffee and a cheese Danish from the employee lounge, Charles took the elevator up the 45th floor. He had the first review meeting scheduled this morning with Billy, who had now been working at his new job for three weeks. Charles caught the eye of the secretary assigned to Billy, indicating for her to accompany him into Billy's office. The office was large, even by private equity standards. It was well furnished, with a cherry wood conference table and a large mahogany desk. On top of the desk sat a 40-inch, high resolution monitor connected to the latest iteration of high-performance laptop. The office enjoyed a view out to the San Francisco Bay from the large windows on one side.

"Good morning, Billy."

"Same to you, Mr. Winters," said Billy, staring down at the floor.

"How have you been?"

"Everyone has been nice to me. Barbara has been terrific at showing me the office and all of the machines and systems."

Billy glanced upwards and smiled briefly at the secretary.

"I see from the files on the credenza that you've been reviewing many of the investment opportunities forwarded to us."

"Actually, Mr. Winters, I've just finished my first report. Barbara helped me load it into PowerPoint. I've never used that software before. It's cool! So many sophisticated features, both visual and regarding audio."

"Good to hear. Can you please email me the PowerPoint file for review? I'll go through it when I get a chance later today or tomorrow."

"Certainly, Mr. Winters."

"So, which investment opportunity are you going to study next, Billy?"

"I'm not sure... There are so many to choose from. Maybe the one from the company trying to collect and recycle plastic from the ocean. Or, perhaps the one working with algae to break down harmful chemicals in the sea."

"Both sound good to me. We're quite focused on the environment with our new Fund. Clean oceans and beaches are part of that. Billy, we'll continue to meet every two weeks to discuss your reports. If there is anything you need in the interim, just let Barbara know."

"Yes, sir, Mr. Winters. Thank you again for this job. I enjoy being able to help out."

Charles then excused himself, explaining that he had several important phone calls to make.

Chapter 29

Monday October 1, 2018
San Francisco, California

The large gong reverberated at 9:00 AM on the 44th floor of the Bank of America building. All of the employees and directors of Blue Planet Investment Company were present, either inside or around the large conference room or via video stream. Steven stepped to the podium and grabbed the microphone.

"It gives me great pleasure to announce that the solicitation period for Blue Planet Investment Fund is now closed. Today marks the first day in the next chapter of our exciting journey. Thanks to the hard work of Charles Winters and the analyst team, we'll have twelve investments funded by the end of this week. Many more are in the pipeline. I look forward to informing our investors of our successes a little over three months from now, when we issue our first quarterly performance report. Thank you all for your dedicated work over these past months. We could never have gotten here without you."

Applause filled the floor.

After it quieted down, Steven continued, "I'd like to especially recognize Shantelle Jones for her excellent work with our investment bankers at Huffman Brothers. They've syndicated a credit facility for the Fund with a sixty percent margin line, much better than the fifty percent typical in the industry. That's yet another vote of confidence in the quality of our team."

The conference room again echoed with applause.

"We're presently working on some favorable media coverage across multiple channels. We'll let you know as soon as we learn the release dates and times. Since we likely won't know all of such in advance, Google Blue Planet periodically to keep fully up to date. Now, let's get back to work making the planet a better place and providing a compelling return to our investors."

A final round of applause filled the conference room.

After Steven spoke with various groups of employees on his way out of the conference room, he signaled to Charles and Samantha to follow him into his office. After the three of them were seated, Steven confirmed the bad news they already knew, and added the latest adverse event.

"You both know that our external capital raise only got to $6 billion, versus the $16 billion target."

Charles and Samantha both nodded affirmatively.

Samantha commented, "I confirm that we pulled out every stop in the sales effort. I can't imagine anything more that we could have done. We pressed hard on our relationships, including Trent Hawthorne and his partners at the law firm. I won't say any more other than that Atlas was utilized to maximum benefit."

"The latest bad news is that the trustees of my wife's trust decided to limit their Fund investment to $1.5 billion, rather than the $4 billion we expected. It seems that they deemed it prudent not to own any more than twenty percent of the Fund. If we had raised the $16 billion, they would have agreed to invest $4 billion, but that's water over the dam at this point. Therefore, we'll initially have $7.5 billion to work with, plus $4.5 billion from the leverage line, for a total of $12 billion, or just forty percent of our original $30 billion plan."

Both Charles and Samantha stared down at the floor. Charles spoke next.

"We're going to have to sweat to make this work. That's of course forty percent of the original target, but with more risk from the relatively higher level of leverage. In addition, the annual management fee on the $7.5 billion of raised capital will only be $56.25 million. We'll need to cut our expense level by about twenty percent just to break even in the management company if we want to be able to provide the planned level of incentive compensation to the high performers."

"I already thought of that. I'd like you each to begin evaluating the staff, identifying the weaker performers for layoff," said Steven, dejectedly.

"While I agree that has to be done, it certainly won't help morale, nor our external image. Maybe we can think of a way to smooth that process," said Samantha.

"I'm open to suggestions, and will consider that further myself."

"I have one other idea," shared Samantha. "Might Atlas be available to help us obtain Fund investments on more favorable terms? The faster we can grow the Fund asset base, perhaps by flipping some of the early investments, the sooner we can ramp up the cash flow from the management fee."

"I didn't want to go there," replied Steven. "The risk of discovery is so much greater in that venue, versus simply encouraging investments into a well-regarded Fund that is also of benefit to society. That said, I'll think about that option as well."

Charles and Samantha returned to their offices to resume their ongoing tasks. Steven sat alone in his office for two hours, thinking through all of the permutations of the present state of affairs. *In for a penny, in for a pound*, he said to himself. He called the Human Resources Department and told them to suspend his salary. That would help save several lower-ranking jobs. Steven then made a phone call that resulted in another $3 million of the dwindling reserve of *his money* being set in motion for transfer to Azure Sky LLC as the initial stop on its journey to Atlas.

Steven informed Charles of his decisions when they ate lunch together later that day at a local restaurant. In between bites of his French- dip steak sandwich and side order of French fries, Charles confirmed his support for everything Steven was doing.

Steven stopped by Samantha's office later that afternoon to communicate the same information. As he sat down waiting for her to return, he noticed that her laptop screen was on an Amazon.com page profiling a variety of whips. He thought better of mentioning anything about that as he shared his latest decisions.

Chapter 30

Friday October 5, 2018
Emeryville, California

Joseph and Bruce arrived at the Soaring Eagle Capital offices 15 minutes before the scheduled 10:00 AM meeting. Emails and phone calls with Ken White over the past week led up to today's in-person meeting. Those communications resulted in the three of them agreeing to sell Environmental Remediation, Inc., including the prototype and all of the intellectual property, to Blue Planet Investment Fund for $10 million in cash. Ken had been instrumental in negotiating the price up from the initially offered $8 million, in addition to obtaining well-paid consulting contracts for Joseph and Bruce for the next six months. These contracts were put in place in order to facilitate the transfer of patents and various technical and operational knowledge.

As Joseph and Bruce waited in the conference room with the large, digital whiteboard, they discussed their decision one final time.

"It's too bad we couldn't find a way to advance the corporation ourselves. The technology is so interesting, and there is so much experimentation yet to conduct," said Bruce.

"I understand your seller's remorse. I have some as well. However, there was simply no avenue for us that was financially viable," replied Joseph. "As Ken explained, there are worse things than being less than thirty years old with about $2.5 million in each of our pockets, after the payment we agreed to for the professor and after paying income taxes. Ken was certainly pleased with the huge return on his firm's investment. I have no doubt that he'd assist us again in the future, should the opportunity arise."

"That's the other thing I can't get off my mind. The future. Where do we go from here?" asked Bruce.

"We have six months of attractive compensation in front of us to facilitate that consideration, not to mention our bank accounts. I'd like us to continue working together if we can identify a suitable prospect."

"Agreed."

The conference room door swung open. Ken was accompanied by three individuals, whom he introduced.

"Joseph and Bruce, this is Jennifer Franklin. She is an in-house attorney working for Blue Planet. Jennifer produced most of the documents we'll be executing today."

"I'm pleased to meet both of you. Congratulations on developing some exciting new technology," said Jennifer.

She distributed her business cards.

"This is Jonathan Martin. He's a financial analyst employed by Blue Planet. Jonathan was the lead evaluator for your company."

The 24-year-old smiled and shook hands, also passing out his business cards.

A tall man of about 50 years stepped forward, not waiting for Ken's introduction.

"I'm Neil Sharpe. I'll be the Chief Executive Officer of ERI pending the Fund's decision whether to combine the entity with one of our other investments in the environmental space. I'm a retired Navy captain educated in marine engineering. I'll be your lead contact, at least at the beginning of the consulting period."

Neil's handshake was firm and lasted a bit longer than usual.

"Let's all be seated. Jennifer, will you please walk us through the documents and coordinate the signing?" requested Ken.

Jennifer explained that the Fund had completed its capital raising period and was now in a position to close on investments in the ESG space. She again complimented Bruce and Joseph on their technology, noting that the management of the Fund was eager to show the investors the type of revolutionary, versus simply evolutionary, technologies that were being funded. Jennifer then commenced walking the attendees through each of the legal documents.

Two hours later, the transaction was completed. Blue Planet Investment Fund would wire the payments to the designated bank accounts. Neil would join Bruce and Joseph at the rented warehouse space at the Berkeley Marina this afternoon to review the prototype and begin transferring files from their laptops to the secure cloud server arranged by Blue Planet.

As the meeting in Emeryville was wrapping up, Bruce asked Neil, "What did you think of the video of the real-world testing of the prototype?"

"I haven't seen that yet. I was finishing another project when this deal came together quickly. I look forward to watching it soon, after I have a couple of days to inspect and better understand the prototype. That way, it will be more meaningful to me."

"I watched the video twice," said Jonathan. "The oil spill cleanup was impressive. The area within the booms didn't look any different to me than the surrounding ocean once the cleanup was completed."

"I was also impressed with the video," added Jennifer. "But I don't understand why the videographer decided to include Joseph's discomfort over the side of the barge. Now that I think about it, perhaps to document that the seas were not placid, thereby lending more credence to the testing."

Joseph blushed. "That certainly validated that Bruce and I did not manufacture the video with CGI."

Ken announced that he had just received a text from Heather Smythe, the local television news reporter. She and her film crew arrived a few minutes later. Heather asked some softball questions of Bruce and Ken, explaining that this would likely be just a one-to-two-minute segment on a forthcoming evening broadcast. A few scenes from the video of the testing would be spliced in.

Later that day, Neil, Joseph, and Bruce rendezvoused at the marine warehouse, with Bruce leading the tour of the facility and the explanation of the prototype. After leaving Neil at 4:00 PM to further study the prototype, Joseph and Bruce each rushed to their flats to shower, shave, dress, and pack a small overnight bag. Sofia and Kathi had informed them to arrive in the lobby of the Claremont Hotel at 5:30 PM. The landmark resort is located high in the East Bay hills above Berkeley and Oakland; often referred to the 'white castle on the hill' by locals.

The women greeted them in the lobby.

"We're all checked in," advised Kathi. "Let's get you two upstairs and prepared for our 6:00 PM appointments."

The men looked at each other, mutually and silently deciding to just follow along with their girlfriends' plans. The four of them enjoyed a 45-minute full body massage in the hotel spa. Neither Bruce nor Joseph had ever experienced anything like it. The spa treatment was followed by a 7:30 PM dinner reservation at the hotel restaurant. While the food was the more standard steak, baked potato, and grilled vegetables,

Sofia did manage to order a bottle of *Nero d'Avola* red wine from Sicily. The women toasted the men's success in completing the ERI deal several times over the course of the dinner. After a *digestivo* of *Amaretto* with cheesecake for dessert, each couple departed for their own rooms.

"Joseph, please get into bed while I prepare something special for you," directed Sofia.

She disappeared into the bathroom. A few minutes later, she emerged wearing an elaborate white lace lingerie outfit that snugly clung to every curve.

"Do you like what you see? It's La Perla."

"The appointments are beautiful, but not nearly as lovely as you."

They made love three times that night.

Chapter 31

Wednesday October 10, 2018
Berkeley Marina, California

Neil Sharpe texted Bruce and Joseph last night to meet him at the marine warehouse space at 10:00 AM. Both men arrived on time and walked into the warehouse together. They observed Neil standing next to the prototype with a laptop open on a nearby table. As they approached, he did not respond. Neil was staring intently at the laptop and shaking his head.

"Good morning, Neil," broached Joseph.

"Hello, gentlemen. Pull up a chair and help me think through some issues I have identified," said Neil.

After Joseph and Bruce were seated, Neil began a structured set of questions.

"Have you ever measured the aggregate energy consumption of the prototype, including all of the pumps and the centrifuge?"

"No," replied Bruce. "The recent test in the ocean was the first time we activated all aspects of the prototype with more than a token amount of fluid."

"Did you notice how loud it was on the video of the test?"

"Yes, I noticed that," said Joseph. "In fact, the television reporter only used the picture from the video in the television segment, utilizing the Q & A from our interview as the sound overlay. Now that I think about your question some more, there was the tugboat holding the barge in place against the current, the three smaller boats with their engines running, the diesel generators on the barge, plus the prototype. There was a lot of machinery that added up to a cacophony."

"The diesel generators on the barge were designed for use in disaster recovery, and so were phased to fire up in sequence as the amount of power being drawn rose. While I don't have an exact measurement, let's assume that the third diesel generator was running at fifty percent of capacity, with the first two operating at their maximum output of 2,000 kilowatts. That would equate to a total power demand of 5,000 kilowatts."

"I'm following you," said Bruce.

"Therefore, the prototype was consuming 5,000 kilowatts of energy to process one barrel of oil vacuumed through a twelve-inch pipe, with a total recovery and processing time of about an hour."

"Agreed," noted Bruce.

The Exxon Valdez oil spill, admittedly a large one, deposited about 262,000 barrels into the ocean. To simply things, let's assume a 100,000-barrel oil spill. That's not much compared to the size of the ultra large crude oil tankers operating these days. Using your prototype, that cleanup would require 100,000 hours or 4,167 days. That's obviously not practical. Therefore, we need to be able to increase the diameter of the vacuum pipe and also augment the vacuum pressure / flow rate. The flow rate can be increased by using more energy and making pressure and temperature adjustments. However, the temperature and pressure increases will create structural demands on the pipe which will also need to be addressed. Similar engineering considerations also apply the reverse osmosis segment of the prototype. The core physics issue is that these changes result in a geometric, rather than linear or arithmetic, increase in energy requirement. As a rule of thumb, to increase the nominal flow rate by a factor of five, we'd need to increase the energy utilized by the square of five, or 25 times. That means having 5,000 kilowatts multiplied by 25 equals 125,000 kilowatts of energy production available. And that does not count the energy needed to sail the ship or barge, plus other ancillary energy requirements. In summary, our first key issue is the interplay between the laws of fluid dynamics and energy."

"I'm not disagreeing with you, Neil, but I do note that there are many options to increase the efficiency of the prototype, and that I intentionally over-engineered the prototype to ensure that it could complete all phases of the test," responded Bruce.

"I'll acknowledge that, but let's keep in mind orders of magnitude. Let me move on to the second key issue: the laws of electromagnetism. These laws follow a geometric or exponential pattern as well. If we increased the fluid flow by five times, we'd need a many times larger magnetic field in conjunction with your chamber 'A'. In fact, I'm not sure if a sufficiently large electromagnetic field could be created outside of something along the lines of a supercollider. In addition, the weight of the required shielding to avoid disrupting the ship's systems would be considerable."

"There is the potential to utilize elements such as neodymium to augment the efficiency and strength of the magnetic field," noted Bruce.

"I understand your point, but think of the amount of magnetism necessary to suspend hundreds of gallons of iron infused crude oil at the same time, recognizing that only the iron molecules in the slurry are magnetically responsive."

"I comprehend what you're saying. That would argue to focus on the chemistry of the bonding agent in order to help address that aspect," shared Bruce.

"True, but let's again keep in perspective orders of magnitude. Now, let me present the third key issue, displacement.

The prototype processed 200 gallons of seawater / oil spill in order to recover just shy of 40 gallons of oil, about 100 gallons of potable water, and around 60 gallons of brine, not to mention the residual chemicals. If this ratio of five to one between fluid vacuumed and the oil spill continued through the other potential changes and enhancements we've discussed, an oil spill of 100,000 barrels of oil at 42 gallons per barrel would require processing and capturing 21,000,000 gallons of fluid. Assuming for simplicity the weight of a gallon of water at just over 8 pounds, that would equate to 168,000,000 pounds or 84,000 tons at an again simplified 2,000 pounds per ton. The ship or barge would therefore have to displace that amount of water, plus more in order to float the engines, crew, its own fuel supply, etc."

"I understand your math, but couldn't the displacement issue be minimized by intermediate transfer of the recaptured fluids to another barge or vessel?" asked Bruce.

"Correct, but that transfer would further increase the amount of energy needed for the operation, circling us back to the energy issue," responded Neil. "But there is one more law of physics to consider. To timely respond to an oil spill, the remediation vessel needs to arrive quickly, before the spill has time to disperse too widely. This means that a ship must be used, rather than some type of barge. For a given ship's hull configuration, ship's depth in the water, and ship's mass, the amount of energy required to increase the speed of the ship again increases geometrically. As an easy example, a ship that needs 50,000 kilowatts to travel at twenty knots would need perhaps 125,000 kilowatts to go thirty knots and about 225,000 kilowatts to speed at 40 knots. This law of nature is one reason even U.S. Navy ships rarely exceed around 30 knots."

"So, we'd need a carefully designed ship that can achieve a relatively high rate of speed without adding to our issue of energy consumption," concluded Joseph.

"That's correct as far as it goes. However, to spin a propeller faster or to spin a larger propeller or both requires progressively stronger and generally heavier metallurgy. This then adds to our displacement problem," advised Neil.

"I'm now understanding how all of these laws of nature interact. Scaling the prototype therefore presents a challenging and multidisciplinary engineering problem," said Joseph.

"I'm glad that you're seeing my point," replied Neil. "However, I believe I can fast forward to a proxy of the eventual solution."

Joseph and Bruce both leaned forward in their chairs with rapt attention.

"The U.S. Enterprise," said Neil.

Joseph was confused. "Forgive me, but is that a joke? A starship with Captain Kirk and Mr. Spock? I don't get it."

This gave Bruce a few moments to think on his feet.

"I believe Neil is referring to the nuclear-powered aircraft carrier sailed by the U.S. Navy."

"That's right, Bruce. While the exact specifications are secret, it is widely believed that the U.S Enterprise's two nuclear reactors produce a combined 200 megawatts, or 200,000 kilowatts of electricity. That is about one-fifth of a large, land-based nuclear power plant. The Enterprise also displaces about 100,000 tons, and can travel somewhere between 30 and 40 knots. In summary, relatively speaking, a ship somewhat like the Enterprise would solve the physics challenges we've discussed this morning."

"Let me try to make amends for my Captain Kirk reference," followed Joseph. "The final law that makes our technology extremely challenging is the law of economics. Even without the armament and related systems, a nuclear-powered aircraft carrier would likely cost about $6 billion to construct, not to mention the operating costs. Even if such a ship cleaned up two oil spills of 100,000 barrels a year at value per barrel of $60, that's only $12 million worth of oil at a 100% recovery rate, plus the value of the potable water. No one is going to build such a vessel to earn less than a 2.00% gross return on invested capital, before operating costs, even if saving the environment does present some economic value in a social sense."

"Well stated, Joseph," opined Neil.

"On the one hand, we could eliminate the desalinization aspect of the protype to reduce demands on the amount of energy and the displacement. On the other hand, we haven't yet factored in the cost, energy demand, and displacement of the significant volume of powdered iron and bonding agent that would be required to be transported and dispersed," noted Bruce.

"I thought of all of that as well," said Neil. "The environmental approval process would likely be more challenging if we're going to dump all of the residual fluids back into the ocean."

The three men sat quietly and stared at each other.

Neil eventually broke the silence.

"I'll spend a couple more days working through various permutations to see if there is not some economically viable application of your technology. I'll keep you apprised, and also forward to you for advance review the report I'll draft for Blue Planet. You two did develop some cool technology and chemistry. There may be opportunities to license some of that intellectual property for applications that we're not even aware of."

"That's professional of you, Neil. We appreciate that and will continue to be of any assistance we can to you. In hindsight, we should have added a marine engineer to our team right at the start. We were just so enthusiastic about the laboratory test results, and then we and our angel investor ran out of capital," shared Joseph.

"I believe you two operated with only good intentions. These things happen. Many technologies don't translate from the laboratory to the real world. Remember the super-sonic transport or SST airplane? Cool technology that never really had a pathway to profitability, not to mention the sonic boom issues."

The three men shook hands, with Neil remaining at his laptop and Joseph and Bruce deciding in the parking lot to visit their favorite bar on Shattuck Avenue in Berkeley to have a drink. Or three.

Chapter 32

Tuesday October 16, 2018
San Francisco, California

Charles Winters was already at his desk on the 44th floor by 7:30 AM. He grabbed several bagels, two schmears, and a container of lox on this way in, along with a venti of coffee. He knew this was going to be a very long day. An email marked *URGENT* with a report from Neil Sharpe arrived late last night while he was sleeping. He had his regularly scheduled meeting with Billy this morning. The afternoon schedule included a session with Steven and Samantha to discuss layoffs. On top of all that, there was the pipeline of potential investments to evaluate in order to fully deploy the Fund's capital and the money to be borrowed on the leverage line of credit.

Fortified with the first bagel and half the venti, Charles opened the email from Neil Sharpe. The Executive Summary section of the report was at the front and very clear. The Fund's investment in Environmental Remediation, Inc. was worthless, or nearly so, due to the impracticality of scaling the technology for real-world application. Charles continued reading the subsequent ten pages of analysis, with some of the math beyond his understanding. However, the key conclusions were evident. The laws of physics would prevent the technology from ever being profitable. Neil recommended that Blue Planet ensure the perfection of the intellectual property rights and then dissolve the entity. To his credit, Neil recommended also timely concluding his services in order to save money.

Just great, thought Charles. The investment we trumpeted on the local television news turns out to be a dud. Thank goodness the wind farm in Minnesota is progressing even faster than planned. We'll need to play that up and hope that no one remembers ERI. He made a note to update Steven and Samantha regarding both investments at their meeting this afternoon.

After reviewing several potential new investments, Charles took the elevator up to the 45th floor for his 10:00 AM meeting with Billy and Barbara.

"Good morning, Mr. Winters," greeted Billy, looking up a bit from the floor in Charles' direction.

"How are you both doing today?" asked Charles.

"Really well," said Billy. "The latest PowerPoint presentation from Barbara and me is the best one yet."

"I've got to agree with Billy," added Barbara.

"That's good to hear. I haven't had a chance to review it yet. I'll look forward to doing that. Billy, how is the new job working out for you?"

"This is the best job I've ever had. I know I've only had a couple, and none in a nice office building like this. The people are all friendly and I've enjoyed looking through all of the submissions for investment. Barbara has shown me how to research the investments on the Internet using some quite sophisticated websites. Way more than just a Google search."

"So, you're happy working here?"

"Oh, yes, Mr. Winters."

"Very good to hear. Well, I'd better get back to my office. We have a large number of potential investments to consider for Blue Planet."

"Good-bye, Mr. Winters," said Billy.

Upon entering the elevator, Charles' focus switched immediately to the upcoming meeting with Steven and Samantha. Because of the disappointing level of capital raised for the Fund, they'd need to cut staffing by about twenty percent. There were going to be some difficult decisions made later today, decisions that would affect peoples' lives, and those of their families. The Human Resources Department for the management company had provided an employee census to the three senior executives that included information on base salary, incentive compensation, benefits expense, and total cost for each employee.

Steven Shaw was at his desk at 1:30 PM. He had just made his final pass through the employee census information. It pained him to have to lay off employees who had only fairly recently been recruited to join the new Blue Planet team. However, that wasn't the only stress on Steven today. The deployment of the Fund capital was proceeding slower than desired, in part due to the difficulty of evaluating and benchmarking some of the ESG related opportunities. In addition, the cost of organizing and carrying the management company, plus the expenditures through Atlas, had consumed the vast majority of Steven's discretionary money. He shivered at the prospect of having to admit this to Veronica, not to mention the potential need to ask her for money from her trust.

At 2:00 PM, Steven, Charles, and Samantha met in one of the conference rooms. Charles was the first to speak.

"Steven, before we get started, there are three things I would like to share."

"The floor is yours."

"The construction of the Minnesota windfarm is proceeding ahead of schedule. We should be able to start receiving initial cashflows by the first of the month."

"Excellent," replied Steven.

"Second, on the other hand, the Fund's $10 million investment in Environmental Remediation, Inc. is likely worthless. I just received a detailed report from the Navy captain and marine engineer we retained to evaluate and integrate the corporation."

"Were we defrauded?" asked Samantha.

"The report says that was not the case. The technology works on a small scale, but because of various laws of physics, can never be expanded to commercial application. The retired Navy captain believes the principals who sold us the corporation acted in good faith."

"Let me ask the next question," insisted Samantha. "Who worked that deal for us?"

"Jonathan Martin was the analyst and Jennifer Franklin was the attorney."

"And they did not identify any of the issues raised in the report?" said Samantha, with frustration in her voice.

"No, they did not. Jonathan is 24 and Jennifer is 25. As a result, they're not that experienced. They're too young to remember Solyndra. In hindsight, we should have assigned a more senior employee to the deal. It was one of our smaller transactions. The information supplied, including a video of a recent live testing, was compelling."

Steven slammed his fist on the conference room table.

"Fuck! Dammit! That's the investment we had broadcast on television. And you know the rule of sequence on aggregate compound investment returns."

Charles nodded his head affirmatively.

Samantha cocked her head, saying, "Just to be sure that I'm completely following you, can you explain that a bit?"

Steven replied, "If you're aiming for a, say, fifteen percent compounded annual rate of return over seven years, which would equate to a 166% gain due to the effect of compounding, and you lose money the first year, the rate of return for the subsequent six years must increase significantly in order to achieve the same nominal gain. For example, if we lose just ten percent in year one, we'd need to then earn a twenty percent compounded rate of return for years two through seven just to generate the same about 166% overall gain. Said another way, we'd need to increase our level of annual profitability by a third, from fifteen percent to twenty percent, to offset the initial loss. That's a tall order."

"In other words, you never want to start a process like this with a loser," simplified Charles.

"I intuitively knew that, but thank you for the more detailed explanation," said Samantha.

The conference room went quiet for several minutes.

Eventually, Steven looked at Charles and said, "Didn't you say that you had three things to share?"

"We're meeting here this afternoon to determine whom to fire, affecting their lives and those of their loved ones. This income is really important for some of our employees and their families. I met with Billy as usual this morning. His mother has an enormous trust fund that he will inherit as the sole heir. Billy hardly needs the income. Do we keep paying Billy and about one-half FTE of secretarial support for him while we lay off employees who are actually contributing?"

"Has his review of the unsolicited investment proposals been of any value whatsoever?" posed Steven.

"Billy's PowerPoint files are visually beautiful, with good audio. He definitely has an artistic sense. However, his analytical abilities in regards to finance are limited. He doesn't have education or experience in that arena. So, I don't see much value in his work. Plus, playing the role of his interested and supportive boss takes up some of my time that could be put to better use elsewhere."

Steven put his head in his hands.

"I hear you, Charles. You raise a valid point. However, I've promised my wife that I'd help Billy with a job. Veronica and I never could have children, and Billy is her only nephew. If we terminated Billy, my relationship with my wife would be stressed. You two should also remember that my wife's trust fund controls twenty percent of the capital in the Fund."

"Enough said," shared Charles.

"Understood," added Samantha.

Steven directed their attention to the large screen with the employee census.

"I think we can all agree on the first two layoffs."

Steven highlighted the names Jonathan Martin and Jennifer Franklin. Charles and Samantha nodded in agreement.

The meeting concluded two hours later. The headcount cuts were all decided. Steven would email the information to the Human Resources Department to commence processing the layoffs. Charles was exhausted as he returned to his office. He decided to check his email before heading home. Included in his inbox was the latest report from Billy. Charles simply clicked 'delete'. Charles therefore never read about the opportunity to invest in a small semiconductor company that had just been awarded a contract to produce microcontrollers for the new Tesla Model 3 electric car.

Chapter 33

Thursday October 18, 2018
Burlingame, California

It was 10:30 AM in the morning and Jennifer Franklin had not yet summoned the will to get out of bed in her small, one-bedroom apartment in Burlingame, located south of San Francisco. Yesterday afternoon had been a brutal surprise. First, a representative from the Human Resources Department presented her with a termination letter plus all of the usual forms and documents for employee separation, including the notice regarding the option to elect continuing medical coverage under COBRA. As Jennifer was still packing up the personal effects from her office, Steven Shaw entered, closed the door behind him, and railed at her. How could she have been so stupid as to do the Environmental Remediation, Inc. deal? How could she have totally missed that the technology was not scalable? Jennifer tried to keep her composure and respond professionally, pointing out that she was the attorney for the transaction and that all of the documents had been proper. This only enraged Steven. He then increased the volume of his voice, eventually yelling at her that not only was she terminated, but that he would see to it that she never got another job in the financial services industry. He then stormed out of her office.

By 11:00 AM, Jennifer finally composed herself enough to get up and make some coffee. Here she was, just one year out of the Hastings Law School, fired, and blackballed by a powerful and influential industry executive. What would she put on her resume? How could she explain this event to a prospective employer without its sounding bad in some way?

Her energy level bolstered by a second cup of coffee, Jennifer sat down at her laptop and began to update her resume. Later that day, she commenced an online job search. She also made a list of contacts in her network who might be able to give her a lead on a new job.

At 6:00 PM, she stopped working on her job search and prepared her first food of the day, a mixed salad. As she was eating, another wave of reality flowed over her. She was heavily indebted with student loans taken out to fund law school, plus a car loan. Although she had selected an apartment in Burlingame, rather than San Francisco, in order to keep her expenses down, she only had enough savings for two months of rent, utilities, food, and other basic costs. She returned to the online job search with added intensity as soon as she finished eating.

Chapter 34

Wednesday November 7, 2018
San Francisco, California

Charles Winters had just taken a bite of his bear claw pastry when his office phone rang.

"Hello, Charles Winters speaking."

"This is Hal Horst from St. Paul. Mr. Winters, have you been watching the Weather Channel?"

"Can't say that I have. Why do you ask?"

"A polar vortex traveled south from Canada last night. Temperatures here in Minnesota fell to as low as negative twenty-five degrees Fahrenheit, with wind gusts up to fifty-five miles per hour."

"Wow. That sounds like one hell of a storm, even by upper Midwest standards."

"Mr. Winters, it's the wind turbines. The extreme cold solidified the lubricating fluid, while at the same time the high wind velocity pushed hard against the blades. The gears are shredded."

Charles paused and took a deep breath.

After composing himself, he asked, "Did the insulation fail? Was there a manufacturing defect?"

"The turbines didn't have much insulation. It never freezes in Southeast Asia."

Charles then remembered that the Minnesota company had

sourced the turbines from a manufacturer in Ho Chi Minh City, in southern Vietnam. The turbines were purchased at a great price, which was one reason Blue Planet had found the investment so attractive.

"Can you check to see if any of the turbine gears are salvageable? Also please contact the manufacturer to see if we can obtain replacement gears, plus more insulation or a heating element for each turbine. I'll request Shantelle Jones, our CFO, to coordinate communication with the property and casualty and general liability insurance companies. I'll start an email string on this topic so that everyone involved can be informed each step of the way."

"Got it. Will do. Good-bye, Mr. Winters."

"Good-bye, Hal."

Charles texted Steven and Samantha, asking if they could meet in his office. While awaiting a response, he emailed Shantelle and copied the various individuals who would be involved in trying to ameliorate this disaster. An hour later, the three executives were in Charles' office with the door closed. Charles recapped his phone conversation with Hal Horst.

"None of our investment evaluation team thought to ask about insulation or heating elements on the wind turbines?" asked Steven, still incredulous about what had occurred.

"Evidently not. We didn't have an engineer on the evaluation team. In hindsight, that was obviously a huge mistake."

"Let's focus on where we can go from here," said Samantha, trying to turn the conversation towards damage control. "How soon until Hal can give us an inventory of the situation?"

"He didn't say, but that will likely take several days. Each turbine needs to be climbed and inspected."

Charles then saw a text from Hal arrive on his iPhone. It

explained that there was insufficient space within the hoods of the turbines to add more insulation. However, the manufacturer was willing to try to design a heating element that could be attached to the outside of the cover. Charles shared the text with Steven and Samantha.

Steven immediately responded, "How long is it going to take to design the heating element, including some type of automated thermostat, manufacture the element, and then have it shipped from Vietnam and installed in Minnesota?"

"I don't know," replied Charles. "I'll follow up with Hal and get some more information."

"Even a best-case scenario would be ugly," opined Steven. "We've got $200 million invested with no cash flow for the foreseeable future, an upcoming default on our contract to provide electricity, unknown repair costs; and all on a project that we presented as one of our leading investments in the ESG space."

"Shantelle will be thorough with the insurance companies. I have no doubt that she'll get us every dollar possible from that source," said Charles.

Steven sighed deeply.

"This is strike three for us. First, the fiasco with the oil spill clean-up company. Then the issues with the caustic elements in the steam tapped by our geothermal energy investment. Now, a polar vortex shutting down our windfarm. When the lending syndicate hears of this, they're going to move to curtail our leverage line, either by marking down the value of our collateral or reducing the advance ratio, or both. Our investment capacity is going to shrink from the already disappointing $12 billion to perhaps around $10 billion."

The three executives were silent for several minutes. Samantha spoke next.

"Is there perhaps some way to make lemonade out of these lemons?"

"What are you saying?" asked Charles.

"How much is left in Atlas?"

"About $500 thousand," replied Steven.

"What if we put lipstick on these three pigs and motivate some unprincipled buyers?" suggested Samantha.

"I can help with the makeup, if you'll handle the motivational aspect," pitched in Charles.

"For plausible deniability, Charles and I do not want to hear anything else in regard to motivation. I'll advise the Board of Directors that we're parallel processing. While we determine the costs and timeframes for the windfarm reconstruction, we'll also be marketing all three investments for sale or trade. There almost always is a greater fool."

"Let's hope this situation is no exception," wished Samantha, with worry in her voice.

Chapter 35

Friday November 9, 2018
San Francisco, California

Joseph and Bruce were surprised to receive the email yesterday requesting their presence for a meeting with the Chief Marketing Officer of Blue Planet at the San Francisco headquarters. The men had read the report about their prototype and technology written by Neil Sharpe and then had a final conversation with Neil where he opined that there would likely not be much for them to do during the remainder of their consulting contracts, although that was of course up to Blue Planet.

They were both wearing their best business clothes as they rode the elevator up to the 44th floor of the Bank of America building. Upon stepping into the lobby at 3:30 PM, they advised the receptionist of their appointment with Ms. Moore. The receptionist showed them into a conference room.

Both Joseph and Bruce were surprised when, a few minutes later, a stunning woman entered the conference room and introduced herself as the Chief Marketing Officer for Blue Planet. She was about the same age as the men, about 5'11" tall, with long, shimmering blond hair that had a bit of a wave. Joseph and Bruce couldn't help but notice that her blouse was open at least one button further down that normal, providing insight into substantial cleavage. Upon introducing herself, her perfect and dazzling white teeth garnered their full attention.

"Blue Planet is considering re-marketing Environmental Remediation, Inc. While Blue Planet is not positioned to be able to fully take advantage of the technology you developed, other entities might be. I've asked you here this afternoon to discuss your roles in assisting us with the marketing of the corporation and / or the sale of its intellectual property."

Joseph spoke first. "We're under the consulting contract for several more months and would be pleased to be of service and fulfill our obligations. However, to be perfectly candid, given the analysis and report from Neil Sharpe, I can't fathom an entity that would be interested in acquiring the corporation, or using the technology."

"Not to sound uncooperative, but I'm having trouble seeing that as well," said Bruce. "I performed quite a bit of research following receipt of Mr. Sharpe's report. I believe he is well-grounded in his conclusion that our technology is not scalable."

"Who's to say that your technology might not have other applications that you have not yet identified? It's a big world out there, with countless teams of inventors and engineers working to solve all flavors of environmental challenges. There might be some key value to at least some aspect of what you have developed," retorted Samantha.

"I see your point," replied Joseph. "We don't know what we don't know."

"Exactly. So, I'll coordinate the marketing of the corporation and the intellectual property, but want you two available to join me on sales calls, either in-person or virtually. I'm hardly a scientist, so I could really use your support."

Samantha casually stroked her hand across her chest as she made the last comment.

She then continued, "We're prepared to offer you an incentive bonus of $25,000 each upon the close of the sale of the corporation and / or all or substantially all of the intellectual property. That would be on top of your existing consulting contracts. We won't want to charge the Fund for that, so we'll pay the incentive from one of our subsidiary companies."

The men had no idea that the subsidiary company referred to by Samantha was Atlas.

"That's generous of you, thank you," said Bruce.

"Just one key point. You can't mention the report from Mr. Sharpe or any of the conclusions therein. I'd like you both to operate just as you did immediately following the test on the open ocean, consistent with the video. We don't want to discourage potential buyers. Plus, in the corporate world, the rule is *buyer beware*."

Joseph and Bruce stared at each other, each uncertain of what to say.

After an uncomfortable pause, Joseph said, "Ms. Moore, might you please give us a few minutes alone to discuss your proposal? It was quite unexpected for us this afternoon. We'd like a chance to talk it over with each other."

"Of course, I'll be back in twenty minutes."

As Samantha existed the room, she ensured that the men got a good look at her taught ass, accentuated by the tight fit of her skirt.

"What do we do?" asked Bruce. "And was it my imagination, or was she coming on to us?"

"Let me answer the easy question first. My guess is that Ms. Moore views her sensuality as a resource to deploy, just as you and I use our brains at work and you use your height in volleyball. I don't think she particularly finds either of us to be sexual magnets, so to speak."

"That seems like a reasonable interpretation of what just happened. Now, what about the requested professional services?"

"While I hear what she is saying, I just can't operate that way. We studied professional ethics as part of the MBA program. In fact, this could be a case study. It wouldn't be appropriate to act as if it were a past point in time, thereby ignoring information gained since then. Omission is another form of lying. I don't want my career stained by that type of behavior."

"Nor mine," added Bruce.

"The incentive bonus and Ms. Moore's physical attributes are temptations. My opinion is that we must resist them."

"I agree. We're together on this. We'll perform the marketing support, but only with full latitude to respond fully to any questions regarding the chemistry and the technology."

Just as Joseph was nodding his head in agreement, Ms. Moore re-entered the conference room. She leaned against the edge of the table, dipping her shoulders slightly to squeeze her bust, and looked at the men with a quizzical expression. Joseph explained their decision.

"I must say that I am disappointed with your decision. I'll share that if you persist in that perspective, you will be violating the terms of your consulting contracts to provide requested support," advised Samantha.

Joseph and Bruce looked at each other and paused. Joseph eventually continued the conversation.

"Meaning?"

"Meaning that all payments under the consulting contracts will cease as of today, as allowed in the document following your failure to perform as required."

Bruce then rose from his chair, stretching to his full 6'4" height.

Looking directly into Samantha's eyes, he simply said, "So be it."

Joseph followed his partner's lead out of the office. Bruce had just spiked a shot down the line.

Chapter 36

Saturday November 10, 2018
San Francisco, California

Veronica and Steven were each seated in plush, oversized chairs in the library of their mansion, reading. It was after dinner.

Frederick the butler entered the room and inquired, "Sir and madam, is there anything I might bring you before retiring for the evening?"

Steven immediately responded, "A glass of the aged single malt scotch. Make it a double."

"Right away sir."

Veronica lifted her gaze from her reading with a concerned look. Her husband had been drinking more and more these past several months. She decided to initiate the conversation gently.

"Steven, how has Billy been at work? I haven't heard you mention much about him lately."

"Charles supervises Billy, so I have limited interface, which is proper decorum since I'm a relative. That said, Charles has shared with me that Billy is very happy with the situation."

"Good to hear. I'll share that with Maureen tomorrow. She worries so much about her son."

Steven returned to his reading. About five minutes later, Frederick arrived with the glass of scotch, served on a silver tray in a crystal glass with a single ice cube formed from Rocky

Mountain mineral water. Veronica used this interruption in Steven's reading to continue their conversation.

"Darling, how are you doing at work? You've appeared a bit more stressed than usual the past several weeks."

She wisely avoided any direct confrontation about his drinking.

"It's been difficult. Several of the initial investments are not working out well, although Samantha is working diligently to salvage them."

"It's not unusual to have some underperforming invest-ments in a Fund that large. In fact, such is functionally im-possible to avoid. With the team you have supporting you, I have no doubt that the law of averages will swing in your favor soon."

"Kind of you to say, dear. The other source of stress is working in this new ESG space. It's so much different than the consumer products industry of Opticore. Much less defined, much less traditional, many more players, and a lot of emer-ging technology."

"I appreciate what you're saying. The Blue Planet environ-ment presents challenges that are quite different from what you worked on previously."

"You can say that again."

"Honey, I'd like to help you, be a sounding board for you. I'm not the financial wizard that you are, but I do have some good business experience. Moreover, I *am* the daughter of Blake Hopkins, after all."

"Your father was an icon."

Veronica smiled wistfully and nodded her concurrence.

"Why don't we set aside some time for some walks on the

Marina Green. That has always been one of my favorite parts of the city. The views and the smell of the Bay are invigorating. The chauffeur can drive us down so we don't have to worry about the parking. We both could use the exercise and fresh air, plus the opportunity to chat."

"My schedule is pretty packed, but let's see if we can work that in."

Steven then took a large gulp of the scotch and returned to his reading. Veronica hoped that her husband would follow her suggestion. It would be a much better approach than continuing the trend toward increasing alcohol consumption.

Chapter 37

Monday November 19, 2018
Burlingame, California

Jennifer Franklin sighed over her morning tea as she read the email with the most recent rejection of her application for employment. In the month since she was terminated by Blue Planet Investment Management, she had applied to over fifty law firms. Only two had granted interviews, with each of those quickly following up with the standard communication advising that while her interest was appreciated, there were other applicants who presented a better fit for the position. Jennifer thought to herself, the reach of Steven Shaw and his cronies must be even more extensive than she imagined. She might have to relocate out of the San Francisco Bay Area, or maybe even California, to get a job. Her grim reality then set in. She barely had enough money for another month, maybe two, of living expenses. She had canceled her cable television service, downgraded her cell phone plan, and cut her food budget. At 5'6" tall and now just 115 pounds, her clothes hung on her like a sack. How could she ever afford a relocation out of state?

Sipping more of the tea, she contemplated her potential options at length. Her parents had died in an automobile crash when she was an undergraduate, leaving her with a small estate that had been spent on law school tuition. She didn't have any other family, and couldn't see herself taking money from friends. If she declared bankruptcy to avoid, or at least postpone, her loan payments, that would be a further obstacle to again being employed by a law firm. She did not have the resources to start a solo law practice and hang out her shingle.

A thought then occurred to her. What if she pursued employment outside of law firms and the business world? There were other types of legal work. Although she concentrated in commercial law at Hastings, she was licensed to practice law of substantially any type in the state. She commenced an online search of open legal positions with non-profits and municipalities. By the end of the day, Jennifer had submitted twelve new applications. After a meager dinner of generic canned chili over rice, she fell asleep while praying for just one opportunity.

Chapter 38

Friday November 23, 2018
Oakland, California

Quinton Jackson, known as 'QJ' in the local neighborhood, woke up at 10:15 AM following his usual late night. He immediately reached for his burner smartphone.

"Yo."

"Leon, this is QJ. You set to shadow the container from the port to the warehouse this afternoon?"

"Yeah, boss. Our guy inside the port will ring me when the box is loaded onto the truck."

"Good. We got five men at the warehouse ready to process."

"Got it."

"You call this number if you see any problem."

"Yes, boss."

After Quinton hung up, he used the toilet and walked into the kitchen to start his coffee. This was a key day for him. The cocaine shipment stuffed inside the shipping container from Thailand was his largest order yet. The drug was concealed in the cushions of rattan furniture, the nominal contents on the import bill of lading. Quinton had timed its arrival for the day after Thanksgiving for two reasons. First, customs enforcement would likely be lax, with minimal staffing. Second, he wanted to boost his inventory before the holiday season, when his clients were generally in the mood to spend more money. The Port of Oakland handled several million shipping containers each year, with the new mega-ships capable of carrying as many as 20,000 containers at one time. Despite these good odds of his shipment not being caught, he was worried. He had expended most of his capital on this buy. Its seizure would set him back years, financially speaking.

Several texts from his gang arrived on his other smartphone as Quinton threw four frozen waffles into the microwave. It took a fair number of calories to fuel a 6'7" tall man weighing over 300 pounds. The betting book for the upcoming Super Bowl was running fifteen percent ahead of last year. While selling drugs was Quinton's primary source of revenue, he also ran a bookie operation and had two pimps managing twenty prostitutes. These ancillary businesses helped generate excess cash for the recurring bribery payments he made to help protect his turf just east of downtown Oakland.

Quinton searched for the powdered sugar in his kitchen. He eventually found it in the drawer behind a loaded .45 caliber handgun. A man in his line of work could not be too careful. The landline phone rang just as he bit into the third, sugar-coated waffle.

"Hello."

"Good morning son, how's my pride and joy?"

"Doing fine, mama. How about you?"

"We got two new residents in the facility. They both like to play bunco. I'm so happy here. Thank you again for arranging this for me."

"You know I'd do anything for you, mama."

"I knew sending you to college was worth it. How's your business doing?"

"The manufacturing plant is humming. Orders are rolling in."

"I never want to be a burden to you."

"Don't you worry about that. Everything is good."

"Are we going to share Christmas dinner?"

"Yes, just as we spoke about before. I'll drop off a letter with the details to help you remember."

"You're such a good boy."

"Got to go now, mama. Good-bye."

Quinton's mother had a stroke a little over a year ago that had resulted in vascular dementia. Her short-term memory was permanently impaired. Quinton moved his mother into the best assisted living facility specializing in memory-care in the entire East Bay. He had no second thoughts about paying the significant monthly fees. His mother had worked two jobs to pay for his education at the nearby Cal-State campus. It was the least he could do, plus he could afford it with the cash flow from his operation.

The manufacturing facility was just one of the diversified front businesses utilized by Quinton to launder the money from the drug sales. He was better educated, and more intelligent, than his competition. His prostitution operation employed a steady mix of Anglo, Black, Hispanic, and Asian girls, allowing him to better meet demand and charge higher prices. His drug operation benefitted from his knack for technology. All email was conducted through an encrypted virtual private network. New email accounts were established weekly. Burner smartphones were rotated every three days. All unofficial records were stored on an offshore server that was also encrypted. These practices cost more money, but had resulted in Quinton's building a significant operation over the last decade.

As he finished the last waffle, Quinton texted the leader of the warehouse crew to text him back when they received the container. $5 million of cocaine at wholesale prices was almost two tons of product.

Chapter 39

Saturday December 8, 2018
Berkeley, California

Kathi arrived at Bruce's flat in north Berkeley just after 6:00 PM. They had arranged to share dinner and watch the latest Netflix release together this evening. As usual, Kathi greeted Bruce with a warm kiss. She was the liveliest of the four of them, apparently blessed at birth with an extroverted, bubbly personality. That was just one of her many attributes that Bruce found so attractive.

"Good evening, lover," said Kathi.

"Dinner's almost ready. Can you help me with the salad while I finish the cheeseburgers?"

Bruce never succeeded in translating his extensive knowledge of the interactions of molecules into the related application of cooking. Cheeseburgers were about the limit of his skill in that regard. Once they were seated, with the wine open and the food served, Kathi, as usual, led the conversation.

"It's great that you and Joseph both got new jobs so soon, and ones that you both like so much."

"I took a risk on joining a small start-up focused on developing solid-state batteries. If we can optimize the chemistry, there is the prospect of much greater energy density, faster recharge times, and lower fire risk than the batteries used, for example, in Tesla cars today. This technology could be one of the key solutions to global warming. Imagine being able to fuel every car with the sun."

"Taking that job must have been a big decision. I'm sure you could have earned a lot more money by working for one of the large chemical manufacturers or some other big business."

"True, the salary isn't great, but I did get a load of stock options. Those could be quite lucrative if the company succeeds. I thought this was the right time to take a gamble on such a job, with the money I have in the bank from the ERI sale."

"Makes sense to me," replied Kathi. "Speaking of the money from the ERI sale, have you considered spending some of it on an upgraded flat? Not to be insulting, but your apartment is on the small side. It would be great to have a bedroom large enough for a king-sized bed, maybe even with its own bathroom. I don't think this place has changed much since its original construction many decades ago. Maybe get something more modern with enough closet space for some of my things."

"Actually, I haven't given much thought to moving," said Bruce.

After finishing their cheeseburgers and salad, Kathi went to her purse and removed a small bottle of Strega Liqueur. Bruce immediately remarked about the bright yellow color.

"Sofia turned me on to this. It's been made in the same Italian town of Benevento since the mid-1800's. It contains over fifty ingredients and has a unique flavor. Are you game to try?"

"Upon your recommendation, of course."

The liqueur was incredibly aromatic, flavorful, and high in alcohol. Kathi poured Bruce a second serving, stating that they could share that during the movie. The film turned out to be highly overrated. Both Bruce and Kathi questioned the intelligence of the Netflix subscriber base. They stopped the movie about half-way through. Kathi again initiated the conversation.

"Bruce, do you ever get lonely living alone? We only see each other a couple of times a week, plus I know you miss working every day with Joseph like you did at ERI."

"Yes, from time to time. But I've gotten used to that over the years."

Kathi rested her head on Bruce's shoulder.

"I didn't mean to insult your apartment earlier. I admit that the one Sofia and I share isn't that great either. It can be noisy on the weekends."

"Yeh, I've noticed that," responded Bruce.

Kathi took two of her fingers, dipped them in the last of the glass of Strega, and rubbed them across her lips. She then sat on his lap facing him and initiated a particularly lengthy and passionate kiss. Afterwards, she paused and looked penetratingly into Bruce's eyes. He remained silent, a bit hazy from the wine with dinner and the two glasses of Strega.

"Okay, I give up! What does a woman have to do? You're so intelligent and well-educated, but can't read an open book!"

"What are you saying?" asked Bruce, now confused.

"I've been trying to communicate that I'd like us to live together," said Kathi.

A wave of revelation flowed through Bruce's consciousness. How could he have been so dense? He could validate the equations used by Neil Sharpe in analyzing ERI, but he couldn't pick up what a woman sitting on his lap was telegraphing.

Quickly composing himself, he said softly, "That would be wonderful."

His reply elicited another passionate kiss, followed by the

most intense sex they had yet shared.

Chapter 40

Wednesday January 2, 2019
San Francisco, California

Steven, Charles, and Samantha gathered in a conference room at Blue Planet Investment Management after the last of the other employees had departed for the evening.

"How did we end up?" asked Steven.

"Subject to final adjustments, it looks like finished 2018 down about eleven percent," replied Charles. "It would have been worse if Samantha had not salvaged some money from our pigs. The loss was also mitigated by a strong performance from our investment in lithium miners."

Steven punched into his laptop. "The final number for the S&P 500 Index for 2018 is down 6.24%. We'll get a bit of political cover from that. Still, our more astute investors are going to be concerned that we lost almost double the S&P drop despite only investing for part of the year."

The three of them were silent for a few moments.

"I know what you're thinking," said Charles to Steven. "The mathematics of sequential returns. Now that we're down eleven percent, we're going to really need to outperform prospectively in order to furnish a reasonable risk-adjusted return on capital to our investors by the end of the funds retention period."

"Yes, Charles, that and the fact that I just lost $165 million of my wife's money."

The room again fell silent.

"Do we have anything else up our sleeves?" inquired Samantha.

"Atlas is tapped out," replied Steven.

Charles stood up and walked back and forth, staring at the ceiling.

"What about Jim Jordan?" asked Charles.

"Who's Jim Jordan? I haven't heard that name before," said Samantha.

"He's a private eye that we've used several times in the past in conjunction with research and motivation," advised Steven.

"If Atlas is a carrot, Jim Jordan is a stick," added Charles.

"I get it. Everyone has their vices. Those can be leveraged as a source of competitive advantage, like getting more favorable terms than normal on asset purchases coming in and asset sales going out."

"Do we have to go there?" asked Steven.

"We're eighty percent invested and behind the curve. The syndicate led by Huffman Brothers has cut our line of credit to $2.5 billion. Even with the layoffs we implemented, the management company will be lucky to break even. I don't see an alternative," opined Charles.

"I'd be willing to work with Jim Jordan, perhaps being caught in a compromising position with influential men or women. I'm bisexual when it comes to extortion," smiled Samantha.

"I'll put you in contact with Jim. As with Atlas, Charles and I are not to be informed of your actions with him. We must maintain plausible deniability."

"Understood," said Samantha.

When Steven arrived home later that evening, he didn't wait for Frederick, but rather went directly to the bar closet and poured himself a hearty serving of scotch. The strain from his work at Blue Planet was eating him alive.

Chapter 41

Monday January 7, 2019
Oakland, California

A gaunt Jennifer Franklin reported for her first day on the new job of being a California public defender working out of the office in the City of Oakland. She had finally found a corner of the legal profession where Steven Shaw evidently had no influence. The salary was less than her prior position at Blue Planet, but the paid vacation and health and retirement benefits were excellent. Also, the work hours were much more regular. Maybe she could finally devote some time and energy to building a relationship…

Her supervisor, Maxine Scott, a tall and robust African-American woman, about forty years old, welcomed her as she entered the department.

"Good morning, Jennifer. Welcome to the team."

"Glad to be on board, Ms. Scott."

"Call me Maxine. We're informal back here. Helps offset being so formal in the courtrooms."

Jennifer smiled. She had responded positively to Maxine during the interview process. She could tell that Maxine was a direct and *what you see is what you get* type of person. That would be refreshing after working with wealthy individuals who were often overly concerned with appearances.

"You'll shadow me for two weeks to help you learn the ropes. Hastings is an excellent law school, but there are practical aspects of this job that one has to learn on their feet. The system is just that – something you've got to figure out how to work within and through."

"I understand. I appreciate your offer."

"First up this morning, we have initial consultations with a prostitute and a man accused of selling ecstasy. They're both repeat customers."

"Does that happen often?"

"Oh, my dear, yes. The California jails are overflowing, the courts are backlogged, not to mention the political pressure to avoid apparent discrimination if too many minorities are prosecuted. We often refer to the processing for minor offenses like these as 'catch and release'. Follow me and we'll meet our first client of the day."

Chapter 42

Saturday January 19, 2019
Las Vegas, Nevada

George Tang had reluctantly agreed to meet with Samantha while he was in Las Vegas attending an ESG convention. George had a PhD in chemistry and was the founder of a small company focused on a new technology aimed at capturing carbon from the air. If successful, the technology presented the potential to meaningfully reduce global warming. The technology was, however, still in a nascent phase, but showed theoretical promise. The company needed an infusion of capital to fund the next steps in the development of the technology, including for sourcing components and conducting testing. George had received an indication of interest for investment from a venture capital firm, plus one from the Blue Planet Investment Fund. The financial terms of Blue Planet's offer were the least attractive of the two preliminary proposals, but Ms. Moore had insisted on meeting to flesh out the mutual opportunity.

At 6:30 PM, George arrived at the small meeting room reserved by Ms. Moore in the hotel hosting the convention. He was already tired from the long list of events and presentations attended earlier that day. Upon entering the room, he observed the credenza filled with various plates of appetizers, plus a well-provisioned tray of assorted beverages, both with and without alcohol. Ms. Moore joined him just a couple of minutes later. She was professionally dressed in a gray business suit, although the skirt fell a good four inches above her knee, and the off-white blouse was snug around her chest.

"Good evening, Mr. Tang. Thank you again for agreeing to meet with me."

"You were quite insistent. I did disclose to you that Blue Planet's pricing indication was at the low end of those I have received to date."

"I appreciate your directness. I have more information to share with you this evening. Before we get started, would you like to get some food and drink?"

"Actually, I would. The buffet lunch today was less than appetizing, to use polite terms. I guess I'm spoiled by my wife's cooking."

"So, she is quite the chef?"

"Not initially, but over fifteen years of marriage and multiple cooking classes, she's become accomplished in most things culinary. Our two teenage boys never go hungry, which is saying something."

Samantha gave a small laugh and replied, "You're a lucky man. Can I pour you a drink? I see that they have Chivas and Grey Goose."

"I'm not much of a drinker. Maybe just one dry gin and tonic to sip on. It *has* been a long day."

Samantha was less than pleased with that response, but smiled and served George the requested beverage. After they each had a few bites, Samantha launched her pitch.

"Mr. Tang, while anyone can offer your firm capital, only Blue Planet can provide access to our unique ecosystem of ESG oriented companies, augmented by our internal staff expertise. If you accept us as your investor, we will introduce you to the many scientists and technologists we have under our umbrella. Think of the resources you'll have access to and what that could do for your company."

"I acknowledge what you're saying. However, the technology that my firm is pursuing is relatively unique, with limited overlap to other disciplines. In addition, the venture capital firm which has presented a better priced expression of interest has made similar points."

"I see. Let me get some mineral water and then I'll move on to my next key consideration. Can I freshen up your drink? Maybe a bit more tonic, and a fresh squeezed lime wedge?"

"That would be refreshing. Yes, thank you."

Although it was January, the desert air in Las Vegas was still parching. As Samantha stood up to approach the beverage station, she stretched and rubbed her shoulder, further tightening the blouse around her breasts. To her frustration, George registered only the slightest of responses. She would probably have to fall back to her third line of attack. Watching George carefully, she dropped a tablet of gamma-hydroxybutyric acid (GBH) into his glass. The relatively strong taste of the lime would mask any taste from the date rape drug. She also added some more gin.

"Mr. Tang, might you please describe for me, what you would desire from Blue Planet in order to render us the preferred investment offer? Please feel welcome to be as specific as possible, including financial terms, intellectual property rights, and ancillary support. We strongly believe in the opportunity presented by your company."

Samantha wanted George to speak as much as possible, thereby increasing the likelihood that he would drink the entire glass.

George commenced listing his ideal set of parameters. Samantha interrupted him several times, asking for more detail or clarification. She also stood up to bring him a salty snack from the credenza, dropping her smartphone as an opportunity to bend down and better display her legs and ass. Again, no more than a quick glance from George and no verbal comment. After about twenty more minutes of conversation regarding potential offer terms, George had finally finished the gin and tonic.

"Excuse me, Ms. Moore, but I'm suddenly not feeling all that well. Might we finish this matter via a phone call next week when I am back in my lab?"

"Of course. I understand."

As George attempted to stand, he experienced vertigo and began to wobble. Samantha jumped up and steadied him, squeezing him tightly.

"Let me help you back to your room. What number is it?"

George handed her the electronic key and mumbled, "1257".

Samantha helped him stumble to his room, holding him firmly against her the entire way.

Once she had George back in his room and passed out on the bed, she called Jim Jordan. Jim arrived from his room in the same hotel a few minutes later. Together, they undressed George, pulled back the sheets and blankets from the bed, and laid him on top of the mattress, with his head propped up on two pillows for better visibility. Samantha quickly removed her clothes. She then posed in multiple positions, including simulating having intercourse with her on top and her performing fellatio. They ran an ice cube across George's face on several occasions to briefly get his eyes open. Video was also taken, with Samantha lying on George's shoulder, dreamily saying what a great lover he had been. Once Jim signaled that they had enough material, Samantha dressed, put the room key on the bedstand, and departed with Jim.

Chapter 43

Tuesday January 22, 2019
Los Angeles, California

George Tang was back in his lab located a few miles outside of downtown Los Angeles. He had managed to make his return flight Sunday afternoon after awaking groggily that morning. As he was catching up on his email, a message arrived from a Yahoo account with a subject line of 'Your Infidelity'. The email was purportedly from a private investigator hired by another, unspecified firm also working on carbon capture. Attached to the email were photos and short videos. Upon looking at them, George could not recall the events. He did remember meeting with Ms. Moore to discuss business terms, but nothing after that. The email stated that the competitor firm wanted to receive the preferred venture capital funding, and so would forward the attachments to his wife if he did not decline their offer. The email also noted that Ms. Moore was not aware of having been filmed, but would be informed if George did not cooperate.

George cupped his head in his hands. *What have I done? I love my wife and have never cheated on her.* He realized that the photos and videos would be devastating to his family. Was the business world really this cutthroat that a competitor, likely also led by well-educated scientists, would stoop to such behavior? Would law enforcement be of any use? He knew that the email account could easily be abandoned and was likely opened under a false name. Law enforcement would surely contact Ms. Moore, which would only make matters worse. He imagined that she would be quite upset with having been filmed because of him.

After another hour of anguish, George walked back to his laptop and typed the following brief return email: 'I will decline the VC funding'.

Chapter 44

Saturday January 26, 2019
Berkeley, California

Joseph arrived at Sofia's apartment at 6:15 PM. He was carrying a small bouquet of red roses and an expensive bottle of Italian wine sold to him by the local wine shop. He hoped it was good. As soon as Sofia opened the door, the hallway was filled with a delicious aroma.

"Wow! That smell is awesome. What have you prepared for us tonight, chef Sofia?"

"It's a famous dish from northern Italy, *risotto Milanese*. You'll see the special color in a minute. The key ingredient is saffron."

Joseph presented the flowers and the bottle of white wine.

"For you, my love."

Sofia bent down and responded with a kiss. They had long since determined how to best maneuver given their discrepancy in height.

"The roses smell wonderful. And you brought a *Grechetto* wine from the province of Umbria. That should pair excellently with the risotto."

"I'll again admit that my expertise flows from a costly relationship with the proprietor of a local wine shop. I think I've funded orthodontia for his kid by now."

Sofia smiled, "Have a seat at the table and open the wine. I'll serve dinner in a moment."

The apartment seemed bigger now Kathi had moved out to share a newly rented townhouse with Bruce. Sofia opened the lid to the serving dish to display the *risotto Milanese*. It had a rich, yellow color and smelled ever better up close.

Joseph raised his wine glass to signal a toast, saying "*Salute, cent-anni* (to your health, and may you live to be 100 years old)."

Sofia responded, "*Anche a te* (also to you)."

After finishing dinner, which also included some *bietole* sauteed in olive oil, onions, and garlic, Joseph cleared the dishes to the sink while Sofia brought out the dessert. When Joseph saw the baked good and the Strega liqueur, he took a deep breath to steady his quickening pulse. Bruce had shared in detail how Kathi had proposed their cohabitation. To buy himself some time, he immediately asked Sofia how her job was going.

"While there are some difficult days, and some frustrating days, I'm really enjoying the work overall. We're using the latest developments in artificial intelligence to sort through vast amounts of information to both identify patterns and build machine learning. The next leap in computer chip processing power should allow us to approach real-time analysis. The possible applications of our technology are almost limitless. Our team is great. I feel fortunate to be on the forefront of a new age. Bill Gates and Paul Allen at Microsoft must have felt something like this in the late 1970's and early 1980's."

"That's one heck of a comparison, but I understand what you're saying," replied Joseph.

Sofia poured the yellow Strega liqueur, saying, "This also contains saffron. I thought it would be an interesting complement to the *risotto*."

Joseph sipped the Strega. The flavor was strong and complex. Following Sofia's example, he then took a bite of the baked good. Its soft texture and gentle flavor were a smooth offset to the taste of the Strega.

"I like this. Thank you for introducing it to me."

"I'm gradually indoctrinating you into your heritage," grinned Sofia.

"And what a pleasant education it has been."

After taking another sip of the Strega, Sofia looked into Joseph's eyes and said, "What might you think about accelerating that indoctrination?"

Joseph thought to himself, that was certainly an open-ended comment! I've been thinking about what Kathi and Bruce decided for almost two months now, intently so since the Strega made its appearance tonight. Sofia is by far the most amazing woman I have ever met. I always look forward to being with her. I love her. Why would I hold back now? Joseph, don't be a fool!

"That would be a capital idea. What do you have in mind?"

"I'm thinking nightly cultural and language lessons, offered in this apartment."

She again looked deeply into Joseph's eyes.

"*Si. Sono d'accordo* (yes, I agree)," said Joseph, pulling her toward him in warm and lingering embrace, followed by a long and passionate kiss.

Chapter 45

Monday January 28, 2019
Oakland, California

After three weeks on the job, and with Maxine's mentoring, Jennifer Franklin was now well into the rhythm of her new responsibilities as a public defender. Many of the cases were similar, with a steady stream of arrests for prostitution and selling drugs. Violent crimes were less frequent, but too often flowed from family issues. While the street gangs generally respected each other's territory and business, occasional overstepping resulted in attempted and sometimes successful homicides. Those cases were handled by more experienced attorneys in the Oakland office.

Arriving at her desk with a cup of tea from the lunch room, Jennifer punched up her assigned consultations arising from arrests over the weekend. Her first client meeting this morning was with a man named Leon Hayes. She walked over to the adjacent building with the holding cells and waited for Mr. Hayes to be brought into the small meeting room. A deputy eventually did so, handcuffing the man to a rigid bar attached to the wall next to his seat.

"Good morning, Mr. Hayes. My name is Jennifer Franklin and I've been assigned as your public defender. Do you know what that is?"

"Call me Leon. Yeh, I know."

"Good. I see from the file that this is your first arrest. You evidently tried to sell some cocaine to an undercover officer late Saturday night around Lake Merritt."

"That's what the brother accused me of."

"Are you saying that you're innocent?"

"He planted the drug on me. It looked like half an ounce. Even if I were selling, who'd push such a small bag?"

"I haven't yet seen any of the video of the arrest. I'll be careful to examine it for what you are saying."

"Good. Can I make bail?"

"I don't see any reason why not. There's no indication that you're a threat to the community."

"Got that right."

"Is there a phone number where I can reach you?"

Leon provided Jennifer with the number for one of his smartphones. Jennifer pressed the button which signaled to the deputy that they were finished.

One of Quinton Jackson's associates bailed out Leon later that morning. Jennifer finally obtained access to the video of the arrest late that afternoon. The lighting was very poor, so it was impossible to observe what happened between the two African-American men. The audio on the recording was primarily of a rubbing or scratching sound. Jennifer inferred that the microphone had either malfunctioned or fallen between parts of the officer's body that were actively moving. She immediately sent an email to the assigned prosecutor.

The next morning, Jennifer called Leon's smartphone.

"Yo."

"This is Jennifer Franklin, the public defender."

"Yeh, this is Leon."

"I got the charges against you dropped. Nothing more for

you to worry about."

"You be good. Thank you."

Leon hung up, thinking to himself that he'll need to be more careful in the future. Quinton usually had all of the cops in his territory paid off, but there must be a few who he hasn't gotten to. Thank goodness the officer approached him when he was almost out of product.

Chapter 46

Friday February 1, 2019
San Francisco, California

Steve, Charles, and Samantha met in the conference room at the management company for a working lunch. After Charles piled four slices of the deep-dish pizza on his plate, they began the review of the Fund's performance in January.

"While some of the investments have been by necessity valued at their purchase price, since they're new additions to the portfolio, our best estimate is that the Fund's value increased two percent last month," reported Charles between bites.

"While that's not bad for one month, we're still well underwater over the Fund's life. In addition, the S&P 500 Index rose 9.2% last month, so our relative performance is terrible," advised Steven.

"Trump's approach to low regulation and low taxation is fueling the economy. Look how far down the unemployment rate has fallen," noted Charles. "If only he could stay off his damn Twitter account."

"You're not the first person I've heard say that!" said Samantha.

Steven refocused the conversation. "The Fund investment total is at about $8.5 billion, including a $1 billion draw on the leverage line. We still need to identify another $1.5 billion in investments."

"I have some good news," smiled Samantha. "We're about to

close on the company with a new technology for carbon capture from the air. We got a *very* good price," said Samantha with a wink.

"That sounds like an investment we could publicize," shared Charles.

"I agree. In fact, I've been thinking that we should share stories regarding some of our most interesting investments on our website. Focus our investor attention on the good we are doing in advancing ESG concepts. That might buy us some more time to catch up with regard to our financial performance. In addition, a few of our investors are more concerned with our social good than our financial returns in the first place," said Samantha.

"Couldn't hurt," responded Steven. "Thanks for making that happen."

After several bites of his one slice of pizza, Steven made a suggestion.

"There may be another way to make up our financial deficit, but it's somewhat outside of our expertise and also risky, particularly with borrowed money on the credit line."

"I'm all ears," said Charles.

"We establish a trading desk within the management company. We then use our internal information gathered across all of our investments regarding ESG topics to buy and sell debt and equity securities for related firms."

"While the offering documents for the Fund do state that it can own securities issued by firms meeting our ESG criteria in lieu of buying the entire companies, a full-scale trading operation might be pushing the envelope in terms of allowable activity," opined Charles.

"Securities trading is not expressly prohibited," countered

Steven. "What if we pay Greene, Robinson, and Sanders their typically exorbitant fee to write us a supportive legal opinion. They'll use the usual language which renders the document functionally meaningless while also protecting them from potential liability. However, that will give us some cover from an optics perspective."

"That sounds good," said Samantha.

"We'd also need to build out a trading desk with high-speed telecommunications and some Bloomberg terminals, not to mention hire a couple of traders and an operations support person. However, the management company is not exactly swimming in extra cash flow right now," sighed Charles.

Steven grimaced. After a pause, he continued. "I just don't see any other way for us to work ourselves out of our situation. The laws of sequential returns are brutal. Charles, how about you monitor Billy's work and his behavior, aiming to identify a reason to terminate him and his secretary."

"We've discussed this before. You convinced me to avoid going down that path," reminded Charles. "Think of the potential repercussions with Veronica."

"The repercussions couldn't be much worse than managing a losing fund focused on a hot segment of the market in the middle of a booming economy. We'll fully justify and document Billy's cause for termination, even if we have to manufacture something. We have time, since it will take a while to prepare the trading operation."

"Charles, if you need me to help with the Billy situation in any way, just let me know. I'm working very well with my new associate," added Samantha.

"Let's get back to work," said Steven, "but first I need a drink."

Chapter 47

Monday February 4, 2019
San Francisco, California

Samantha noticed that Steven was even more stressed than usual this morning. He had developed a nervous tick, constantly running his hand back through his hair. She surmised that his spending the weekend with his wife knowing that he had ordered Billy's termination was eating him alive. The nervous tick was on top of greatly increased alcohol consumption, which she observed as correlated with the relative performance of the Fund. She knew that Steven was now keeping a bottle of Macallan scotch in the lower drawer of his desk. Wanting to protect her income, plus genuinely caring about Steven, she entered his office to propose an idea.

"Steven, we've all put so many hours into our endeavor, especially you. What do you think about a quick break to help us relax and recharge? My treat."

"I usually say that *time is money*, but I'll admit to being exhausted, and receptive to your suggestion. Anything in particular?"

"An associate recently told me about a local yacht business, Bay Tours. Their specialty is a gourmet dinner on the Bay, touring around Angel Island and Alcatraz, and then watching the sun set through the Golden Gate Bridge. It's only a four-hour event, but from what I hear quite relaxing. Being out on the water is a great way to take your mind off day-to-day responsibilities. You, Charles, and I could book the yacht for the evening. They usually take four to six people at one time, but I think they would accommodate us."

"My wife's going on a girl's weekend with her sister, Maureen, starting Friday morning. They're planning on a full set of spa treatments at the Post Ranch Inn in Big Sur. So, the timing is good for your suggestion. I'm in; if the calendar also works for Charles."

"I'll check with him and make the arrangements."

Chapter 48

Saturday February 9, 2019
San Francisco Bay, California

They boarded the Bay Tours yacht at the Alameda Marina. It was a beautiful boat, modern in design, sixty-five feet in length, with a canopied deck on the bow and a hot tub in the stern. Samantha took the lead, making introductions and greeting the crew, comprised of the captain (John), a first mate (Duane), a chef (Paula), a bartender (Suzanne), and a waitress (Tracy). Samantha quickly noticed that all three women were in their mid to late twenties and quite attractive.

After receiving a brief safety instruction, the three guests were seated on the bow, and the ship departed the dock. It was 3:00 PM on an unseasonably warm day, with the Santa Anna winds blowing from the east.

"What can I bring you to drink?" asked Suzanne. "We have substantially every type of premium spirit on board, plus an extensive inventory of beers and wines."

Steven and Charles opted for 18-year-old Glenfiddich. Samantha requested a glass of *Pinot Grigio*. Tracy soon thereafter arrived with a tray of assorted hors d'oeuvres, including caviar and freshly sliced *prosciutto* with melon. John pointed out visual highlights as the yacht traveled a round-about path toward the Golden Gate Bridge. Suzanne never let their glasses become more than half empty, while Tracy piped requested music over the speaker system when it was not in use by John.

Ninety minutes into the cruise, Paula announced, "Dinner is served.".

The meal was presented on fine porcelain plates and included pheasant *cacciatore, polenta*, and mixed vegetables that had been sauteed in white wine. A crisp, chilled vintage chardonnay was poured to accompany the food. Everything was delicious.

At 5:30 PM, John again came over the speaker and announced that most guests enjoyed having dessert and watching the sun set out the Golden Gate and into the Pacific Ocean while seated in the hot tub. A wide variety of swimsuits were available in the cabins below deck. After looking at each other with a 'why not' expression, Steven, Charles, and Samantha headed below. The selection of available swimsuits was extensive, with several even large enough for Charles. Samantha selected a more modest cut than she usually wore. Once they were in the hot tub, Paula, Suzanne, and Tracy arrived at the stern carrying a bottle of Dom Perignon, champagne glasses, and plates of *tiramisu*. The three women were in bikinis, serving the surprised guests from within the large hot tub. No one objected. The women were good-looking and all three of them were by then well lubricated.

As they finished the *tiramisu* and watched the sun drifting lower in the western sky, Duane approached the hot tub and asked Samantha if her party would like some complementary cocaine. He showed her a decent sized bag from his pocket.

Samantha thought for a moment, and then responded. "Why the hell not. That will really get our mind off the office."

Steven and Charles heard this, and did not object. Like Steven, Charles had also sampled various pharmaceuticals over the years, particularly in college. Any resistance the men might have had was worn down several glasses of alcohol ago.

The six of them in the bubbling and warm hot tub each partook of the drug while admiring the incredible view and steadily laughing among themselves. Steven was now totally relaxed, for the first time in a long while. He relished the feeling.

As John began to turn the yacht around for the return trip, Paula, Suzanne, and Tracy each gently whispered into Steven's, Charles', and Samantha's ears, respectively, that they would be pleased to conclude the voyage with some time alone in the staterooms below deck. Tracy also asked Samantha if she would prefer Duane.

"No, not tonight. I'm up for something different."

Paula led Steven below deck, removed his swimsuit, and began to stimulate him. He was too cognitively impaired to recognize her professional behavior.

At 7:15 PM, the three Blue Planet employees stepped back onto dry land after extending their thanks to the crew. Little did they know that Bay Tours was indirectly owned by Quinton Jackson. He had started the company after scoring huge profits with his most recent cocaine shipment. The company was part of Quinton's broad diversification plan to attract wealthier clientele. As a new business, he had authorized a period of free samples in order to build buzz. He was also counting on the addictiveness of cocaine to generate repeat customers, especially among the rich who could afford the expense of a cocaine habit.

As Steven passed out in the back seat of his chauffeured sedan on the way back to his mansion, he had no inkling that he had just contracted chlamydia.

Chapter 49

Saturday February 23, 2019
Berkeley, California

Kathi, Bruce, Joseph, and Sofia were sitting down to dinner in the apartment now inhabited by Joseph and Sofia. Sofia had once again cooked a delicious meal paired with a suitable wine. The main course was *polpette*, large meatballs comprised of three different cuts of meat, seasoned spinach, and two types of aged, dry cheese.

As they started eating, Kathi, ever the live wire of the group, asked, "So, tell me Sofia, how's my replacement working out?"

Sofia smiled, "Well, he takes less time in the bathroom in the morning than his predecessor, so I haven't been late to work in while. On the other hand, he hasn't been much help in the kitchen, unless you count making leftovers disappear."

"Isn't that a bit of a stereotypical answer?" needled Bruce. "*I Love Lucy* went off the air in the fifties."

"Perhaps certain things never change," laughed Joseph.

"Speaking of change, Kathi and I have been talking. We want to float something by you two," said Sofia.

Bruce and Joseph both opened their eyes wide, then turned to each other with quizzical expressions. They each raised their hands palms up, indicating that neither of them knew what to expect next.

"Sophia and I are both working on cutting edge technologies. Between us, we've gained quite a bit of knowledge regarding artificial intelligence, machine learning, and data mining," explained Kathi. "These technologies are likely to become more mainstream in the next several years, facilitated by the ready availability of cloud computing."

"You're both way beyond Bruce's and my understanding in those fields, but we have a general idea of what you're talking about," noted Joseph.

"We were wondering if there might be a related entrepreneurial opportunity. You two made a tidy profit on ERI. Maybe there's another new company to be formed here," suggested Sofia.

"If you two could have access to near-instantaneous information from the Internet, not just web page content and posted files, but also macro trends across multiple social media platforms, what would you do with that capability?" asked Kathi.

"We're also talking about the ability to monitor changes to web pages and data mine the content from those changes through AI. Think of it as having you finger on the pulse of the Internet," added Sofia.

"The whole, global Internet?" asked Joseph?

"Eventually, potentially yes, to at least a meaningful extent. Initially, a more defined subset of the Internet might be targeted. Likely the subject of our business objective," replied Kathi.

"One idea might be a sort of faster and more comprehensive news service," said Bruce. "Or, maybe some type of early warning system, such as for adverse weather."

"We also thought that there might be some political value in the technology we're talking about. Politicians could be informed in almost real-time of the country's reactions to various statements or events. Sort of like a more advanced version of Hilary Clinton's reviewing the latest polls to determine her position on various topics," added Sofia.

They all shared a laugh at Sofia's last comment.

She then said, "Think about this some more while Kathi and I finish preparing dessert."

While the women were in the kitchen preparing the servings of *sfogliatelle* and the *nocciolo digestivo*, the men shared ideas back and forth. Once the four were all again seated at the table, Bruce spoke.

"One thing we learned from ERI is to start with a small prototype for ease of construction and testing, but to also evaluate that the technology and engineering can likely scale to a real-world application. We also learned that it's often best to conduct more frequent and more incremental tests, carefully analyzing the results along the way. ERI exhausted most of its funding with the single test outside of the Golden Gate Bridge. We probably could have more quickly appreciated the impact of the laws of physics with more gradual stages of development."

"That sounds logical to me," said Kathi. "That's a good process and approach, but we still don't have a well-defined business opportunity."

"One of my professors in the MBA program had a pet phrase, *information is power*," said Joseph. "One place where information has the most power is the stock market. Think of the huge daily trading volume and the enormous sums of money on the New York Stock Exchange and other platforms. If someone had access to better and / or faster information about company earnings, new patents, testing results for new medications, changes in executives, mergers and acquisitions, or customer reaction to a new product, to name just a few topics, they could buy or sell ahead of the general market and potentially make a fortune."

"I understand what you're saying," advised Sofia, "but we don't have huge sums of money to deploy in buying and selling large numbers of stocks."

"I would recommend focusing on a single industry as an initial step, to echo Bruce's earlier comments and to respond to your point. In addition, I'd recommend conducting the trading primarily through the options market. Smaller amounts of capital would be needed," explained Joseph.

"I don't know much about stock options. Can you explain them to me?" asked Kathi.

"Sure. In the most basic form, there are two flavors. A *call* option gives you the right to *buy* a specific equity at a specific price within a defined time period. A *put* option gives you the right to *sell* a specific equity at a specific price within a defined time period. In essence, you want to own a call option if the stock's price is going to rise, and vice-versa for a put option," detailed Joseph. "You can also sell options rather than purchase them, with your desired price change inverting from my earlier explanation."

After a few sips of the *digestivo*, sourced from Italian hazelnuts, and several bites of the flaky and creamy *sfogliatelle*, Sofia presented an idea.

"What if we convert Kathi's old room from a guest bedroom into an office. We can upgrade our Internet service to the fastest available speed and buy a couple of high-end laptops. We can also purchase some time on one of the cloud services, which includes access to certain AI and other technology tools. Kathi and I can then do some coding after work and on the weekends. The idea would be to see if we can glean information from the Internet that would be advantageous in trading options. Bruce, perhaps you could research where to target our efforts in terms of industry or market. We'd also need to figure out how to prioritize potential data sources. Joseph, we'd need your help in deciding how to integrate our mined data with the options market. I'm thinking that we do this on a small scale as an initial test, running a simulation and recording our theoretical results."

"Aren't we fortunate fellows, dating such intelligent, and attractive, women," grinned Bruce.

"I'd like us to be able to relatively quickly gain an insight as to whether this idea presents any true entrepreneurial opportunity. I don't want to burn too much time if this isn't going to lead anywhere," shared Kathi. "I have competing priorities in my life."

She then looked into Bruce's eyes.

"To echo what Kathi said, I'm happy to contribute, so long as this night and weekend work does not foreclose certain other highly valued activities," said Joseph.

"Of course not," said both women in unison.

Chapter 50

Friday March 1, 2019
San Francisco, California

Steven, Charles, and Samantha were again gathered in one of the conference rooms on the 44th floor of the Bank of America building. The tabulation of their results for February had just been completed.

"Charles, how did we do last month?" asked Steven.

"Pretty close to last month, up about another two percent."

"How does that compare to the S&P 500 Index?" inquired Samantha.

"That was up just shy of 3.00%," responded Charles.

"Just great. The Fund is still negative life to date, and we've now fallen further behind the general market. If this keeps up, our investors are going to seriously question why they ever agreed to pay us a 0.75% annual management fee when they could have purchased a better performing S&P 500 Index Fund with an expense ratio of 0.05%," whined Steven.

He ran his hand through his hair and stared at the ceiling before continuing.

"If the Fund's performance does not materially improve relatively soon, the directors are going to start pounding on me."

Charles and Samantha knew to stay quiet, giving Steven some time to digest the latest information.

Steven eventually repositioned himself forward in his chair

and said, "This only further supports our need to advance the trading platform. What's our status on that, Charles?"

"The tenant improvements to build out the trading desk and related technology should be completed within two or three weeks. The Bloomberg terminals are ordered and will arrive soon. We've identified a recruiting firm to use in sourcing the two traders. The Human Resources Department has completed the job descriptions, including for the operations support person. In summary, we should be ready to go in between two and three months."

"That's quick work. Thank you, Charles. And where are we on terminating Billy and laying off his secretary?" asked Steven.

"I really haven't found a way to do that," replied Charles. "He's punctual, never misses a day in the office, submits a new PowerPoint file to me every week, and has become well-liked by the team on the 45th floor. While his work product is not superior in terms of financial analysis, it has improved over time. I just don't see a sufficient reason to terminate him, especially given the relationship with Veronica."

Steven's face contorted in frustration.

"We don't have enough cash flow in the management company to simply absorb all of the added costs of the trading operation. We have to develop a solution."

After a pause, Samantha spoke.

"California has some of the most stringent laws in the country regarding sexual harassment. What if we document Billy's sexually harassing a woman; likely on two different occasions with two different victims. That way, we can claim a pattern of unlawful behavior and have no choice other than to terminate him."

"That would work in theory, but Billy is hardly a sexual harasser. His autism makes it difficult for him to even look at people he does not know well," expressed Charles. "I just don't see Billy sexually harassing anyone, even if placed in an environment of high temptation."

"I believe two occurrences could be manufactured, one with myself and one with another woman. I have someone in mind for that role. She is attractive and in need of extra money to pay for medical treatments for her child. I have a bit of cash left over from the final disbursement from Atlas."

Samantha paused and waited for Steven's response. She observed his discomfort. Each step of trying to render the Fund successful was layering on more challenges and more stress.

He ran his hand through his hair, eventually saying, "That's an excellent plan. Veronica believes strongly in human rights, including a woman's right to not being in fear of abuse of any type. See what you can set up."

"Will do. As usual, I won't share any details with you or Charles. The harassment will be reported through the Human Resources Department, and will occur in an environment where all evidence can be tightly controlled," said Samantha.

"So be it." Looking up at the clock displaying 3:00 PM, Steven added, "It's time for a drink."

Chapter 51

Wednesday April 24, 2019
Oakland, California

After a long morning in court mounting a spirited defense of one of her clients accused of opioid trafficking, Jennifer Franklin was approached by a short, stocky man right after the judge called for a recess for lunch.

"Here's my card. Call me."

Looking down at the card, Jennifer saw the name of Troy Stapleton, Esquire; and a phone number. The name did not ring a bell. Flipping the card over, she did recognize the law firm of Harrington & Harrington. That was one of the premier criminal defense firms in the Bay Area, with a provenance dating back to right after the second world war.

Jennifer mulled the request over in her mind as she nibbled on a Greek salad at a deli located down the street from the courthouse. Was the invitation personal or professional? Could a law firm of the caliber of Harrington & Harrington possibly have an interest in one of her indigent clients? Harrington & Harrington had successfully defended some upper-echelon members of the various crime families over the past decade. That type of legal assistance was extremely expensive.

After concluding her closing argument to the jury at 4:00 PM, the judge declared that deliberations would commence tomorrow morning. Jennifer returned to her office to catch up on her email and messages. Just before 5:00 PM, she decided to call Mr. Stapleton.

"Hello, Troy Stapleton speaking."

"Good afternoon. This is Jennifer Franklin. You handed me your business card earlier today."

"Yes, Ms. Franklin. Thank you for responding. I wanted to share that several of our attorneys have been most impressed with your work on behalf of your clients, particularly given the limited resources available to the public defenders' office. They've witnessed your performance while waiting in the courthouse for their sessions with the various judges."

"Oh, I see. Well, thank you for the kind words."

"I'd like to extend you more than a compliment. My firm is interested in interviewing you in consideration of future employment."

Jennifer paused for a moment to collect her thoughts.

"That's more than a bit unexpected. I've only worked in criminal defense for about four months."

"I'm surprised to hear that in light of the favorable comments I've received about your work. What did you do beforehand?"

"I worked in corporate law, primarily in negotiating and documenting merger and acquisition transactions. That was my first licensed position following graduating from Hastings. I also performed some clerk work while pursuing my law degree."

"At Harrington and Harrington, we value attorneys with a spectrum of legal experience. With our variety of defense cases, one never knows what background might prove valuable in serving our clients."

"That makes sense from what I know of a few of your firm's higher profile cases. Some of that defense work was clearly enormously complicated, with a wide scope of expertise needed to conduct research, assemble the defense, and educate and convince a jury."

"Now it's my turn to thank you for a compliment. Tell you what, please think about whether you might have an interest. If so, please contact me again. Needless to say, our firm's compensation structure is a multiple the state's. You'd also benefit from the opportunity to work with fellow professionals who are among the elite in our industry, plus have the chance to apply yourself to work that is much more intellectually challenging than what you typically address in your current position."

"Thank you again for reaching out to me. I will give this conversation some consideration and get back to you."

"Goodbye, Ms. Franklin."

Well..., thought Jennifer. That was certainly an unexpected turn of events! All of the advantages presented by Mr. Stapleton were valid. On the other hand, the hours would be more demanding, and Jennifer would potentially be defending some individuals accused of much more serious crimes than her current clientele. Countering that thought, she reminded herself of her strong belief in the American justice system and everyone's right to a defense and a trial by their peers. While not perfect, the American system had proven itself far better than alternatives in most other countries.

Jennifer contemplated the potential new opportunity all the way through the Chinese take-out dinner eaten in her small apartment. After finishing her meal, she signed on to her personal laptop and checked out her favorite social media sites. At 7:00 PM, a message flashed in her browser. She had an invitation on Match.com. The gentleman was two years older than her. His profile displayed a photo of a handsome man. The biographical information included being a graduate of the University of Santa Clara and five years working for the FBI.

His name was Matthew Haddock.

Jennifer poured a glass of *Pinot Grigio* and sat back down in front of the laptop. She had been lonely these past months, leading to her posting on several dating sites. She worried about being a defense attorney potentially dating someone in law enforcement, but then convinced herself that the Bay Area was a big place, with little likelihood that their professional lives would ever intersect. Plus, he was really cute, apparently quite fit as far as she could determine from the photo. After one more sip of wine, she replied affirmatively to his interest and commenced the initial electronic communications.

Chapter 52

Saturday April 27, 2019
Oakland, California

Steven awoke with a headache. Yesterday afternoon had been brutal. Two investors called to rake him over the coals after reading the Fund's first quarter performance report. Then, at the end of the day, Shantelle Jones, the management's company's CFO, had requested an immediate appointment. Blue Planet Investment Management barely broke even on a cash flow basis last quarter. Any further increases in operating costs would cause the company to have to choose between a number of unpalatable options, such as delaying settling its payables, cutting salaries across the board, or seeking an operating line of credit. Given the company's financial profile, any such credit facility would be expensive and would likely require the personal guaranty of Steven.

Steven crawled out of bed, being careful not to awaken Veronica. She had been out late last night at another fundraiser for her non-profit. Steven felt guilty that he had failed to contribute time or money to his wife's efforts to benefit disadvantaged children.

As Frederick brought him a freshly brewed cup of cappuccino, Steven opened the calendar on his smartphone. Argh, he thought. He had a lunch meeting in downtown Oakland with one of the Fund's larger, smarter, and more vocal investors. He would likely be verbally pilloried for the failure to install adequately insulated wind turbines in Minnesota, leading to an early, significant loss for the Fund despite Shantelle's thorough pursuit of insurance claims. Steven knew there was no defense, no carefully crafted words, that might soften the conversation. He was going to carry the whip to his own lashing.

By 1:30 PM, Steven exited the skyscraper located near the 12th Street BART train station. The luncheon had proceeded even worse than expected, with the investor even bringing up the loss on the ERI investment and Steven's apparent inability to operate within the laws of physics. Now thoroughly depressed in addition to being stressed, a thought came to mind as he ran his hand through his hair. The one time he had not felt bad in recent months was aboard the yacht. He longed for that sense of relief from his troubles. He was in the vicinity of Lake Merritt, a well-known area for purchasing drugs. He decided to walk to the park and at least observe things. Sitting on a bench by the water, he soon witnessed multiple individuals making exchanges. The drug sales were being conducted with only a minimum of concern. There were no policemen in the area.

After watching one particular African-American man conduct several transactions without interference of any kind, he decided to approach.

Leon picked out the rich white guy more than thirty yards away. The clothes were a dead giveaway, especially the Italian leather shoes. He mentally quickly adjusted his pricing upwards. Leon also signaled his lookout.

"Yo."

"Afternoon."

"Interested in something?"

"Something white."

"How much you got?"

"Five hundred."

Leon reached into his left coat pocket and by feel picked up two small bags of his premium cocaine, not the excessively cut product sold to the junkies. He smoothly reached his hand into Steven's jacket pocket and deposited the product. Leon then looked into Steven's eyes and then down to his right coat pocket. Steven understood and deposited the cash, quickly walking away afterwards.

Later that evening, Steven did two lines in the greenhouse located in the back of the mansion's garden. He hid the remainder of the cocaine in a long-unused box in a garden shed. He was finally able to feel better, temporarily released from his demons.

Chapter 53

Sunday April 28, 2019
Berkeley, California

About two months had passed since Sofia, Kathi, Bruce, and Joseph had decided to pursue the technology-related entrepreneurial opportunity involving artificial intelligence, data mining, and machine learning. The second bedroom in Sofia's and Joseph's apartment had been converted into the headquarters for their as yet unnamed venture. A central table was surrounded on all sides by laptops, a high-capacity, high resolution color laser printer, a new Internet modem, cat 6 ethernet cables, uninterruptible power supplies, whiteboards, and a projection screen.

At 6:30 PM, the four of them sat around the table to discuss their progress to date and share a bottle of *Catarratto Bianco* wine from Sicily selected by Sofia.

"The software we've coded looks like it's integrating well with the technology tools we've accessed through the cloud service," advised Kathi.

"In the past few days, we've been able to discern live trends in our targeted market well before any mass-media news reports. Bruce's idea of leveraging his knowledge from his work at the solid-state battery startup to focus on companies in the emerging environmental technology space was a good one. That helped concentrate our data mining and speed obtaining results," added Sofia.

"That was a good summary, Ms. Jobs," said Kathi.

"Thank you, Ms. Wozniak," replied Sofia.

The women laughed.

Seeing the perplexed look on the men's faces, Kathi added, "The founders of Apple. Jobs was the taller one."

The men grinned broadly. Bruce then refocused their discussion.

"My perception is that we'll have a Democrat for President in 2021. Trump just can't avoid antagonizing too many constituents with his off-the-cuff communications. If we have a Democratic President, there will likely be a shift in government emphasis toward climate change and related matters. I think we've therefore selected a growing target market, where we can leverage our technical expertise and where there will likely be evolving technologies which present significant financial opportunities."

"The key next step is linking our interpreted Internet information into actionable trades in the options market," added Kathi. "We can identify trending matters on the social media platforms and also monitor company press releases and regulatory filings for keywords and specific subject matter. What we're not sure of is how to convert that to buy and sell orders."

"This is untouched territory as far as I know," explained Joseph. "I was thinking of possibly developing some type of point scoring system. Certain positive or favorable observations in the mined data would be scored into points, perhaps with some type of relative weighting. Companies that accumulate a certain number of points within a given timeframe would be flagged for purchasing a call option and / or selling a put option. The inverse would apply to companies that accumulate a certain number of negative points."

"I like that idea," said Sofia. "Joseph, please think about examples of positive and negative keywords, topics, and phrases. We'll also need the parameters for a simple scoring system, perhaps beginning with assigning 1, 2, or 3 points based upon the relative importance of the information. We can observe what other keywords, topics, and phrases are correlated with the ones you supply to enhance the system. Kathi and I will code the scoring formulas. Our system will produce a recap report or score sheet each day. We can then compare that output with the actual change in equity prices," presented Sofia.

"This all sounds good, but I have one primary concern with our approach. What about the potential impact of a systemic event on the overall capital markets? If a major war breaks out, or there is a financial meltdown like in the late 2000's, or some other large-scale unfavorable event occurs, we'll lose money even if we pick the best stocks. We may lose less than the average, but we'll still lose," detailed Bruce.

"A falling tide sinks all ships," added Joseph. "I see what you mean. I agree. We should add some front-end or macro market monitoring to our technology that advises us when to either avoid investing in the first place; or to sell index call options or purchase index put options if we still want to put some capital to work in an adverse overall environment."

The other three nodded their concurrence.

Sofia verbalized their agreement with, "Sounds good. We've got a plan!"

After they relaxed a bit and enjoyed the last of the wine, Kathi spoke, "This has been a lot of work. We're doing our day jobs, and also advancing our potential venture. I don't want all of this to crowd out time for our relationships."

When Bruce did not react, still thinking about the earlier conversation, Kathi jumped onto his lap facing him, gave him a lingering kiss, and smiled.

"Oh, that's a good point. How about if we set aside an upcoming weekend for just socializing, no work performed or even mentioned," suggested Bruce.

"I've always wanted to spend a weekend at a bed and breakfast on the north coast, near Mendocino," said Kathi. "I've heard it's beautiful and peaceful."

"Sounds wonderful," replied Bruce.

Joseph looked at Sofia, expecting a similar suggestion.

Sofia observed this and said, somewhat mysteriously, "I have something a bit different in mind for us."

Joseph knew better than to pursue further questions in that regard, and remained silent.

"Well, we should be going," said Bruce. He stood up, easily lifting the much smaller Kathi to her feet. They departed for their townhouse with their arms around each other.

Chapter 54

Wednesday May 8, 2019
San Francisco, California

Samantha mentally reviewed her plan one last time. Now ready to proceed, she closed the door to her office and removed her panties. She was already wearing her most extreme push-up bra, having been sure to camouflage that by wearing her suit jacket all morning. Her skirt fell four inches above her knee even when pulled down to her hips. She took the elevator up to the 45th floor and walked into Billy's office.

"Good afternoon, Billy."

"Oh, hello, Ms. Moore."

Billy had become acquainted with Samantha via the executive profiles loaded on the management company's intranet. They had never previously met in person.

"We're low on office supplies downstairs. Might you please help me borrow some from the 45th floor supply room?"

"Well, okay."

On the way to the supply room, Samantha attempted to set up Billy.

"Billy, have you ever had a girlfriend?"

"I went on two dates with an autistic girl in high school. They were arranged by the parents. She was never really a girlfriend."

"I see. Do you like women, Billy?"

"My mother has been really good to me, despite my problems."

"I mean liking women in a more personal way, such as a girlfriend."

"I've watched videos about that on the Internet."

Somewhat encouraged that her plan would work, Samantha asked Billy to get a box from the far side of the supply room. She used that distraction to unbutton her suit jacket and open her blouse down about six inches. She then grabbed and climbed a stepladder, ostensibly to select office supplies from the top shelf. She was careful to keep her back to the security camera in the room, and to choreograph her movements so that Billy would be facing the security camera.

"Let me hand you some supplies to place into the box," said Samantha.

She gestured for Billy to bring the box closer and lift it up, thereby ensuring that his gaze could not possibly avoid traveling up her skirt. In passing down the office supplies, Samantha positioned her cleavage as close to Billy's face as she could while still making the scene appear legitimate from the angle of the security camera.

Samantha slowly passed Billy various office supplies while using her peripheral vision to monitor his groin. Running out of a reasonable amount of time in light of the planned future review of the security footage, with her back still to the camera, Samantha withdrew a handkerchief from the pocket of her jacket and blotted her face and neck, commenting that it was warm in the room. She then slowly ran the handkerchief across her cleavage, counting on a standard visual response to result in Billy's following it.

Samantha again used her peripheral vision to monitor Billy.

Success! In fact, the young man appeared to be particularly well endowed. She turned back towards the shelving to button up her blouse and jacket, out of the view of the security camera.

As she descended the ladder to collect the box of office supplies, she pointed at his erection, saying "What is that?"

Samantha acted aghast, gesturing several times to ensure that the video would be conclusive.

Embarrassed, Billy darted from the room, but not before giving the camera a profile shot of his protruding penis.

One down, one to go, thought Samantha.

Chapter 55

Saturday May 26, 2019
San Anselmo, California

It was the Saturday of the long Memorial Day weekend. Bruce and Kathi were traveling north up the 101 Freeway to Mendocino to a B&B. Joseph and Sofia were about to leave their Berkeley apartment to a destination that only Sofia knew. Joseph was intrigued by the mystery; even more so after Sofia told him to buy a bottle of *Trebbiano* white wine from northeastern Italy and dress in his best casual clothes.

"It's almost noon. Should we have a bite to eat before we depart?" asked Joseph.

"That would be a big mistake," replied Sofia, smiling.

Sofia drove them over the Richmond Bridge and into Marin County, located to the north of San Francisco, eventually stopping in the town of San Anselmo.

"The suspense is killing me," said Joseph. "When are you going to tell me what you have planned for today?"

"We discussed taking some time to focus on our relationship. I planned today to help you get to know me better."

Sofia parked the car in front of the Green Meadows retirement community. Joseph followed Sofia into the assisted living portion of the complex. They stopped at one of the apartments on the second floor. Sofia knocked on the door. A short woman, apparently in her nineties, opened it.

"Ah, Sofia, *nipotina, benvenuta*. Come in, come in." Joseph immediately noticed the extensive hand gestures.

Sofia approached the elderly woman, bent over, kissed her on each cheek, and said *"Nonna, come sta?"*

"Not so bad for over ninety. And who's this good-looking gentleman?"

"He's the boyfriend I told you about, Giuseppe."

Quickly realizing that Sofia had planned his introduction to her beloved grandmother, Joseph searched his memory for the right phrase to use. He approached her, also kissed her on both cheeks, and said, *"Sono lieto di fare la sua conoscenza* (I am pleased to make your acquaintance)."

"Handsome and also speaks Italian!" grinned *signora* De-Marco. "Please, have a seat at the table."

The dining room table was already set with plates, glasses, silverware, and napkins.

"Signora, while Sofia's been educating me in my cultural heritage, I must admit to being far less than fluent in Italian," shared Joseph.

He then presented the *signora* with the bottle of wine.

"Molto buono!" exclaimed the *signora* after looking at the label.

While the *signora* walked into the kitchen, Joseph caught Sofia's eye. She simply smiled at him.

"Ecco, we have *antipasti misti* to start," said the *signora* as she slowly brought one plate after the other to the table, the best she could do in light of her age and physical limitations. "Giuseppe, can you please open the wine? Sofia, please pour the mineral water."

The *signora* said grace in Italian. Joseph only understood about every third word. They starting eating from the plates of cured meats, assorted cheeses, and preserved peppers kept in olive oil with garlic. The *signora* was hardly shy in asking Joseph a lengthy series of pointed questions.

"So, Giuseppe, do you come from a good family?"

"Not famous or wealthy, but honest, hard-working people."

"There's no shame in doing a good day's work," opined the *signora*. "Speaking of work, Giuseppe, what do you do for a living?"

"I work in finance. My first job out of graduate school was with a start-up company, which we eventually sold. I'm currently working for a mid-tier investment bank."

"You earn good money? Stable job?"

"I'd say yes to both."

"Good to hear."

The *signora* raised her glass of wine in a toast, saying, "*Cent'anni* (may we live to be 100 years old), which in my case isn't too much longer!"

Joseph and Sofia both laughed. The *signora* circled back to her investigation.

"Giuseppe, do you like children? Any nieces or nephews?"

"I'm an only child, so I would actually like to have a family on the larger side. I really enjoy sports – the teamwork, the exercise. I'm looking forward to teaching my children how to play whatever sports appeal to them."

"It's important for a father to set a good example for his children, and sports provide many opportunities for that. Do you know that Sofia was a basketball star in high school?"

"Not really a star, *nonna*, just a tall girl with lots of energy," blushed Sofia.

After they finished the antipasti dishes, Sofia cleared the plates to the kitchen and re-filled their wine and water glasses. This gave the *signora* enough time to bring out a basket of freshly baked, sliced bread, while Sofia carried a piping hot dish of baked ziti, fresh from the oven.

"*Mangiamo* (let's eat)," said the *signora.*

About half way through the pasta, the *signora* returned to questioning Joseph.

"Giuseppe, do you go to church?"

"I did while growing up. However, I've been remiss in that regard in recent years."

"The good Lord bestows many gifts, but only if you are there to receive them," advised the *signora.*

"You have a good point. Now that we're talking about it, I *have* missed the spirituality and peace present in mass," noted Joseph.

"I would like us to join a parish and attend mass more frequently," shared Sofia. "It's important to have a balance in life between the corporal and the spiritual. You taught me that, *nonna.*"

"You were always such a good student, Sofia, especially in the kitchen. Do you remember the other big lesson?"

"To take time in life to live and love," responded Sofia.

"My dear Enrico and I ensured we ate Sunday dinner together every week, without distraction. No phone calls, no television, just focused on each other. We also took two weeks each summer to rent a house on *Lago di Como.* Such beauty is inspirational."

"I wished I had more time to get to know *nonno,*" said Sofia.

"He was a good man, a blessed soul, passed too young," commented the *signora*, with a sadness in her voice.

She then stayed quiet for the first time since Joseph walked in the door.

Sofia eventually broke the silence with, "*Nonna*, I have no doubt that you've prepared a delicious dessert."

"Of course!" She turned to Joseph and inquired, "How about some *dolce*?"

Although Joseph was now already more than full, he responded with, "Based upon the desserts you taught Sofia to make, I can hardly wait to see what you've prepared."

Sofia cleared the dishes from the table and brought dessert plates and a bottle of *Frangelico* to the table along with two small glasses for the *digestivo*. She explained to Joseph that since she was driving, she would skip the cordial.

The *signora* emerged from the kitchen carrying a plate with some type of elaborate-looking cake, presented on a highly decorated, raised dish.

"*Signora* DeMarco, please forgive my ignorance, but what is this cake called?" asked Joseph.

"*Nadalin.* It was invented in Verona, Italy in the 13th century. It pairs well with the *Frangelico*."

As the three of them were enjoying the dessert, the *signora* honed in on her final line of inquisition.

"So, Giuseppe, tell me about your plans for my granddaughter."

Joseph took a deep breath. He looked at Sofia, who indicated that she would not be jumping into this part of the conversation.

"Well, *signora*, let me begin my answer by saying that I love Sofia. She is the most marvelous woman I have ever met. Smart, fun, attractive, and the second best cook I have ever met, after you of course."

The *signora* smiled from ear to ear.

Joseph continued, "Every moment with Sofia is a blessing. I remind myself every morning how fortunate I am to have met her."

"That's a good answer, Giuseppe. Don't ever forget that the richness of life is in relationships, both with God and with other people. Anything you can buy eventually breaks, wears out, or becomes obsolete. The warmth in one's heart from a good relationship is eternal."

"I told you that my *nonna* is the family's resident philosopher," grinned Sofia.

At the conclusion of the meal, Joseph received a call on his smartphone from one of his co-workers at the investment bank. While he was talking, Sofia helped her *nonna* wash the dishes. When they were side by side at the kitchen sink, the elderly woman signaled for Sofia to bend down.

She whispered into Sofia's ear, "*Approvo. Mi piace lui* (I approve. I like him)".

"*Sono molto felice* (I am very happy)", replied Sofia.

After multiple hugs, kisses, kind words, and good-byes, Joseph and Sofia started the return drive back to Berkeley. Sofia stayed mostly silent, giving Joseph some time to integrate everything he had seen and heard during the afternoon.

Joseph finally stated, "Thank you for arranging today. Your *nonna* is one hell of a person, and at her age! I can't imagine what she was like at twenty-five years old... I now have a much deeper appreciation for your family's background and your childhood."

"Mission accomplished," joshed Sofia.

Chapter 56

Monday June 3, 2019
San Francisco, California

Steven, Charles, and Samantha met in Steven's office at 7:00 AM, before most of the management company staff would arrive. Charles brought in two jelly doughnuts and a venti of coffee, while Samantha carried a small mug of hot tea. Steven had downed an espresso while being chauffeured to the building.

"Let's recap where we are," said Steven. "First, the latest performance results."

"The Fund is now in the black, up a cumulative one percent. That's quite a comeback from our poor start. We flipped the investment in the company working on carbon capture from the air to a hedge fund for a fifty percent profit. That was a great buy."

Samantha grinned, but maintained her silence, continuing to keep the details of her activities with Jim Jordan secret from her fellow executives.

Charles continued, "The new trading operation had an excellent first week."

"I'm sure glad to hear that. I had to give the two traders a piece of my return as part of their compensation packages. The savings from firing Billy and Barbara were not enough. By the way, Samantha, never let me fall on your bad side. I was pleasantly surprised when the Director of Human Resources called me to advise that the company had no alternative but to terminate Billy due to repeated incidents of sexual harassment. It seems that he has difficulty controlling his erections."

Samantha simply smiled, then asking, "While the Fund's having a positive return is good news, where are we versus benchmarks?"

"The S&P 500 Index is up over eleven percent year-to-date, so we're still lagging badly," advised Charles.

"Where are we on the exposure limits for the trading operation?" inquired Steven.

"Still at level one. We want to monitor their performance some more before we raise the allowable value at risk. They're still obligated to take small losses in order to avoid a potentially large loss. That approach does, of course, also limit our upside potential," advised Charles.

"How much is available to borrow on the leverage line?" asked Steven.

"About $800 million. However, even with the value at risk limits in place to control our exposure, we've only turned over $100 million to the traders," replied Charles. "The information flow from the rest of the team regarding promising new technologies has been effective."

"What's the latest management company cash flow projection from Shantelle?" asked Samantha.

"Not good. Remember that we also had to hire an operations support person for the traders, plus the ongoing expenses of simply running a trading desk. In addition, now that we've been open a year, we need to give cost of living raises to the staff outside of the incentive pool. While the improved Fund performance is gratifying, that doesn't do much for the revenues into the management company. Even with stretching our payables, the management company will run out of cash in six months unless we take some other action."

"I can't see laying off any more employees at this point," opined Charles. "If we do, we'll endanger our ability to run the Fund successfully."

"I agree," said Steven.

"The last of the Atlas cash was spent on the Billy matter," shared Samantha. "I've had to pay for Jim Jordan's recent services from my own pocket."

"I'm willing to take a pay cut," offered Charles.

"I won't have you do that, especially when I might have to ask you to help Samantha fund Mr. Jordan. Instead, I've decided to scrape up whatever cash I can on a personal basis and then book that as a loan to the management company. The loan will be a zero-coupon instrument, with no payments due until we unwind the Fund. I'll accrue the minimum interest rate allowable under the applicable IRS regulations."

"That's generous of you, after all you've already put on the line," commented Charles.

Samantha nodded her agreement.

What Steven did not share was that his personal financial assets, distinct from his wife's trust, were nearly exhausted. In fact, he had already started selling personal property from their mansion, starting with his Rolex, gold cufflinks, and other items he thought Veronica would not miss. This had only further increased his stress level, resulting in his having made two more trips to Oakland to meet with Leon.

Chapter 57

Monday June 17, 2019
San Francisco, California

Jennifer was a bit nervous entering the law offices of Harrington & Harrington on her first day employed with the firm. She had gotten emotional last Friday on her last day on the job as a public defender. Saying goodbye to Maxine Scott was particularly difficult. Maxine had been a great mentor; patient, supportive, and encouraging. However, the compensation package from Harrington & Harrington was simply too much to decline, especially if Jennifer ever wanted to live somewhere other than her tiny apartment in Burlingame. The new position was also closer to that apartment, with the primary office located on California Street in downtown San Francisco.

"Good morning, Jennifer."

"Good morning, Mr. Stapleton. Nice of you to greet me on my first day. I appreciate that you have more important matters to address."

"No problem at all. At Harrington & Harrington, we take the onboarding process seriously. There's nothing like a good start to a new career. Let me show you to your office. After Alexis has assisted you with all of the human resources and technology set-up, call me and I'll introduce you to Robert Anderson. You'll be riding shotgun with him in his defense of one of our clients accused of money laundering."

"Sounds great. Thank you."

The day proceeded quickly for Jennifer. The pace of activity in the law office was much faster than in the public defender office. Part of that was due to the pedigree and education of the attorneys. That was also due to the greater complexity of most of the cases, leading to a much more substantial volume of documents and depositions to review. 6:00 PM arrived before Jennifer knew it. She hurriedly left her office and took the BART train down a station. She had agreed to meet Matthew Haddock at a highly regarded wine bar for their third date tonight. Since their initial electronic communication via the dating site less than two months ago, they had first met for coffee, then for lunch. This was their initial evening encounter.

"Hello, Jennifer. Nice to see you again. Please have a seat."

Matthew was already seated at a table when Jennifer walked in. He stood up and gestured for her sit across from him.

"How are you this evening?" asked Jennifer.

"Good, if somewhat mentally worn down, to be honest. Among the projects I've been assigned to is a new technology platform that analyzes incoming bill of lading data to identify potential importation of contraband. It's a massive system that collects and reviews data from air, rail, truck, and ocean freight. There are a lot of data elements, such as type of cargo, weight, volume, exporting site and entity, importing site and entity, frequency of shipment, final destination, etc. Our FBI team is tasked with developing criteria among the data elements to flag specific shipments for inspection. Not all of the source systems use the same terminology, nor employ exactly the same data elements. On top of that, there is just a huge amount of information to process."

Matthew then paused, realizing that he had gone on too long.

He quickly said, "But you probably didn't plan on spending the night discussing FBI computer applications," smiling and looking into Jennifer's eyes.

He certainly is handsome, thought Jennifer. Apparently fit, with a slight wave to his dark blonde hair. He's two years older than I am, well educated, with a budding career. This is definitely an upgrade from most of the men I've dated. She tried to make him feel better about his lengthy project description.

"I can understand what you're saying. For example, with many thousands of containers being offloaded from a single ship at each port call, it's physically impossible to inspect many on a percentage basis. Therefore, some type of probabilistic analysis is critical to effectively utilizing the available enforcement resources."

Matthew was once again impressed with Jennifer's quick uptake and grace in communication. No wonder she was such a successful attorney. And cute.

"Well said. Now, how about we consider what wine to taste tonight?"

"Do you have a recommendation?" asked Jennifer.

"I'm Irish by ancestry, so whisky and cordials are more my areas of expertise. I'll defer to you."

"Hmmm... The *Prosecco* from the Veneto region of Italy sounds delicious. Let's start with that."

The evening progressed smoothly. Two well-educated professionals sharing their perspectives and opinions, sometimes gently arguing, always respectful of each other.

At 9:00 PM, Jennifer looked at the time on her smartphone and said, "Tomorrow is my second day at the new law firm, so I need to get my rest. Might you be interested in sharing a delicious dinner next Friday or Saturday? I know a special place. My treat."

She opened the calendar app on her phone.

Matthew smiled at Jennifer's spunk. She was livelier than most of the women he had dated. He found that quite appealing.

"I was hoping you might suggest something like that."

Chapter 58

Saturday June 29, 2019
Berkeley, California

Sofia, Kathi, Bruce, and Joseph were again together in Sofia's and Joseph's apartment to share dinner and discuss their AI project.

"Let's sit at the table," said Sofia. "Tonight, we're having a sort of Italian smorgasbord. First, we'll try three different types of *arancini*, stuffed balls of risotto rice that are deep fried. That's a dish from southern Italy. Then, we'll share a plate of pasta that is a specialty from Rome called *cacio e pepe*."

"No shortage of carbohydrates tonight, I see," joshed Kathi.

"I knew we'd need our energy to decide what to do with our potential venture," smiled Sofia.

"I bought of bottle of highly recommended *Soave* wine from the Verona area, courtesy of my now wealthy local wine shop owner," joked Joseph.

After they were about half way through the meal and had caught up with the latest news in each of their personal and professional lives, Bruce said, "So, where are we with the testing of the AI application?"

Joseph responded, "We spent two weeks noting the system's recommended buys and sells of options based upon the data mining, analysis, and scoring criteria we've developed. Each time, we captured the prices at the time of recommendation, and then compared the prices a week later. In seventy percent of the simulated trades, we broke even or made money. That is an astounding result."

Sofia added, "Kathi and I studied the thirty percent of the simulated trades where we lost money. We identified various patterns in those trades, such as the source of raw information from the Internet used in the analytics. We then fine-tuned the coding to reduce the likelihood of a repeated loss."

"After that step, I interfaced my smartphone to the system and spent one week making actual trades from my online brokerage account. All of the buys and sells of options were conducted in small dollar amounts. I closed out all of the positions at the end of the trading this afternoon."

"And the answer was? Don't keep us in suspense!" exclaimed Kathi.

"I generated a profit on sixty-five percent of the trades, broke even on ten percent, and lost money on twenty-five percent. In aggregate, a very profitable week on a percentage basis, even if the nominal dollar amounts were small."

"While that is a great success, we have to be careful not to extrapolate too much from just one week's trading. There may be important variables that our system cannot evaluate, which just did not happen to be meaningful in this particular week," noted Bruce.

"Agreed," said Joseph. "We learned a lot about the risks of extrapolation with ERI. We also have not yet had the system generate a macro avoidance flag. In addition, we need to recognize that the equity markets rose strongly during June. There was hardly a reason to avoid being invested."

"So, where do we go from here?" inquired Kathi. "More testing?"

"I don't think it's fair to have Joseph take all of the financial risk with the live testing," opined Sofia. "I'd feel bad if he took losses simply because our heuristics have shortcomings."

"Why don't we form a limited liability company, or LLC," suggested Bruce. "Based upon what we learned in working with Ken White while at ERI, LLCs are relatively simple and low cost to establish. We can each be members, or partial owners, of the LLC. We can also each contribute an initial funding for the LLC. The LLC can open an online brokerage account for conducting the option trades recommended by our system. The income or loss from the LLC would be passed through to our individual federal and California income tax returns. That way, we'd all share in the financial aspects, rather than putting that all on Joseph."

"We could contact Ken for recommendations for an attorney to help with the LLC formation documents and a certified public accountant to assist with the tax information reporting," suggested Joseph. "But, there's one more key aspect we need to discuss."

Sofia, Kathi, and Bruce each stared at Joseph as he paused to finish his last *arancini*, this one stuffed with a tomato and meat sauce.

"I can only take so much time from my job to punch in the trades recommended by the system. In addition, the lag time between the system recommendation and my entering the trades introduces an element of risk. In other words, the options may reprice by the time I can get online. Is there any way we can directly interface the system to the online brokerage account?"

"Hmmm…," said Kathi. "I'd need to perform some research to see which online brokerage accounts would support an automated API, and what the technical and administrative criteria are for that."

"I can help program the API. From what I've seen with

Joseph's option trades, there are a limited number of data elements to pass through, such as the specific option contract, the quantity of options, and a maximum or minimum execution price. Joseph, I'd need your help in building a database of the option contracts available on the exchanges from time to time in order to allow the system to generate the specific trade information," said Sofia.

"No problem. Now that Bruce has helped us narrow our field of investments into the environmental technology space, we have a manageable number of companies and option contracts to consider," replied Joseph.

The conversation paused while the four friends considered everything that had been discussed. Sofia used this opportunity to serve dessert.

"Have any of you ever tasted *stracciatella gelato*?"

Kathi, Bruce, and Joseph all shook their heads in the negative.

"It's heavenly. Fine chocolate integrated into Italian-style vanilla ice cream," explained Sofia.

As they were indulging in the delicious dessert, Bruce brought the conversation back around to their venture.

"How about this as a follow-up plan. I'll contact Ken White regarding the LLC, attorney, and CPA. Joseph can continue the testing of the system with small dollar amounts. Kathi and Sofia can work on fine-tuning the system algorithms based upon Joseph's trading results while also working on the API. We'll continue to keep each other apprised via our text string."

"That sounds good, but there is one other aspect we should discuss," interjected Kathi. "If we decide to proceed with our enterprise, Sofia and I don't have that much capital to contribute to the LLC. I wouldn't want to take advantage of you and

Joseph having the cash from the ERI sale."

"That's needlessly considerate of you, Kathi," said Joseph. "The way I look at it, you and Sofia have contributed enormous sweat equity via all of your time programming. Your intellectual property contribution is enormous. I vote we count that as an equal capital contribution to the LLC, making us each twenty-five percent owners."

"I second the motion," jumped in Bruce.

Sofia raised her wine glass in a toast.

"To the four entrepreneurs! Blazing new trails together!"

After they clinked glasses and finished the last of the *Soave*, Joseph said, "That reminds me. We'll need a name for our LLC. Something that has not been used before."

"Didn't Sofia just suggest Blazing Capital LLC?" smiled Kathi.

"I'll verify that name is available, but that sounds great to me," responded Bruce.

And so Blazing Capital LLC was conceived. Little did the four parents know how appropriate that name would become.

Chapter 59

Thursday July 4, 2019
San Francisco, California

Veronica and Steven were dressing for the afternoon's event, a fourth of July fundraiser hosted at their mansion in support of Veronica's non-profit. Attendees would include quite a few 'A-List' socialites and captains of industry, augmented by a couple of mid-level celebrities.

"Steven, I don't mean to be insulting in any way, but you look terrible. Have you been sleeping? Perhaps you should make an appointment with your physician."

Veronica in particular noted his thinning hair and the dark circles under Steven's eyes.

"Managing the Fund's operations has been more difficult than I ever would have imagined. We're dealing with so many cutting-edge technologies in a rapidly evolving space. At the same time, the S&P 500 Index is on a tear, up almost nineteen percent during the first six months of the year. That has made our relative performance appear disappointing, which in turn has increased the pressure from the Board of Directors and from our investors."

"They should understand that the Fund is an intermediate-term venture, with some of the capital allocation toward small and illiquid entities. It takes time for investments like that to produce profits."

"You're of course correct, but the Fund is only up about two percent cumulatively at this point. The fast rise of the S&P 500 Index and other equity markets has been front page news. You know how people focus on what we've done for them lately, concentrated on the short term."

"I've encountered some of that perspective in regards to the non-profit. Donors want to see results quickly. They often don't understand that we're fighting the teachers' unions and their paid-for politicians."

As Steven finished putting on his tuxedo, he noted how loose the waist had become. His diet of coffee, alcohol, and cocaine wasn't providing much nutrition.

"Steven, you know that Maureen will be attending today."

"I think you mentioned that to me, yes."

"She's still quite upset about Billy's firing. I must admit that I was very disappointed, in fact angry, as well, until you showed me the video excerpts of his approaching women with an obvious erection. However, I don't think you should share that video with his mother. It would be too personal."

"Agreed. I'll try again to explain that it was a decision by the Human Resources Department and that I had no involvement whatsoever."

"She may not be satisfied with that. She loves Billy as only a mother can. She'll also have a difficult time imagining that an autistic, socially introverted individual would have the chutzpah to sexually harass women."

"I'll do the best I can with Maureen."

As Steven and Veronica descended the main staircase to the foyer, they saw the caterers assembling a tent, a sound system, serving stations, tables, and red, white, and blue decorations in the meticulously maintained garden. The forecast was for a sunny day, with afternoon temperatures in the city in the mid-70's, moderated by the cooling effect of the fog bank outside of the Golden Gate. Steven thought to himself, thank goodness I hid my cocaine stash so carefully in the gardener's shed. Over the past months, he had become increasingly addicted to the powerful drug.

Chapter 60

Friday September 13, 2019
Chicago, Illinois

Brian Compton, Esquire, was sitting at his desk in his one-man, Chicago law office when six FBI agents walked in, showed him a search warrant, told him not to touch anything, and placed him under arrest after reading him his Miranda rights. Two of the large international banks had recently upgraded their software for monitoring financial transactions for potential money laundering. The enhanced technology flagged funds transfers conducted by entities controlled by Brian, including Azure Sky LLC. This resulted in the filing of Suspicious Activity Reports with the Financial Crimes Enforcement Network, a bureau of the U.S. Treasury Department. Those reports led to a referral to the FBI and several weeks of probing and research. Late yesterday, the regional FBI office decided to move on Brian, before he became aware of their investigation and potentially destroyed important records.

After Brian was led away, FBI agents collected boxes of paper documents from his office, along with his smartphone and laptop. A second FBI team was doing the same at Brian's home. Unsurprisingly, all of Brian's devices were encrypted.

Under questioning later that day at the FBI regional office, Brian refused to speak other than to demand his right to meet with a defense attorney. In particular, Brian denied the FBI's requests to divulge the encryption keys to his devices.

The further investigation of the case was assigned to lead FBI Special Agent David Morton. David met late in day with the regional FBI chief, Stuart Alsop.

"What do you think so far?" asked Stuart.

"I think Brian Compton was well prepared for an event like today. The encryption used on his business and personal laptops is high grade, much more advanced and with a longer key than is employed in most business software. We'll have to see if our technology team can crack it. At the same time, we'll digitize and then sort through all of the paper documents. That said, I'm not hopeful in that regard. Compton has an undergraduate degree in criminal justice in addition to his law degree. I just don't see his being careless enough to leave any type of physical paper trail."

"Sounds like this case is going to take a while," opined Stuart.

"You can say that again. I just heard that Compton has retained one of the top criminal defense law firms in Chicago. The U.S. Attorney's office can plan on encountering every roadblock allowable under the defense procedures."

"Well, keep me informed. And let me know if I can be of any assistance, including with prosecution team. This case could open up a lot of avenues for us. We don't have any idea how extensively Compton is connected, although the size of the fund transfers described in the Suspicious Activity Reports indicates that Compton has been playing in the major leagues. In fact, we may need to provide protection for him. It wouldn't be unusual for his types of clients to ensure that he could never be deposed, much less testify at trial."

"Good point. I'll keep you updated regularly," promised David.

The fund transfers through Azure Sky LLC through to Atlas were thus secure for the time being. Of course, Steven Shaw had no way of knowing about today's events.

Chapter 61

By 6:30 PM, Bruce, Kathi, Joseph, and Sofia were all gathered in Joseph's and Sofia's apartment. Dinner tonight was simply a pizza from Gino's Restaurant and a bottle of California chardonnay. The team had been putting in many hours over the past two weeks completing the setup of Blazing Capital LLC. There had been no time to cook. Bruce began the discussion.

"The LLC is legally formed and registered with the California Secretary of State. The online brokerage account has been opened and funded with some of the profit from the ERI sale. Ken White linked us up with a good, local CPA."

"Great work, Bruce," said Joseph. "I've continued conducting the option trades in small dollar amounts as recommended by the system. With the ongoing fine-tuning performed by Sofia and Kathi, our success rate has improved by another two percentage points."

"We've completed the API from the system to the online brokerage account," added Kathi.

"And also coded in risk-control parameters based upon the financial algorithms supplied by Joseph," said Sofia.

The four of them looked at each other at this point, each waiting for the other to speak.

Finally, Joseph asked, "Does anyone know of a reason why we shouldn't go live?"

The room was again silent for several minutes.

Bruce eventually spoke, "I can't think of anything we've missed, other than a live test of the macro circuit breaker. The S&P 500 Index is slightly up thus far this quarter. There haven't been any dramatically down days in the stock market in quite a while. While Trump is certainly a loudmouth, his economic team has engineered a very strong economy. Look how low the unemployment rate is."

"The system did flash from green to yellow a couple of times this quarter. A paring back of exposure was indicated, which Joseph executed," noted Sofia. "I know that's not a valid test of the coding's being able to protect us from a dramatic drop in the stock market, like in 1929 and 1987."

"I have a lot of confidence in the coding that Sofia and Kathi have developed. That said, the real world is a large and complex place. The capital markets also evolve constantly. I'd vote to proceed to activate the system on an autonomous basis, but with initially restrictive risk exposure limits. We can all monitor the results daily via the VPN. If anyone identifies an issue, we quickly pull the plug," suggested Joseph.

"That sounds good to me," echoed Bruce. "If anyone notices an unfavorable trend or some other issue, we'll all have the access to suspend the system. We'll also all have access to the online brokerage account, so that we can close out positions separately from the actions of the system."

"I think that's a prudent approach," shared Kathi.

"I agree with what's been proposed," added Sofia.

"Well then, a toast to the opening bell at the stock market on Monday morning!" said Kathi.

The glasses full of wine were clinked, with all four of them excited about what the future might hold.

Chapter 62

Thursday September 30, 2019
Oakland, California

Customs Officer Ben Taylor was on duty at the Port of Oakland this morning. He flagged a specific incoming container for inspection. Ben had been advised to search the forty-foot steel box based upon a tip from the FBI, which in turn resulted from the new database system that Matthew Haddock and others at the FBI had been developing for the past several months. The system identified the weight of the container as being two standard deviations outside of the mean for the cargo classification of rattan furniture. Ben waited patiently on the dock as several thousand containers were unloaded from the huge ship by the enormous overhead cranes. Finally, the designated container was dropped onto a truck chassis and driven over to the customs inspection station. Ben rode in the truck with the driver.

A co-worker of Ben's started the video recording. That would be part of the evidence should any contraband be found. The video would also document that the customs agents followed procedure and did not plant anything. Another co-worker approached with one of their trained drug-sniffing dogs; this one a German Shepherd named Max. As soon as the container was opened, Max started barking. Ben entered the container with Max, who pawed several of the cushions tied to the rattan furniture. After carefully cutting open one of the cushions, Ben removed a shrink-wrapped block of white powder, holding it up for a clear video shot. He inserted a pocket knife into the powder and placed some into a plastic bottle. The container was then closed and sealed with special locks bearing the U.S. Customs and Border Protection logo.

Ben ran the sample from the plastic bottle through the chemical analyzer in his office. The result came back as high-grade cocaine. Ben picked up his cell phone and called Matthew Haddock, whose contact information had been provided on the initial email.

"FBI Special Agent Matthew Haddock speaking."

"Hello Agent Haddock, this is Ben Taylor from U.S. Customs here at the Port of Oakland. I received an email from your office requesting inspection of a specific incoming container."

"Yes, I understand. Our new system just went live a few days ago."

"Turns out you were right. We found cocaine. Don't know how much yet. We just sampled one of the cushions. The container is stacked eight feet wide by 9 and a half feet tall with the furniture. I figured you'd want to have some of your team on site before we perform any further investigation."

"That's appreciated. My partner and I can be there in about an hour if that works for you."

"Sounds good. You can text me on this number when you arrive."

"See you soon."

Once Matthew arrived on site, the U.S. Customs Officers began unloading the furniture into a secure warehouse located adjacent to their offices at the Port. Max was again brought in. He signaled every cushion. Four hours later, almost two tons of cocaine in shrink-wrapped packages was stacked in the warehouse.

"This has to be associated with a large operation," said Ben. "Someone invested a lot of capital to import that much product."

"We'll start the trace immediately and will coordinate with your office and the U.S. Attorney's Office. Shipments of this size are typically associated with multiple shell companies. It usually takes a while to sort through the layers, sometimes requiring the assistance of overseas intelligence agencies," said Matthew.

"I've seen situations where the goods producer, in this case the furniture factory, has no idea that their exports were being used for drugs. Sometimes the truck drivers divert the containers on their way from the factory to the port. The contraband is hidden in the legitimate export good. The importer may be involved or not. Sometimes the shipment is diverted on this side, with the drugs removed prior to the delivery to the buyer."

"I'm sure that the exporter and the importer will both claim no knowledge of the cocaine, regardless of whether they are guilty or not. They know how to use our procedures and laws to their advantage. That's why it usually takes so long to investigate and build a case for prosecution. I'm sorry, I don't mean to diminish in any way your work today, Ben."

"No offense taken. The representatives we send to Washington often stack the deck against us and then complain that we're not doing our job. Just look at the periodic border crises. Some of my colleagues work down south. That's a tough life."

Matthew shook Ben's hand after arranging to be emailed today's video. FBI Special Agent Haddock knew that he had a long stream of work ahead of him.

Chapter 63

Tuesday October 1, 2019
San Francisco, California

Charles and Samantha joined Steven in his office at 3:00 PM, closing the door behind them.

Steven looked up from his laptop and asked, "Where did we end up for the third quarter?"

"Based upon our latest estimated valuations, the Fund is now up a cumulative five percent. Our trading team did really well this quarter. That's been a financial lifesaver for us," replied Charles.

"The stock market has been on a tear this year," noted Samantha. "Where did the S&P 500 Index finish the quarter?"

"Up over twenty percent year-to-date," advised Charles.

"So, the good news is that the Fund has managed to recoup our initial losses, including on that fucking Minnesota windfarm. The bad news is that we're still badly lagging the overall market, we haven't lined up much of a profit-sharing payment for us, and the management company is just barely getting by in terms of cash flow," said Steven. "Any ideas on where we go from here?"

"We've identified an early-stage S corporation that is working to field test some potentially revolutionary technology for generating powerful magnetic fields. I don't fully understand the details yet, especially the chemistry, but it appears that, if successful, there could be substantial applications in terms of the green energy industry," shared Samantha.

"Why another firm involving magnetic fields?" asked Steven. "We lost our shirt on that bullshit oil spill remediation company that utilized magnetism."

"Two reasons. First of all, I think we could buy and quickly flip the company for a nice gain given the increasing political pressure about climate change," replied Samantha.

Both men nodded their understanding, awaiting her second reason.

"Secondly, the principal is a forty-five-year-old man with a wife and four children who is apparently experiencing a midlife crisis. He just bought an expensive sports car and has had hair plug surgery. He may be a perfect target for an episode with me and Jim Jordan."

"Don't worry Steven, I'll pay Jim's fee for this. It's the least I can do after everything you've devoted to the Fund," said Charles.

"Sounds like it's worth a shot," concluded Steven.

"Jim's going to get very tired of filming my naked ass," smiled Samantha.

The three executives all shared a laugh at Samantha's last comment. Then Charles spoke.

"I think we should raise the value at risk exposure limits on the two traders. They've proven their effectiveness. That's the fastest way for us to pump up the Fund's return."

"While that's true, they've been operating in a hot segment of a strong bull market," said Steven. "The traders have not really been tested by a difficult environment."

"You're of course correct. On the other hand, the economy is roaring, unemployment is at a record low, and Trump's policies have been pro-business. I'm thinking we should strike while the iron is hot," opined Charles.

"I'm with Charles on this," said Samantha. "From everything I've read, I don't see the Federal Reserve taking away the punch bowl by implementing an overly restrictive monetary policy. Pretty soon, we'll be into the election season. The Federal Reserve almost never dramatically adjusts interest rates during an election. They don't want to be viewed as interfering with politics."

"Okay. You two have convinced me. Let's triple the value at risk limits for the two traders, but continue to monitor their performance closely," decided Steven.

As Samantha exited the meeting, the discussion of the Fund's quarterly results reminded her that it was about time for Mistress Moore to book another performance review with Herman Phillips. She also remembered that she needed to order a yet more painful device to maintain Herman's interest.

Chapter 64

Friday October 5, 2019
San Francisco, California

Shantelle Jones, the Chief Financial Officer of Blue Planet Investment Management, was waiting for the elevator on the 44th floor when Roger Suffolk, the Chairman of the Board, also arrived at the elevator bank. Roger had just completed a Board committee meeting.

"Good afternoon, Shantelle. How are you today?"

"Personally fine, but, frankly, worried on the corporate side."

"About what?"

"We've taken on a significant amount of risk, which as a CFO, I'm by nature concerned about."

"Please, tell me more."

"Well, first of all, the Fund is investing in nascent technologies in a relatively new sector, ESG. That presents a notable amount of risk in and of itself. Then, we've added the leverage line syndicated through Huffman Brothers. While leverage can amplify our returns, it also has the potential to magnify losses."

"I understand everything you've said," advised Roger.

"To top it off, we're now running a trading desk, another operation that's fundamentally risky."

"It's my understanding that we have established risk exposure limits for the trading operation, and that results to date have been favorable."

"True. However, what I worry about is the *cumulative* risk across the *aggregate* operations of the Fund. Each risk component I have mentioned is, by itself, manageable. It's the potential interplay among these three sources of risk that I don't feel is well enough understood, and also sufficiently controlled."

"I see your point," acknowledged Roger.

"Has there been any discussion among the directors to enhance the Fund's risk management practices?" asked Shantelle.

"A couple of the directors have brought up similar concepts over the past several months. However, we're not in a good position to do much about it."

"Mr. Suffolk, I don't want to come across as unprofessional or unduly negative. That said, can I ask why not?" inquired Shantelle.

"You know that Mr. Shaw owns the management company, and in fact funded it from his own pocket. As the sole owner, he has the right to appoint and terminate each of the directors. In addition, his wife's trust represents twenty percent of the investment in the Fund. Absent something egregious, the best the Board can do is communicate and work to influence things in the right direction. This is a much different situation than the typical publicly traded corporation listed on the NYSE."

"I understand that, and everything else you've said. I'll also try to influence Mr. Shaw in a prudent direction."

"Shantelle, this has been a good conversation. Please know that I am always available to listen to your concerns. That's inherent in my role as Chairman of the Board."

"Thank you, Mr. Suffolk."

Roger and Shantelle entered the next arriving elevator heading down. Once on the ground floor, they each went their separate way.

Chapter 65

Brian Compton, Esquire, had made bail almost immediately following his arrest more than four weeks ago, facilitated by the arguments presented by the top-flight criminal defense law firm he had retained. Brian and his lead defense attorney, Richard Pennington, were meeting this morning at the regional FBI office with Stuart Alsop and David Morton.

"Good morning, gentlemen," said Stuart. "I'm Stuart Alsop, the regional FBI chief here in Chicago."

"My name is David Morton. I'm the Special Agent assigned to Mr. Compton's case."

"I'm Richard Pennington, the attorney for Mr. Compton, whom you both of course know. Before we commence this meeting, I would like stated that the usual terms and conditions apply. This is a meeting to discuss a potential plea bargain and settlement. Nothing discussed here this morning will be admissible in any future court proceedings."

"Acknowledged and agreed," replied Stuart.

David then took the floor.

"We've worked with FinCEN and identified five other suspicious funds transfers associated with Mr. Compton or entities he controls, directly or indirectly. All of these transfers were to entities legally domiciled in the Cayman Islands and other tax havens."

"It's not illegal to facilitate the purchase of real estate in the

Caribbean," replied Richard. "Many wealthy individuals desire some beachfront property for rest and relaxation."

"We were able to follow a couple of the paper trails," shared David. "It appears that the price paid for the real estate being transferred was well above market, as if to justify the transfer of funds offshore."

"The real estate market in many of the island countries is less than liquid. Comparative valuations are few and far between, especially for parcels with ocean frontage. Beauty is in the eye of the beholder," responded Richard.

At this point, David realized that the negotiation was going to be as difficult as he feared. He stood up to pour himself a cup of coffee from the carafe on the credenza. The FBI had not been able to crack the encryption used on Brian's devices. Therefore, the only evidence they had been able to assemble by this point were some meager leads from the paper documents seized from Brian's office and the records of the fund transfers sourced by FinCEN. He decided to try a different approach.

"Mr. Compton, you enjoy an enviable lifestyle. You live in a five thousand square foot house in one of Chicago's toniest neighborhoods, belong to a premier country club, and drive a BMW 7 Series, all while paying private school tuition for three children. That's an impressive feat for a one-person law office."

"There's no law against success," countered Richard.

"That's of course true. This is America after all," said David. "However, we've pulled Mr. Compton's federal tax returns for the past three years. His adjusted gross income has never exceeded $150,000. It's hard for me to understand how anyone could pay federal and the high Illinois state income taxes on that income and still have enough money left over to finance Mr. Compton's lifestyle."

"Mr. Compton may have access to assets other than the

cash flow from his business, such as an inheritance or income earned by his wife."

"We did notice that Mr. Compton has consistently filed his income tax returns as 'married filing separately', which is unusual," said David.

"Not all that unusual, and certainly not illegal," retorted Richard.

At this point, Brian spoke for the first time, asking to have a few minutes alone with his counsel. David and Stuart exited the meeting room.

"It's clear that they did not crack the encryption, or this conversation would have been much different," said Richard.

"That makes sense. However, I see where they're headed. They're going to push for a full IRS audit covering all tax years still open for examination. That will take a year or more to conduct. In addition, I won't be able to continue to keep this matter secret from my family. They'll also try to pull my wife's tax returns and subject her to deposition. There's also the risk that their technology team cracks the encryption code in the interim. A year is a whole generation in terms of computing power. Even a 1,024-bit key can be broken with enough brute force, technologically speaking. Things will be much worse for me if they access the files on my devices. Why don't we see what they might offer?"

"I don't generally like to go down that road so early in an investigation," replied Richard. "But if you insist, I'll do so."

"I've got three kids ages eight through twelve. I don't want to stain their childhood with this, if at all possible," said Brian.

Richard texted David and Stuart to rejoin them.

"Gentlemen, if you'll coordinate with the U.S. Attorney's office for a proffer agreement, my client and I would be willing to discuss alternatives for a plea bargain. The usual provisos would apply. Anything communicated in the plea bargain discussions would not be admissible in any potential future trial or at sentencing, if applicable."

David and Stuart looked at each other, as neither had expected that comment. Stuart spoke after a brief pause.

"We'll follow up in that regard through channels and get back to you."

"This meeting is now concluded," advised Richard.

He stood up, quickly mirrored by Brian. They departed the office.

"Well, that was certainly a surprise," expressed Stuart.

"My gut tells me that he does not want his wife to become involved," shared David.

"It never ceases to amaze me how some people are more afraid of their spouses than of the FBI."

Chapter 66

Friday October 25, 2019
Chicago, Illinois

Brian Compton, his defense attorney Richard Pennington, FBI Special Agent David Morton, Helen Barksdale from the U.S. Treasury Office, and U.S. Attorney Arlene Bishop met together in a conference room at the U.S. Attorney's Office. Ms. Bishop began by introducing herself and Ms. Barksdale. She then extended the proffer agreement to Richard. After reviewing it, he advised Brian to sign it.

"So, what offer are you willing to make to my client?" inquired Richard.

Ms. Bishop responded, "After reviewing the file over the past several days, it appears that Mr. Compton was just a conduit for money laundering, and likely not a principal in the associated illegal transactions. Should Mr. Compton plead guilty to misdemeanor money laundering and provide his full cooperation, including giving us the encryption key to his devices and testifying at trial regarding his knowledge of his clients' activities, we can offer one year of home confinement followed by three years of supervised release. A fine of $50,000 would be paid by Mr. Compton. The U.S. Treasury and the Internal Revenue Service will not pursue claims of underreported income. We would also not seek revocation of Mr. Compton's license to practice law in the State of Illinois."

Ms. Barksdale chimed in, "I confirm that the U.S. Treasury Office is willing to forego the tax enforcement as part of an overall negotiated agreement."

"The offer is not reflective of the potential value of Mr. Compton's records and testimony. You've already obtained information from FinCEN regarding the size of some funds transfers," responded Richard.

"Well, counselor, what do you have in mind?" asked Ms. Bishop.

"I acknowledge that your superiors will want, from a political perspective, some evidence of punishment. That said, six months of home confinement and followed by two years of supervised release would be more than adequate. No tax enforcement *and* no fine. There is no reason to punish my client's innocent wife and children. We will agree to the misdemeanor plea. And, of course, there would be no action on your part to pursue revocation of Mr. Compton's license to practice law. He is the primary support for his wife and three children," countered Richard.

"I will agree to those terms with the clear requirement of Mr. Compton's full cooperation in our investigation of his clients. If we discover that he has held anything back, the deal is off," presented Ms. Bishop.

"Another consideration," interjected Richard. "Due to the potential response of some of Mr. Compton's clients, which we cannot predict nor control, we'd require two additional components. First, that Mr. Compton's name be omitted from the public portion of the prospective prosecution to the degree possible while still pursuing the cases. Second, that the FBI will provide personal protection to Mr. Compton and his family upon his request, at no cost, and for as long as he reasonably desires."

Richard smiled inwardly to himself. He knew that the request for protection would only whet the appetite of the feds to obtain a plea bargain, and therefore surrender to more favorable terms for his client.

After a pause, Ms. Bishop spoke, "I can agree to the pursuit of limited confidentiality."

"The term 'reasonably desires' is quite open-ended," noted David. "I believe I could get FBI approval for protection ending one year following the conclusion of the final prosecution, with of course no guaranty as to the effectiveness of the protection. Everyone here appreciates the reality that certain elements of society are better armed that federal law enforcement."

Brian gulped at David's last comment despite being well aware of criminals often possessing military-grade weaponry. Thank goodness his clients were primarily rich individuals simply seeking to become even wealthier.

Ms. Bishop then stood to attract everyone's attention, turning to Brian and saying, "Mr. Compton, do you fully understand and agree to the terms and conditions as previously discussed?"

Brian stared down at the table in the face of this final question. How had his life come to this? He was in the top third of his law school class. Was wanting to provide a better life for his family so wrong? Maybe that was just an excuse for greed...

Dejectedly, he eventually responded, "I understand and I concur."

The meeting attendees agreed to follow up with the usual documentation and processing. Brian Compton, Esquire, would become the bitch of three law federal enforcement agencies.

Chapter 67

Tuesday December 10, 2019
Oakland, California

After more than two months of painstaking research following the interception of the large quantity of cocaine hidden inside the cushions of the rattan furniture, FBI Special Agent Matthew Haddock believed he finally knew who might be behind the importation. He had contacted international police organizations, requested special Suspicious Activity Report analysis from FinCEN, and poured through stacks of legal documents associated with the various entities at least tangentially related to the seized shipping container. The entities were most often limited liability companies, but there were also a few non-profits and several S corporations. One entity often owned the next one, with the various companies formed in multiple states. The pattern of ownership indicated that someone had an in-depth knowledge of the information collection and organizer disclosure practices from state to state, resulting in making the audit trail as difficult as possible to pursue.

The manufacturer of the furniture in Thailand claimed no knowledge of the cocaine. The importing furniture retailer took a similar position. There was no evidence of large funds transfers either to the furniture manufacturer or from the furniture retailer.

Matthew received a big break when the name Quinton Jackson popped up on an internal FBI system of potential criminals. An attorney in Chicago had provided Quinton's name to the FBI as part of a plea deal. Matthew recognized that name as being associated with three of the entities he had researched, including the trucking company which had been hired to transport the rattan furniture to the retailer. Quinton's name had also been mentioned by a detective on the Oakland police force as an individual rumored to control some East Bay turf in regards to organized crime.

At 7:00 AM, an armed FBI team descended upon Quinton's home. He was still asleep when they entered his bedroom. Quinton offered no resistance. After being read his Miranda rights, he was led away to the San Francisco regional FBI office. Once there, refused to speak other than to demand to call his attorney. While Matthew delayed in providing that opportunity, hoping to get him to say something, Quinton remained calm. He knew that all of the vital records were heavily encrypted, with most of them stored on an overseas server. He also knew that his practice of using burner cell phones for short periods of time would also deny the FBI a source of evidence. His paid-for politicians and individuals in law enforcement would furnish whatever support and cover they could, eager to continue the gravy train he provided. Finally, he had kept Troy Stapleton of Harrington & Harrington on retainer for years. Quinton would have access to the best legal defense team that money could buy.

At 2:00 PM in the afternoon, Troy Stapleton called Jennifer Franklin into his office. Despite all legal research now being conducted digitally, Troy maintained a large bookshelf behind his desk filled with the traditional trial case and statute books. This made a good show to the uninformed, validating his above-average hourly fees.

"We've got a new criminal defense case," advised Troy.

"Accusation?" asked Jennifer.

"Large-scale drug importation for distribution and sale. An existing client who has had us on retainer for years."

"Who's driving the case?"

"SF FBI. My guess is that they don't have much evidence, other than over two tons of seized cocaine."

"That will certainly attract some prosecutorial attention."

"Agreed. Our client is being held locally pending arraignment. We're going to visit him right now."

Troy and Jennifer drove to the cell where Quinton was being held. Jennifer was initially intimidated by Quinton's 6'7" frame and over 300 pounds, much in the apparent form of muscle. She calmed down after Quinton smiled and greeted her. It was immediately apparent that this was a well-educated man.

Quinton began the conversation by explaining that he had not said anything whatsoever to the FBI. The second topic of discussion was how quickly Troy could get him released on bail. Troy commented that he would work diligently on that, but such would likely take at least several days. Quinton shared that he would have no financial difficulty posting bail. The conversation concluded with Troy promising to follow up as quickly as possible with the U.S. Attorney's Office to understand the full scope of the charges and also to schedule a prompt arraignment hearing.

On their way out of the building, Troy and Jennifer passed Leon Hayes walking in. Quinton had called him to bring in his cholesterol medication after receiving approval of such from the FBI. Jennifer and Leon each stopped and stared at each other for a moment, before progressing in their separate ways.

"Boss, I brought the medication you asked," said Leon.

"Thank you. I don't want any artery damage."

Leon raised an eyebrow at these words. Quinton gave him

a small nod. 'Artery damage' was the pre-arranged phrase for Leon to tell QJ's team to shut down operations and destroy anything that could be potentially used as evidence.

"Boss, before I go, that woman attorney that just walked out."

"Jennifer Franklin."

"She good folk. She helped me a while back."

Quinton again gave Leon a brief nod and signaled with his eyes for Leon to depart.

Chapter 68

Friday December 13, 2019
Emeryville, California

At 5:30 PM, Kathi was still in her office at the technology firm. She initiated the planned group Facetime conference call with the other members of Blazing Capital LLC. Once everyone was linked in, Sofia commenced the discussion.

"I just got off the VPN into the system. Everything looks good from that standpoint."

Joseph spoke next.

"The software has exceeded our expectations. The interface to the online brokerage account is operating flawlessly. We've generated a profit or broken even on an amazing seventy-nine percent of our trades. In fact, we've already doubled our initial investment, pre-tax of course. We'll each be paying federal and California income taxes on the LLC's profits, which will likely require a distribution from the LLC. But, that's a nice problem to have."

"Good thing we lined up the CPA," said Bruce. He continued with, "I have one area of concern. Has the macro indicator given us any signals?"

"A few brief yellow lights, but generally green. We've still never seen a red light," replied Joseph.

"That makes sense given the continued bull market. The S&P 500 Index is almost at 3,200," added Sofia.

"The U.S. economy just keeps rolling along," noted Bruce. "It almost looks like a steamroller. 2019 is looking like a third consecutive year of GDP growth between two and three percent."

"So, do we let things ride, perhaps expanding our risk limits since we now have much more capital?" inquired Kathi.

"I'd be okay with a fifty percent increase in our exposure profile," shared Joseph. "I'll continue to monitor the online brokerage account daily. The brokerage firm's app is really well designed."

"We don't know if and when some evolution in the capital markets might render our algorithms less effective," commented Sofia. "So, I agree with Joseph. Let's go for it before we encounter some systemic change and need to reprogram."

"All those in favor?" asked Bruce.

The decision passed unanimously. Kathi and Sofia updated the risk mitigation module of the system over the weekend. Blazing Capital LLC would commence taking larger positions starting with the opening of the stock market on Monday morning.

Chapter 69

Friday December 20, 2019
San Francisco, California

"Almost ready for Christmas, Charles?" asked Steven at the end of the workday.

"Yes. I'm going to visit my brother and nephews. They've got quite a feast planned. My sister-in-law cooks some of the best stuffed turkey that you've ever tasted."

"Turkey for Christmas?"

"I put in a special request after not being able to join them for Thanksgiving."

"Oh, I see. Before we take off, what's the latest from our trading desk?"

"Looking good for the fourth quarter, although I noticed that several of our targeted positions were unexpectedly bid up right in front of our buy and sell orders. It happened several times, and never before this week."

"Might there be a new competitor? Someone who has decided to focus on our target market?"

"Possibly," replied Charles. "I did a bit of research. It looks like whoever is doing these trades can move very quickly, and with sophistication through the options market. There were some interesting, and in fact suspicious, patterns."

"Do you think we have a leak?"

"Could be. However, only the two traders, the operations assistant, and I are privy to the planned and actual trades."

"Might one or both of the traders be front-running us with transactions executed out of brokerage accounts they control, whether for themselves personally or for others?"

"That's more likely. It would be quite lucrative to execute trades just ahead of us, knowing in advance that our volume purchases would likely move the market price. In addition, we trade in a defined space focused on environmental technologies, leveraging the knowledge base of our Fund's investments. A trading coincidence in that space would likely not be."

"Greed sometimes knows no bounds. How about putting Jim Jordan onto the two traders, quietly of course. Have him shadow them. See if any new Ferraris are showing up at their houses, etc.," suggested Steven. "At the same time, you keep a closer eye on the traders at the office. See if you can observe any telling behavior."

"Sounds good. Too bad we can't trust anyone in this world," replied Charles.

"Other than each other," said Steven, putting his hand on Charles' shoulder and lightly squeezing.

Chapter 70

Monday December 23, 2019
San Francisco, California

Veronica returned home just before 5:00 PM. She immediately requested that Frederick bring her a cosmopolitan to drink. She walked upstairs and prepared for Steven's arrival. A half-hour later, she heard Steven enter the front door and met him in the foyer.

"Steven, let's sit in the library. I have something to tell you."

Veronica closed the double wood entry doors to the room filled with books, many of them rare first editions. She did not want Frederick to overhear them.

"Steven, I had three conversations today that I need to share with you."

"Of course, my love. Anything I can do to help."

"The first conversation was with the gardener early this morning. He discovered a bag of white powder in the shed while looking for some material for a new planter. He's street-wise, and advised me that the powder is cocaine."

"I wonder who could have put it there? We have so much help coming and going to maintain the property."

"So, you're denying that it's yours? Despite the weight loss, irregular hours, and periodic erratic behavior?"

Steven quickly analyzed the situation and determined it was best to continue denying that the cocaine belonged to him.

"I know I've been highly stressed at work, but that's quite

different than using cocaine," rebutted Steven.

"Okay, let's leave that topic for now. Would you like to hear about my second conversation today?"

"Yes, you know that you can share anything with me."

"It appears that you've shared with me. I went to the doctor today after experiencing vaginal itching and a discharge. I have chlamydia."

Steven panicked at Veronica's latest comment. He knew in his heart that Veronica would never be unfaithful. It just wasn't in her makeup. He hadn't noticed any symptoms, but he knew from his college days that the STD could be asymptomatic for periods of time. His mind raced. It must have been that evening on the yacht! The one that reintroduced him to cocaine and apparently made his acquaintance with venereal disease.

"I believe that's highly treatable if caught early."

It was the best line that Steven could summon in the moment.

"I've already started a course of antibiotics."

"That's good."

"Steven, do you have a mistress?"

"No. I would never even think of that."

"So, you've just been picking up women for casual sex?"

"Not that either."

"That leaves only one alternative, since I know you're not gay. Whores! Really, Steven, with your good looks and education, not to mention a wife who has always loved you and been faithful to you, you still stooped to whores!"

"You don't understand... I was under a lot of stress, plus the influence of alcohol and cocaine."

"So, the cocaine from the garden shed was yours."

"Yes."

Veronica shuddered, picturing Steven as one of the wealthy and powerful men associated with Jeffrey Epstein and his harem of underage girls. She gulped the last of the cosmopolitan and continued.

"Do you want to hear about my third conversation?"

Steven just stared down at the floor, trying to calculate a way to rescue himself from the situation.

Veronica continued, "My third conversation was with an attorney. He gave me this document to hand to you."

Veronica pulled a one-page letter from the bookshelf. Steven read it slowly, and then again. The document advised Steven that Veronica desired an immediate separation in preparation for divorce proceedings. He was to vacate their house immediately and not return unless invited. Any violation of these terms would result in Veronica's contacting local law enforcement, including in conjunction with the stash of cocaine.

"But, Veronica, I love you. I have since the day we met."

"Evidently not enough to keep your dick in your pants," she screamed, finally allowing her emotions to overtake her. She continued yelling, "Great fucking Christmas present, Steven! There are two duffel bags upstairs. Pack some of your clothes and get the hell out of here." Veronica broke down in tears, sobbing loudly.

Not knowing what else to do, Steven sheepishly left the library and went upstairs to pack the duffle bags. He then had the presence of mind to realize that this would likely be his last time in the mansion, and that his personal financial resources were exhausted. Now thinking more quickly, he went to Veronica's jewelry case and removed two large pieces from the bottom that she did not wear often, yet were particularly valuable. He placed one piece of jewelry into the middle of each duffle bag. He called an Uber to take him to a local hotel.

Chapter 71

Thursday January 9, 2020
San Francisco, California

Quinton Jackson arrived punctually at the law office of Harrington and Harrington in San Francisco to meet with his attorneys Troy Stapleton and Jennifer Franklin. The lawyers had been successful in getting Quinton timely released on bail. Quinton sat on a couch in Troy's office. The chairs would have been a tight, and uncomfortable, fit for the large man.

"So, where are we?" asked Quinton.

"The U.S. Attorney's office is investigating the case with the assistance of the FBI. They know that a trucking firm controlled by you was lined up to transport the rattan furniture. They dug through the historical records and discovered that the same trucking firm was always hired to transport the imported containers from the Port of Oakland to the furniture retailer. The retailer is a national firm that is publicly traded on NASDAQ. There is no evidence that the retailer knew anything about the cocaine," advised Troy.

"That doesn't sound like much."

"There's more. The FBI in Chicago has obtained the full cooperation of a local attorney under a plea deal. The attorney has turned over records of entities controlled by you transferring significant sums of money to accounts in the Cayman Islands, with the transfers washed through entities controlled by the attorney and disguised as real estate transactions."

"That son of a bitch! That asshole Compton promised me that he'd keep things secret! That's why I agreed to his fucking large cut."

Troy and Jennifer glanced at each other. It was clear that Quinton had more than a passing relationship with the attorney, evidently named Compton.

"The U.S. Treasury Office is about to initiate an audit of your federal income tax returns. I assume that you did not disclose your ownership of foreign accounts on your Form 1040 Schedule B?" asked Troy.

"You assume correctly."

"It gets worse. The FBI has developed a matrix of entities controlled by you. The U.S. Attorney is about to pursue a judge's approval to obtain bank account statements, brokerage account statements, and income tax returns for all of those entities."

"I employ several experienced CPAs to perform the accounting and tax return preparation for my entities."

"Do you really think that you'll be able to justify the revenue and cash flow run through all of those entities?"

"It's not my fault if the CPAs make a mistake."

"Actually, it still would be your liability, unless the CPA was personally embezzling from you."

"They wouldn't dare do that."

"Perhaps more critical than all of the foregoing is that the FBI and U.S. Attorney's Office is teaming with the local police department to squeeze individuals who may be in your employ. We've heard from the street that they are offering sweet plea deals to provide evidence that you're a kingpin of the cocaine trade," said Troy, grimly.

"Damn!"

Wanting to give Quinton some time to digest everything that had been discussed, Jennifer said she was getting herself a glass of water. She brought one back for Quinton as well. Quinton took a gulp, leaned back on the couch, and looked at the ceiling. He eventually spoke.

"Looks like it's time to activate my insurance policy."

"I'm not following you," said Troy.

"I've got video, audio, and documentary records on many of the rich and powerful in the Bay Area. You'd be surprised who my clients are. You'd also be surprised at who I have on payroll, especially those hypocritical politicians campaigning on a platform emphasizing law and order. All of that content is stored on an overseas server utilizing advanced encryption. The feds will never access that on their own."

"I'm still not clear on what you are saying."

"See if you can cut me a plea deal. I'm talking full witness protection and relocation, plus allowing me to retain my financial assets --- at least those the feds don't know about and won't try to find under the plea deal. I'll turn over the data, but there's no way I will testify. I'd never make it out of the court building alive. You've got to appreciate the type of people I'm talking about. Trust me. It'll be worth it to the feds."

Troy and Jennifer looked at each other, nodded, and turned back toward Quinton.

"We'll see what we can negotiate," said Troy. "Would you be willing to identify one big fish as an appetizer?"

Quinton looked up at the ceiling in thought.

He eventually responded, "Yeah. How about a State Senator who extolls family values in every campaign, but is actually one of my best customers for both the blow and the ladies? He likes them real young. In fact, this guy would've been on the Lolita Express with Jeffrey Epstein if he had more money."

Jennifer deferred to Troy to respond to this latest piece of information.

Troy simply replied, "Quinton, we'll be in touch. In the interim, keep your head down, if you know what I mean."

"Got that right."

Chapter 72

Friday January 17, 2020
Berkeley, California

Blazing Capital's system flashed a yellow light late last night, leading to its automatically reducing exposure and moving more of the online brokerage account assets into cash upon the open of the stock market at 6:30 AM this morning. Joseph saw the text message from the system about this just after he awoke at 6:45 AM. He nudged Sofia awake.

"Buon giorno, donna bella. Come sta?"

"Your accent is getting better! What's up my *amore*?"

He updated Sofia. They decided to immediately call Kathi on her smartphone.

"Did you see the text from the system last night?"

"Not yet, I was just opening my eyes as you called."

"It flashed yellow and pared down exposure automatically. Do you know why?"

"Not yet. I'll log on and see what happened. Sofia, can you join me on the VPN?"

"Right away."

"Sounds good. Let me know if I can help you two with anything," said Joseph.

Kathi initiated a Facetime call to Bruce, Sofia, and Joseph at 7:00 PM that evening.

"It looks like the system went to yellow based upon the

amount of web traffic devoted to something called a cor-onavirus. The threads indicate a potential negative macro event. We Googled multiple web sites. The biggest news we could find was that the U.S. Center for Disease Control dispatched one hundred people to three American airports to screen travelers coming from Wuhan, China. It appears that the first travel-related case of the virus entered the United States two days ago," said Kathi.

"The politicians and the news media haven't indicated that this is a major risk," noted Bruce. "In fact, the S&P 500 Index was slightly up today. There doesn't appear to be any capital markets concern about this."

"The global Internet is a much better source of information than our government and the media," opined Sofia. "This coronavirus issue appears to be a completely new event. It's unlikely that the big players in the capital markets understand much about it yet."

"We've sold out a number of gain positions and gone more to cash. No one ever went broke taking a profit," said Joseph. "Let's review the system's programmed response if it flashes to red. I'll also try to check in with the online brokerage account more frequently each day to better monitor things and keep everyone well informed."

"Sounds like a plan," replied Bruce. The women concurred.

Chapter 73

Saturday February 15, 2020
San Francisco, California

Jennifer Franklin and Matthew Haddock had continued to occasionally date over the past six months. While they enjoyed each other's company and were sexually compatible, they each had demanding jobs that had limited their time together. In addition, they had intentionally maintained their distance while Jennifer was assisting in the plea deal negotiation for Quinton Jackson, neither wanting to taint the proceedings because of their relationship. With Quinton's plea deal concluded about two weeks ago, they were again free to spend some time together. Jennifer was hosting tonight's dinner in her new apartment in San Francisco. The 2-bedroom apartment was a major upgrade from her meager flat in Burlingame, facilitated by her much higher income working for Harrington & Harrington.

Matthew arrived with a flowering house plant and a bottle of Silver Oak Napa Valley Cabernet Sauvignon.

"A house-warming gift for you. Congratulations again on the new digs," said Matthew.

Jennifer greeted him with a kiss.

"Please put the plant on the counter for now. I'll find a sunny window for it later. Oh, and please open the wine. We both could use a drink."

Matthew nodded affirmatively and said, "I'll say. What are the odds that we'd both work on the Quinton Jackson matter? That was a monster of a case."

"Three days just to complete the plea deal. Then day after day of follow-up to turn over all of the photos, videos, recordings, and documents. I can't even imagine how much data that totaled."

"I have no idea either. Our office and the U.S. Attorney's Office will be digesting that for months. I'm so glad that it's over and we can be together again."

Matthew gave Jennifer a warm hug from behind as she was preparing the salad.

"Talk about a small world, included in the photos Quinton supplied were several of my former boss purchasing cocaine from one of Quinton's men. I took a second look when I saw that being prepared for uploading to the FBI's server. I always thought Steven Shaw was a jerk, and not just for firing me for no reason."

A light bulb went off in Matthew's head. That name, Steven Shaw, wasn't it one of those listed as a client of Brian Compton in Chicago? The same attorney who had helped Quinton launder his drug sale profits through to the Cayman Islands? Not wanting to step over the line, Matthew decided to ask just one follow-up question.

"Where did you work for Mr. Shaw? I don't remember your mentioning that before."

"He's the President at Blue Planet Investment Management, here in the city."

Matthew did not ask or say anything else in this regard. He wanted to share a pleasant evening with a cute and friendly woman, and avoid taking advantage of their relationship in any way. However, on the short drive back to his apartment the next morning, he couldn't help but think to himself. There's a very wealthy individual who was a client of Quinton, and who used the same attorney in Chicago as Quinton to mask the transfer of funds to each of their accounts in the Cayman Islands. Someone must have fronted a lot of capital to import over two tons of cocaine at one time. Could Steven Shaw have been the financier for Quinton? That would certainly explain why he would fire Jennifer for no reason. It wouldn't have been good for him to have such a sharp attorney at his company. Hmmm......

Chapter 74

Monday March 2, 2020
Berkeley, California

Joseph got out of bed early, being careful to avoid awakening Sofia. He had a big meeting lined up at his job this morning and had been thinking about it all night. While at the kitchen table having a cup of coffee, he started looking through the emails and text messages on his smartphone. It wasn't long before his pulse quickened upon seeing the text message from the system. The coding for the macro environment monitoring produced its first red light last night. It was now 6:45 AM. Logging on to the brokerage account, he saw that the system had already sold all long call option and all short put option positions. Two-thirds of the account balance was now in cash, with the remainder allocated to sales of call options which were just barely out of the money (i.e.; with a strike price just above the price of the underlying security) and purchases of put options that were substantially away from being in the money. Joseph recognized that such positioning was the system's programmed response to an anticipated rapid and significant decline in the equity markets.

He returned to the bedroom. Sofia was just getting out of bed. Joseph shared the news. They decided to group text with Bruce and Kathi. The four members of Blazing Capital LLC discussed the event and agreed to allow the system to do its work, while continuing to closely monitor the online brokerage account. Kathi and Sofia would validate what input had triggered the red light and report back to the team.

On a Facetime conference call at 7:15 PM that evening,

Kathi and Sofia confirmed that the web traffic regarding the coronavirus was the primary trigger for the red light. An increasing number of countries had confirmed the presence of the virus in the past forty-eight hours, with the United States today reporting 102 known cases and six known deaths. In addition, the S&P 500 Index was down over twelve percent from its recent peak as of last Friday, which was a financial trend trigger previously built into the system at the suggestion of Joseph.

"In summary, we're positioned for an aggressive bear market," said Joseph.

"How much money will we lose if the system is wrong and the stock market rallies?" asked Bruce.

"We don't have much invested in the out of the money put options, so no big loss there. In addition, most of the account balance is in cash. We could, however, lose money on the sold call options. However, the system sold slightly out of the money contracts and we booked the option time premium, so we could absorb somewhat of an increase in equity prices before losing substantially on those positions. That said, a significant and rapid stock market rally could generate a notable, though not financially devastating, loss," advised Joseph.

"Given that this is our first experience with a red light by the system, I think it would be prudent to be particularly cautious," opined Sofia.

"We can tighten the risk parameters to have the system automatically close out the sold call option positions after a, say, loss of ten percent or more of the account value," suggested Kathi.

"Worst case, we'd therefore lose some of our accumulated profit, but avoid approaching an overall loss," explained Joseph.

After some further discussion, the four agreed to continue following the system's advice, subject to the tightened risk control parameter suggested by Kathi. Joseph commented that he would very closely monitor the system's trades and positions, plus the capital markets in general. Bruce volunteered to perform some additional Internet research about coronaviruses in general, and this apparently new strain in particular.

Chapter 75

Monday March 9, 2020
San Francisco, California

Steven didn't awaken until 8:30 AM. Faced with solely living off the cash from selling Veronica's jewelry, he had relocated to a cheap hotel on the edge of the Tenderloin District in San Francisco. His adjoining neighbors stayed up late last night, loudly partying. Groggily picking up his smartphone, he saw that the equity markets were down big this morning. He immediately called Charles.

"Good morning, Steven."

"Your voice sounds strange."

"I'm on my way to urgent care. Feels like there's an elephant sitting on my chest."

"It *is* flu season."

"I was with the traders on Friday. They were each coughing up a storm. I should have kept my distance."

"Speaking of the traders, do you know our position this morning in light of the drop in the stock market?"

"I haven't heard from them. I'm pulling into urgent care right now. Can you give them a call at the office?"

"Will do. Get yourself taken care of."

"Good-bye."

When neither trader answered his phone calls, Steven called the 44th floor receptionist.

"Blue Planet Investment Management. This is Lisa. How may I help you?"

"Hi, Lisa. This is Steven Shaw. I'm trying to get a hold of either one of our traders. Have you seen them this morning?"

"Now that you mention it, they usually stop by my desk to chat, but haven't this morning. One of them is interested in my roommate. Let me walk over to their area and call you back."

Steven's smartphone rang ten minutes later, just as he was finishing shaving.

"Mr. Shaw, it's Lisa. Neither trader is in the office, nor is their operations assistant. I asked around. One of our financial analysts, Kyle, who is a personal friend of theirs, shared that he received a text on Saturday indicating that the lead trader was on his way to the hospital. That's all I've discovered so far. I'll continue to ask around and call you back if I learn anything else."

"Thank you, Lisa."

Steven finished dressing and made the twenty-minute walk from his hotel to the office. Veronica's trust owed their Lexus and their Mercedes. He had been traveling by foot and using public transportation, Uber, and Lyft since being thrown out of the house.

Upon arriving at the office, he approached the financial analyst, Kyle Stanberry.

"Good morning, Kyle. Lisa shared with me that you received a text over the weekend from our head trader that he was headed for the hospital."

"Yes, Mr. Shaw. He attended a big event in Chinatown the weekend before, and started feeling bad by mid-week last week. I heard all three of them coughing repeatedly on Friday."

"Have you heard anything else?"

"I'm sorry Mr. Shaw, but no."

"Thank you, Kyle."

Steven walked over to Lisa's station and inquired if she had any new information. Lisa had called all of the local hospitals, eventually locating the three missing employees. They were all at San Francisco General.

"Did you get through to their rooms?" asked Steven.

"No. The nurses' station advised that all three are on ventilators. Evidently this new virus is really nasty, and spreading quickly. I even saw on my news app this morning that one of the NBA players was just confirmed with the virus."

"Thank you for the quick work, Lisa."

Steven walked quickly to his office and checked the stock market through the browser on his laptop. Equity prices were still down considerably. Now starting to panic, he texted Charles, inquiring regarding his status. Charles texted back that he was going to be admitted to the nearby Saint Francis Memorial Hospital for treatment, and that he would be quarantined for some period of time.

A panic began to take hold of Steven. While he knew the general nature of the traders' activities, he did not have a detailed tactical knowledge of the technologies they utilized, nor of all of the brokerage accounts. He also had no easy way of quickly ascertaining all of the open positions. The traders were expected to back up each other, with Charles as the contingency plan. That plan had now failed. Steven called the company's IT Department to gain access to the traders' computers and their files stored on the central servers. This was more difficult than it sounded, as the IT Department did not have possession of the passwords and encryption keys used by the traders. In addition, the dual authentication processes used by the brokerage firms all interfaced to the smartphones of the traders.

Reduced to least temporarily operating via old-school methodologies, Steven started pouring through what paper records existed in the traders' offices and making phone calls to the brokerage firms he remembered being used by the traders. It was going to take a while for Steven to assemble a complete inventory of the Fund's trading positions and then execute transactions to mitigate losses in the declining stock market.

Chapter 76

Monday March 16, 2020
San Francisco, California

By the end of the day, Steven had finally completed closing out all of the Fund's trading positions. It had been an onerous process over the past week, like trying to catch a falling knife. The S&P 500 Index declined from 3,090 on March 2 to 2,386 today, a drop of almost twenty-three percent. While the health of the young traders and the operations assistant had gradually improved over the past couple of days, Charles had not been so lucky. His age and obesity stacked the deck against him in his fight against COVID. The virus won. Steven lost his best friend. This deeply saddened and angered Steven at the same time. His anger flopped from being upset with Charles for not taking better care of himself to faulting WHO and CDC for failing to more effectively respond to a deadly virus first identified months ago.

Charles was of course not the only casualty. As Steven tallied up the latest update to the spreadsheet, he blanched at the total. The slow exit from the trading positions had generated a loss of $120 million for the Fund. Steven would need to share this soon with the Board of Directors. In addition, the loss would be disclosed to the Fund investors in the upcoming quarterly performance report. To make matters even worse, a number of the companies in the Fund's portfolio had also suffered adversely from the spread of the coronavirus.

Steven repeatedly ran his hand back and forth through his thinning hair as he contemplated what to do next. He decided to turn his attention to writing a eulogy for Charles. A virtual Zoom session was being organized by Charles' friends and family as a way to remember the man. Now without both Veronica and his best buddy, Steven felt very alone in the world.

Chapter 77

Friday March 27, 2020
San Francisco, California

Steven was about to go downstairs to purchase a sandwich for lunch when Roger Suffolk, the Chairman of the Board, entered his office.

"Hello, Steven, please have a seat."

"Hello, Roger. I wasn't expecting to see you until the regular Board meeting next week."

"We called a special Board meeting this morning via Zoom."

"I don't remember hearing about that."

"That's because the purpose of the meeting was to discuss your future with the company."

"Oh, I see..."

"Steven, there's no easy way to say this, so I'll be direct. While the Board recognizes and appreciates all of your efforts in support of the company and the Fund, we determined that we had no choice but to terminate you. The vote was unanimous. The recent trading losses on top of the early investment losses, especially that damned windfarm in Minnesota, have made it politically impossible for us to continue to support you. If we did not terminate you before the upcoming release of the first quarter Fund performance report, we'd likely be sued by the investors. I know you understand how these things have to proceed."

Steven's head fell into his arms on his desk. He acknowledged the position the Board had been placed in. On the other hand, he had put everything into the company. His money, his marriage; in fact, his total life.

When Steven finally looked up, Roger continued, "We've named Shantelle Jones as Interim President. I have to ask you to now pack up whatever personal items belong to you and exit the premises. I'm sorry, Steven."

Roger departed the office, signaling Lisa on his way out to bring the two cardboard boxes to Steven.

An hour later, just as Steven was about to leave with his two boxes, a man he had never met walked into his office. There were three other men he did not recognize standing just outside.

"Steven Shaw, I am FBI Special Agent Matthew Haddock. You are under arrest for multiple alleged felonies. Please come with us."

Matthew read Steven his Miranda rights. That was functionally unnecessary, as Steven's head was spinning as a precursor to his falling into a deep depression. Steven would not say anything to anyone for several days.

Chapter 78

Monday April 13, 2020
San Francisco, California

The United States was now in the full siege of the pandemic. Domestic deaths had just topped 23,000 and infections were rapidly climbing toward a million. This had resulted in a delay in Steven's meeting with defense counsel. Another reason for the delay was Steven's inability to retain his own attorney. His funds were exhausted, his best friend was dead, and his wife was in the final stages of completing the divorce petition. The U.S. Attorney's Office in San Francisco therefore had to identify a public defender to assist him. The law enforcement team had arranged for a socially distant meeting in the jail this morning, with all parties wearing N95 masks.

"Good morning, Mr. Shaw. My name is Maxine Scott. I'm a public defender who usually works out of the Oakland office, but have been assigned to your case because of my years of experience."

Steven looked up at the robust African-American woman, simply nodding.

"Mr. Shaw, if you can't hear me because of the social distancing and the masks, please let me know. I'll do the same for you."

Steven again nodded.

"I received your case file last night. I must say, we don't get many billionaires in the public defenders' office. Mostly individuals accused of petty theft, drug sales, prostitution, and similar low-level crimes."

Steven shrugged his shoulders.

After a pause, he said, "I'm not a billionaire. My wife is the wealthy one. In fact, I'm dead broke."

"Let me understand this correctly. You are a finance wiz and President of an investment management company, but you're broke?"

"I got fired last month. Not that such makes any difference, financially speaking. I wasn't taking any salary from the company."

"I see. I did some Internet research on you. What about the money you earned over the years, including on the Opticore Products Corporation sale?"

"All invested into Blue Planet and lost."

"Mr. Shaw, let me pause you right there. Do you understand that I am your attorney and that anything you say to me is subject to attorney-client privilege? Nothing from our communications can be brought up in court."

"I understand."

"Do you also understand that if you do not tell me the truth, I likely can't do an effective job of defending you?"

"That makes sense."

"So, let's back up and start again. What happened to all of the money you earned over the years, including from Opticore?"

"I fronted the costs for establishing Blue Planet Investment Management."

"I'm going to give you one more chance, Mr. Shaw. What is Atlas?"

Steven gulped. Maxine noticed this despite the mask.

"How do you know about Atlas?"

"I've received the case file. The U.S. Attorney's Office is charging you with financing the purchase and importation of large volumes of cocaine, among other crimes. It seems that two individuals have struck plea deals to turn over evidence. One of them is Brian Compton. The other is Quinton Jackson."

"I don't know Quinton Jackson."

"So, you do know Brian Compton?"

"Yes. He's an attorney in Chicago that I used to channel funds offshore."

"I'll again ask my earlier question. What is Atlas?"

"It's an entity domiciled in the Cayman Islands."

"And what type of business does Atlas conduct? Is it a manufacturer, a service provider?"

"Actually, it's just a bank account."

"Ah, now we're getting somewhere. Mr. Shaw, the FBI believes that Atlas funded the purchase and importation of cocaine by Quinton Jackson. Mr. Jackson was also a client of Mr. Compton."

"I told you before, I don't know Quinton Jackson."

Maxine sighed. "Let's try a different tack. Mr. Shaw, is this you in these photos? I understand that there are several videos. These photos are just excerpts."

Maxine held up the photos for Steven to see.

"Yes, those photos are of me."

"And what are you doing in these photos?"

"Speaking with an African-American gentleman."

"Really, just having recurring conversations by Lake Merritt on different days with the same fellow? What's his name?"

"I don't know. Is that Quinton Jackson?"

"Hardly. That's one of his employees. So, Mr. Shaw, what were you doing on those days by Lake Merritt?"

Steven was starting to sweat. He answered the question.

"Buying cocaine."

"This is making more and more sense now. You and Quinton Jackson both used the same attorney in Chicago to launder funds to overseas entities. You can't account for all of the money that was transferred to Atlas. You were a customer of Mr. Jackson. The purchase of the cocaine shipments would have required substantial cash. I can see why the FBI is pursuing you."

"I didn't launder any illegal money into Atlas. Those were my funds legitimately earned."

"So, you disclosed your ownership of overseas entities and bank accounts on your federal income tax returns, while also paying income taxes on the bank account interest earned?"

"No. I didn't want to tip off my wife and her team of trustees and CPAs."

"That doesn't make you look very good, Mr. Shaw, not to mention opening you up to prosecution by the U.S. Treasury Department for tax fraud."

"Oh, that would be correct. I understand."

"Now we're back around the circle. Mr. Shaw, if the funds in Atlas were not used to pay for importing cocaine, what were they used for?"

The sweat was now pouring down Steven's forehead. He used his mask to dab the sweat away from his eyes.

"Would bribery and extortion be a better answer?"

"I'd have to think about that. Not an easy question to answer at this point. The devil is in the details, Mr. Shaw. You're quite a character, aren't you?"

Steven resumed staring at the floor. Charles was dead. He had heard that Samantha had recently resigned from Blue Planet to take a marketing position overseas, likely in a country without an extradition treaty to the United States. Samantha was very bright, likely leaving little audit trail. Mentioning her name would not do Steven any good.

"Your silence has answered my question. Mr. Shaw, I need you to listen carefully to what I am about to say."

"Okay."

"The public defender's office does not have the resources to mount an effective defense in a case like yours. We don't have a deep understanding of international capital flows and experts familiar with offshore bank accounts. The feds are going to charge you with multiple crimes, many of which could result in years in prison. From what you've said, even if you did not finance the cocaine shipments, you could be found guilty of bribery and extortion as the FBI follows the trail of bread crumbs. Brian Compton is singing like a canary, so the FBI will know everything he knows. They've got you dead on the income tax related violations. While it's my sworn duty to defend you to the best of my abilities, I'm going to admit that this case is way beyond my scope. It would be like a peewee football team competing with the 49ers."

"I didn't make any money from all of this. In fact, I lost everything."

"Crime is not measured by the financial result, Mr. Shaw, but rather by the intent and the action. Besides that, with the plea deals made for Compton and Jackson, the feds are going to want some scalps. That's how the system works."

Steven was near collapse. On top of everything else, his body was still suffering from alcohol and cocaine withdrawal.

"So, what do you want from me?"

"Authorization to pursue a plea deal of your own. You'll need to serve some prison time. Doesn't sound like there will be any financial restitution. You'll also be of course barred for life from working in the financial industry. It may be easier for you to confess to the drug financing than open Pandora's box about your actual utilization of the funds from Atlas."

"I'll think about that and get back to you."

"That's your decision, Mr. Shaw. I'll know where to find you when you're ready."

Maxine gathered the various documents and photos into her briefcase, and signaled that she wished to leave. Steven was taken back to his holding cell, where he fell into a stupor, drool dripping out of the corner of his mouth.

Chapter 79

Saturday May 9, 2020
Berkeley, California

Kathi, Sofia, Bruce, and Joseph were now all working from home virtually in light of the pandemic. After carefully quarantining themselves for two weeks, they gathered at Sofia's and Joseph's Berkeley apartment for dinner.

"Great to all be together again in person," said Bruce as he and Kathi entered the apartment. "Zoom and GoToMeeting are just not the same."

"Ditto," said Kathi. "As usual, it smells wonderful in here. What's on the menu, Sofia?"

"Since we haven't all been together for a while, I prepared a special menu. We'll start with *frico*, a hot dish comprised of cheese, potatoes, and onions. This is a specialty from the Friuli region of northern Italy."

"Sounds delicious," opined Bruce.

Sofia continued, "Our main course will be *manicotti*. These are stuffed crepes with a complex filling. I'll give you more information when we eat them."

"My contribution was further funding the new swimming pool at the house of my local wine merchant," smiled Joseph. "He recommended a French *Pomerol* red wine for our meal, after explaining to me that Italy does not have a monopoly on great wines."

"That's a topic open for an extensive debate at a later date," laughed Sofia. "The dessert is a surprise."

After catching up with their recent employment-related events and polishing off every crumb of the *frico*, Joseph brought up the topic of the system.

"We made a pile of money through most of March after the system flashed the red light. The rate of return on the out of the money put options was astounding. We all agreed at the end of March to close out all positions and go to 100% cash, based upon our concerns that the pandemic environment introduces a lot of wildcards and a likely structural shift in the behavior of the capital markets. We were correct in our concerns to a certain extent. If we had actually conducted the trades recommended by the system starting in early April, our percentage of trades generating a profit or breaking even would have been down five percent. That would still be a good performance, but highlighting that the system likely needs some ongoing programming. The world evolves, and so would the system need to."

"That's a good summary in English," responded Kathi. "I've analyzed our programming and noticed that the evolution in the behavior of the capital markets has been faster than the machine learning of our artificial intelligence."

"Hence a need for more and faster processing power," noted Sofia, "in addition to fine-tuning our code."

"So, where do we go from here?" asked Bruce. "Do we make some adjustments and go back into the market?"

"That's one option," replied Joseph. "But I'd like to share a quote from one of my finance professors in the MBA program. *One doesn't need to get rich twice.* In other words, don't squander the fruits of your success and need to start over."

"Just how much is in the online brokerage account for Blazing Capital LLC?" inquired Kathi.

"A bit over $12 million. While we'll each have some income tax obligation at the end of the year, we're already in the top percentiles of richest Americans," shared Joseph.

"Did I hear a recommendation forthcoming?" asked Sofia.

"We can continue to operate the system, fine-tuning it on a continuing basis, while controlling our risk exposure. That could be quite profitable," said Joseph.

"I hear a 'but' coming," interjected Sofia.

"More like an 'or'. We could instead market our system for sale. If it is worth a few millions to each of us, it must be worth many, many millions to global investment banks with trillion-dollar balance sheets. While we've developed the system to focus on the environmental technology space, think what our technology could do if applied more broadly. The four of us would never have the time available to do that by ourselves."

"Bruce, where are we with the patents?" asked Sofia

"Should be issued any day now."

"My thought is that we contact Ken White to help us market our intellectual property. He did a great job for us with ERI, and I trust him," shared Joseph.

"There is a related point to consider," said Bruce. "As we're talking about this, I realize that no secrets last forever. Neither do any advantages. Someone else might develop a similar, or even better, system. That technology might be faster and more robust than ours. We'd then lose the trading advantage, and the purchase price for our then inferior system would plummet."

"Well said. The old adage to *strike while the iron is hot* still has validity," said Joseph.

"It can't hurt to test the waters and see what response Ken

White gets to marketing our IP," opined Kathi. "We wouldn't be obligated to sell unless we found the offer to be compelling."

"Ken would also help us protect our IP with the usual screening of potential buyers, along with the execution of non-disclosure agreements," added Joseph.

"So, do we have a decision?" inquired Sofia. "The dessert needs to be eaten immediately following the final step in the preparation, so I can't bring it to table until we're done with this conversation."

The four friends looked at each other and nodded in agreement. Sofia walked into the kitchen and commenced filling the freshly baked *cannoli* shells with flavored *ricotta* cream. The southern Italian sweet was served with a glass of *Vin Santo*.

Chapter 80

Wednesday July 1, 2020
Victorville, California

Steven Shaw was in the second week of his prison term at the minimum-security federal prison in Victorville, located in southern California. Maxine Scott had been successful in negotiating a relatively favorable plea deal for Steven, pushing the U.S. Attorney's office to admit that they had no direct evidence of Steven's funds from Atlas being transferred to cocaine traffickers in Southeast Asia. Steven would serve for two years, followed by three years of supervised release. There was no financial restitution. Maxine had validated that Steven had substantially zero assets. The actual use of the Atlas funds was never discovered due to a combination of the relatively quick plea deal and bank secrecy practices in the Cayman Islands.

The minimum-security prison was actually nicer than the Tenderloin hotel Steven had lived in after being ejected from his home by Veronica. There were three nutritional meals served a day, multiple recreational opportunities, and health care, including for the vestiges of Steven's withdrawal from his addictions. With Maxine's help, he'd already completed the antibiotics course for his chlamydia while being held in jail.

Steven was in the TV room when one of the guards delivered an envelope to him, of course opened in advance by the prison staff. The envelope contained the final documents associated with his divorce from Veronica. Steven would receive no financial benefit from the divorce due to the trusts' ownership of the vast majority of her assets, his admitted infidelity, and his inability to pay for a divorce attorney to represent his interests. In addition, he did not want to have Veronica alert local law enforcement to his cocaine stash or to his theft of her jewelry, something she discovered not long after their separation. Involving local law enforcement would have only further complicated Maxine's efforts for the plea deal with the feds. Steven had no choice other than to accept Veronica's terms and conditions, as harsh as they were. *Hell hath no fury like a woman scorned*, thought Steven, followed by his deep remorse at having destroyed a marriage to a woman he dearly loved.

Steven glumly walked down to the prison library. He'd have plenty of time over the next two years to read. But about what? Should he read for pleasure? He had always enjoyed 'hard' science fiction. What about some of the classics he had not been exposed to in college? Or, should he be reading to prepare for the next stage of his life? He'd only be 46 years old when released from prison, not ancient by any means. He was still bright and well educated. He started with nothing almost three decades ago when his father was killed in Afghanistan. He could rebuild his wealth and eventually his status. In fact, enough money can buy status, mused Steven. But what field should he pursue? He was banned for life from having a securities license and working in the regulated financial industry. Yet, finance was what he knew best. Plus, he was a felon, which would limit at least his initial employment opportunities, if not also his long-term prospects for work.

Later, while eating his dinner from the institutional metal tray, the answer came to him. Cryptocurrency! That was a new and rapidly growing financial field with almost no regulation. It was largely conducted through technology, thereby facilitating some degree of anonymity. The profit opportunities were enormous! Write, or have someone write for you, some computer code that creates a limited number of coins or tokens. Establish a process for mining the tokens, plus for maintaining a record or electronic ledger of their ownership. Then, use social media to create demand for the tokens, with scarcity built in as a means of inciting interest. Monetize the tokens by selling them for actual dollars. In the end, you're selling digital bits or electrons for hard dollars, with the only overhead being some cloud hardware and software, plus the cost of a team to maintain such.

The next morning, Steven commenced reading everything he could about cryptocurrency. The prison allowed inmate access to approved websites, including Wikipedia. The library received a wide variety of printed magazines, including several that specialized in technology articles. In particular, Steven devoured every source of information he could find regarding the genesis and development of Bitcoin. Several of his fellow inmates had a background in technology, although their expertise was generally focused on using such for embezzlement. However, even that aspect helped Steven round out his knowledge base.

As the weeks progressed, Steven's focus on cryptocurrency grew to become relentless. It was almost as if he had developed a new addiction.

Chapter 81

Monday June 14, 2021
Victorville, California

Steven received some very good news this morning. As a consequence of severe overcrowding in California prisons, the white-collar nature of his crime, ongoing concerns about COVID in communal living arrangements, and his good behavior while incarcerated, Steven was approved for early release as of this afternoon. He would still need to be monitored through three years of supervised release, consistent with his plea bargain.

Steven's focus immediately shifted to planning what he would do upon his discharge. Veronica certainly had no interest in seeing him. She had not communicated a single time during his year in Victorville. Maureen would likely never speak to him again in light of Billy's being fired from Blue Planet. Charles died of COVID. Steven had not heard from Samantha since being shipped to Victorville. He had no children. Most of his former colleagues would shun him, not wanting to be associated with a felon who supposedly financed cocaine shipments. Steven came to the conclusion that he would be on his own for at least a while.

He was assigned to a probation officer in San Francisco. The law enforcement bureaucracy had evidently decided that he would want to relocate to the city of his former residence and employment. This did not bother Steven, as he had always loved the city by the Bay, plus was familiar with the geography. Starting over in San Francisco would be more efficient than having to allocate time and attention to learning a new area.

Steven's thoughts then turned to his next challenge. He would leave prison with a bus ticket and a few dollars in his pocket, but no real financial resources to speak of. How would he restart his life without money? He thought long and hard about potential alternatives in this regard through lunch and into early afternoon.

At 2:00 PM, a prison guard approached Steven.

"Shaw, we're ready to release you. Follow me and we'll perform the usual exit procedures."

"Okay."

Steven was given some casual civilian clothing, the contact information for his probation officer, a bus ticket to San Francisco, a small wad of currency, and a bag containing the items with which he checked into the prison. As he was undergoing the final processing, another guard approached.

"Shaw, one more piece of mail for you."

He handed Steven the already opened envelope. Looking inside, Steven was surprised to see a cashier's check drawn on one of the major banks. It was made payable to him, with no indication of the source. The amount was $10,000. Steven wondered who his guardian angel was.

He boarded the next bus for San Francisco, a long and slow trip from Victorville. Upon arriving at the main bus terminal in the city, Steven walked the fourteen or so blocks to the Tenderloin District hotel where he had stayed following his eviction from the mansion. It was good to be home, or at least something close to that.

Chapter 82

Friday July 2, 2021
San Francisco, California

In the two or so weeks since his return to San Francisco, Steven had conducted the initial meeting with his probation officer, opened a checking account with the $10,000 cashier's check, purchased an inexpensive laptop and a cheap smartphone, started a new email address, and opened both an online brokerage account and a cryptocurrency trading account. He was now faced with a dilemma. He wanted to spend much of his time trading primarily cryptocurrency and using online forums to build a network of individuals who might facilitate his wealth rehabilitation plan. However, the $10,000 from his unnamed angel was not sufficient capital to live on plus use for trading. In addition, his probation officer 'highly encouraged' Steven to get a job and rent a more permanent address than the Tenderloin District hotel.

Steven pondered what he should do next. He'd need a job that allowed him to be at his computer during hours when the stock exchanges were open. He'd also need an employer who was not sensitive to Steven's felon status. He couldn't work in any regulated financial business such as a bank, credit union, mutual fund company, security broker / dealer, or investment bank. Unfortunately, financial services were one of the primary industries in San Francisco, along with technology firms. While Steven had familiarity with various aspects of technology, he was not proficient in coding, network management, or information security. His being skilled in Microsoft Office and the similar software made available through the Google network was primarily from a perspective of supporting his financial analyses.

The good news for Steven was that the U.S. economy was bouncing back strongly from the COVID recession, fueled by mass vaccinations, extensive fiscal stimulus from the U.S. Treasury, and a very accommodative monetary policy implemented by the Federal Reserve. There were literally millions and millions of open positions posted online nationally, as companies in almost every industry struggled to meet the reinvigorated demand for their products and services.

Steven applied online for ten different positions which had just one thing in common. The work hours were approximately 10:00 PM to 6:00 AM. This would allow Steven to be at his computer for the opening of the stock markets at 6:30 AM Pacific Time. By the end of the day, he had received only one reply to his applications. It was for an interview for night shift manager at a fast-food franchise located nearby. While hardly relishing the thought of working in fast food following years of being served Dom Perignon by a butler, he recognized that he would likely have few options. Steven confirmed the appointment for tomorrow afternoon.

Chapter 83

Saturday July 3, 2021
San Francisco, California

Steven dressed in casual clothes for the 2:00 PM interview at the fast-food franchise located on the edge of the Tenderloin District. Upon walking in, he asked for Candido, just as he had been instructed in the email.

"You Steven?" asked a thin man with a mustache, apparently about 35 years old and of Hispanic ancestry.

"Yes. Pleased to meet you."

"Follow me into my office."

The office was an eight-foot by eight-foot room in the back of the restaurant with a laptop, multi-function inkjet printer, and an adding machine positioned on top of a repurposed door that functioned as the desktop. The desktop was suspended by two large plastic crates. The office also evidently functioned as a storage room for non-perishable inventory such as napkins, detergent, and toilet supplies.

"Have a seat."

Candido pointed at another plastic crate that apparently was the guest chair.

Steven sat attentively on the crate.

"I got your online application. You ever work in food service before?" asked Candido.

"No, but I have a lot of experience managing people and running an operation. I also have sales experience."

"Where you been the last year?"

"In prison, under a plea deal that my public defender negotiated."

"I know how that works. Move the people through the system. You do anything violent?"

"No, not at all. I was accused of selling drugs."

"Not unusual around here. Why did you apply for the night shift?"

"I have other work that starts early in the morning. Got to string a couple of jobs together to make rent in this town."

"Got that. When can you start?"

"Immediately."

"You'll follow the day shift manager around for a week and then start night shift, Wednesday through Sunday. If you have good performance for ninety days, we pay a $1.00 per hour incentive. Show up here at 3:00 PM tomorrow. Let me get you a uniform."

Candido mentally sized up Steven and tossed him two polyester shirts, a baseball-style cap, and a pair of polyester pants from a cardboard box behind him.

"Here's the paperwork we need to get you on payroll. Bring these documents back completed."

"Will do."

"One more thing. We got a zero-tolerance policy for being impaired on the job or stealing, whether money or food. You understand?"

"Yes."

"Any questions?"

"Is there any online training information available? I'd like to get a head start."

"Yeah, I should have mentioned that."

Candido wrote a URL and temporary ID and password down on one of the napkins and handed it to Steven. He then stood up and extended his hand.

"Steven, welcome to the team."

"Thanks for the job."

On his brief walk back to the hotel, Steven further strategized. He wouldn't have much in the way of wardrobe costs since the franchise supplied uniforms. His food bill would be reduced by the meals at the restaurant. The starting hourly wage certainly wasn't much by Steven's historical standards. On the other hand, this job would get his probation officer off his back and allow him to trade crypto and securities in his online accounts coincident with the opening of the markets. He'd also have all day Monday and Tuesday to further develop his trading strategies.

Once back at the hotel, Steven linked into the WiFi and loaded the web page that Candido provided. The parent corporation maintained what amounted to an online university regarding every conceivable aspect of the fast-food operation. There were many pages dedicated to the food products, including nutritional information and detailed instructions, including videos, regarding how to prepare each item. Other pages provided education regarding cleaning practices, opening and closing tasks, and how to operate the POS system. By 8:00 PM, Steven felt well prepared for his first day on the new job.

Chapter 84

Wednesday July 7, 2021
San Francisco, California

At 9:30 PM, Steven departed his hotel room for his night shift at the fast-food restaurant. Despite the long daylight hours of summer, it was now dark in the city except for the lights from the cars, buses, and staggered overhead street lamps. Most businesses other than the low-end bars that populated the Tenderloin District were closed. The homeless were starting to bed down for the night in the doorways to the buildings, except for those fortunate enough to have a tent pitched on the sidewalk. Over two decades of government initiatives had only resulted in a significant increase in the homeless population. The city even had a 'poop patrol' of employees whose job was to collect human feces from the sidewalks and parks.

As Steven turned a corner, three men jumped him, knocking him to the pavement. The fall scraped a large chunk of skin off his left forearm.

One of the assailants held a knife to Steven's throat, while another demanded, "Let me have your money."

Steven did not move, pinned to the ground and with the knife touching his skin. One of the men pulled Steven's wallet from his pocket and looked inside.

"No credit cards and thirty-seven dollars! Fuck you!"

The man took the cash while another kicked Steven in the gut with three rapid blows. They then ran down a nearby alley into the darkness.

Steven took a few minutes to compose himself and fill his lungs with air. He then slowly completed the short walk to the fast-food restaurant, holding his left arm in the air in an attempt to reduce the loss of blood. Candido was just finishing his evening shift as Steven entered.

"What happened to you?"

"Mugged," replied Steven.

"Happens all the time. The poor preying on the poor. The addicts desperate to fund their next fix. Let me grab the first aid kit and help you clean up."

"Thanks."

Candido first cleaned and disinfected the forearm wound.

As he was finishing bandaging Steven, he said, "Man, you might want to get some protection. We put video cameras all around the restaurant and have an alarm system, but that only helps so much, and not at all when you're down the street."

"What are you suggesting?"

"A friend of mine can sell you a cheap handgun for cash; probably a .22. Won't stop a car, but should be enough to encourage the assholes to find a different victim."

Steven's cuts and bruises were now becoming more tender, as his adrenaline level receded. He thought to himself, on the one hand, I've never even fired a gun before. On the other hand, I've got to make that walk five nights a week. I might not be so lucky the next time.

Turning towards Candido, he said, "Sounds good."

Chapter 85

Tuesday July 13, 2021
San Francisco, California

By 7:00 AM on his second day off this week, Steven had already conducted eight crypto trades. He spent all day yesterday analyzing the trends in the various cryptocurrencies, their correlations to each other and to the equity indices, and their behavior in response to key external news. This led him to develop a sophisticated crypto trading algorithm. Today was the initial test of that algorithm. It employed various long and short positions across five of the cryptocurrencies that were traded in higher volumes.

Steven also conducted several stock option trades in his online brokerage account. He continued to focus on the environmental technology sector, seeking to leverage everything he had learned at Blue Planet.

In between trades, Steven chatted on various crypto-related online forums. He had already made a couple of contacts with individuals who were contemplating starting entities that would mine, trade, develop, and / or invest in cryptocurrencies. Several of these individuals had commented about being impressed with Steven's financial acumen.

After the 1:00 PM close of the stock market, Steven checked his email one last time before getting into bed. He continued the sleep patterns mandated by his night shift job even on his days off. This behavior benefited his mental alertness and therefore his trading results. Just before closing his laptop, an incoming email arrived. The subject line read: 'Mutual Opportunity'. Intrigued, Steven opened the email after ensuring that his malware software was active. The short email presented an invitation for a Zoom video call next Wednesday morning at 4:00 AM Pacific Time. The sender was only identified as 'cryptoman777', who used a Yahoo email account. Steven pondered why someone would schedule a call at that hour. At least he would be awake anyway, as part of his typically daily cycle. Curious, and with nothing to lose, Steven confirmed the meeting via a brief email reply.

Chapter 86

The night shift manager job at the fast-food restaurant had been an eye-opener for Steven. His clientele at 2:00 AM on a Monday morning were an assortment of late-night partiers, third shift blue collar workers, junkies, homeless, and prostitutes. He could smell some of them when they walked in the front door. The employees working his shift were primarily recent immigrants, generally with limited English language skills. While Candido kept the employee files locked in a cabinet in the office, Steven guessed that a fair number of his co-workers used fictitious social security numbers. Who would take a physically demanding, low-wage position with lousy hours during an economic boom? Illegal immigrants and felons. As he cleaned the dining room portion of the restaurant for the third time on this shift, Steven contemplated just how far he had fallen from the upscale neighborhood of Pacific Heights. He vowed to himself that he would one day return.

During the typically slow period between 3:00 AM and 4:00 AM, Steven took the opportunity to train his staff on how to increase sales. There were two primary approaches. The first was to recommend an auxiliary or complementary item for each food order. Steven had his shift team practice saying *would you like some fries with that* in the best English they could muster across their range of accents. The second avenue was to mention that a larger drink size was available for just a small price increment. When taking the online training class, Steven quickly understood that the marginal product cost for the larger beverage size, including adding more ice, was negligible, thereby providing an attractive gross margin.

At 5:00 AM, Steven helped the cooks shift to the breakfast menu. With that completed by 5:30 AM, his thoughts turned to his planned trading starting an hour from now. There had been some significant news about cryptocurrency by a celebrity over the weekend, so trading volume and volatility would likely be high at this morning's opening of the capital markets. That was good news for Steven, as greater price fluctuations expanded trading opportunities under his algorithm. Volatility was also favorable to his stock option trading. Steven had already built his account balances up to $20,000 from their meager beginnings. His paycheck covered his modest living expenses, allowing him to reinvest all gains from his trading activity. In another month, he'd be able to apply to add a margin line of credit to his online brokerage account, giving him more liquidity to work with.

Steven's prediction about the cryptocurrency market this morning was accurate. The recent news produced big price swings. The stock market also displayed particular volatility. At 11:30 AM, Steven was still glued to his laptop, executing trade after trade. He had barely moved in the last five hours. He finally got up to use the toilet.

Just after the 1:00 PM market close, Steven collapsed into the bed. He had been awake for sixteen straight hours between the shift at the fast-food restaurant and the trading period in the capital markets. He fell asleep with a smile on his face. His trades today had been quite profitable. It wouldn't be long before he could relocate out of the hotel and start moving back up in the world.

Chapter 87

Wednesday July 21, 2021
San Francisco, California

Steven activated the link to the Zoom video call at 4:00 AM, as directed in the email he received about a week ago. While he had performed multiple online searches and made inquiries in various online forums, he still had no idea who cryptoman777 might be. Once the session organizer admitted Steven to the virtual Zoom room, Steven saw the round and bearded face of a man he estimated to be in his forties. The background behind the man was a plain white wall. Steven noticed from the Zoom settings that the video recording feature was deactivated and that the encryption feature was on. The man on his laptop screen was identified in the Zoom software as cryptoman777, with no other information.

"Hello, Steven. I am cryptoman777. Pleased to meet you."

Steven detected what he thought was a slight Russian accent.

He replied, "Pleased to meet you as well."

"Let me be direct. We have identified you through the online crypto forums as someone evidently possessing both extensive knowledge regarding cryptocurrencies and advanced financial education. Would you say that is true?"

"Not to sound egotistic, but, yes, I'd say that is true."

"We search for individuals such as yourself and stake them with crypto trading accounts on a number of the exchanges, along with an initial investment in various cryptocurrencies."

"I wasn't aware of that business model," advised Steven.

"We in fact have a quite robust business model. Our employees benefit from having almost 24 / 7 access to the crypto markets around the globe, trading on all of the major exchanges, and being able to take long and short positions in all of the primary cryptocurrencies. Access to our technology infrastructure is provided through an encrypted virtual private network that utilizes some of the most advanced security features. Our employees receive a twenty percent commission on their trading profits, paid of course in cryptocurrency to the account of their choosing. Any employee losing money for three consecutive months is automatically terminated. Do you have any questions about what I have said thus far?"

"What order of magnitude of trading stake are you talking about?" asked Steven.

"We start employees with the crypto equivalent of two hundred fifty thousand U.S. dollars. Employees who display particular success are often entrusted with larger trading accounts."

"I take it from the nature of the email I received and this conversation, that the employment relationship is, shall we say, unofficial," assumed Steven.

"Do you have an issue with that?" asked cryptoman777.

"Not at all. In fact, avoiding income taxes would allow me to much more rapidly accumulate wealth."

"I see that we think alike."

Cryptoman777 gave his first smile of the video conference.

"We'll monitor your activity through our technology infrastructure. That allows us to calculate your twenty percent share of the trading profits. If you would like to pursue this opportunity, send another email to the Yahoo account that I contacted you with. That email should simply state your agreement to proceed and provide us with your crypto account information for payment. After that, or in seven days if we do not hear from you, the Yahoo email account will be deleted. From then on, we will get in contact with you if we need to. You will have no way to initiate contact with us. Do you understand everything I have presented?"

"Yes."

"One more point. If we catch you front-running the trades on our behalf, the consequences will be very, very serious. Do you clearly comprehend what I am saying?

Steven gulped. His imagination ran through all of the permutations of what 'very, very serious' might mean. Given the profile of the conversation, Steven concluded that, at minimum, great physical harm might be involved; or worse.

Taking a deep breath, he responded, "Yes, I clearly comprehend what you have said."

"Excellent. Good-bye."

Cryptoman777 terminated the Zoom session.

Steven thought through the pros and cons of this new opportunity. This was an avenue for him to more quickly generate wealth, one that dovetailed with the focus on cryptocurrencies that he had pursued since early in his prison term. The opportunity to avoid income taxes was attractive. While that could create an issue down the road, Steven had learned in prison that the justice system meted out comparatively small penalties for white collar crime. For many white-collar criminals, any penalties assessed were just an affordable cost of doing business. Trading in cryptocurrencies in and of itself was not illegal. None of the new trading accounts would be in his name. He would only have online trading access;

and no funds transfer authority. Steven guessed that his prospective employer was some entity located in Russia, based upon cryptoman777's accent and the difference in time zones leading to the 4:00 AM video call. That did not bother Steven. The investments made by Blue Planet were located in multiple countries. With the technology available today, business was now truly global. Steven laughed to himself as he thought about this further, remembering all of the 'no customer service' help lines for American companies that rang in India.

Steven would need to keep his job at the fast-food restaurant to satisfy his probation officer and to provide a visible source of income. While doing both jobs would be exhausting, Steven knew that he had to do something more dramatic if he was to timely return to the lifestyle he coveted. At 6:00 AM, before the opening of the stock market, Steven sent an affirmative reply to cryptoman777. By 7:00 AM, he liquidated all of the cryptocurrency trading positions in his accounts and initiated the transfer of the funds to his online brokerage account. He would now concentrate his personal trading solely in the equity and stock option markets. This would eliminate any possibility that he might be perceived as front-running cryptoman777. Steven was highly motivated to avoid 'very, very serious consequences' from his new employer.

Chapter 88

Friday July 23, 2021
San Francisco, California

Steven arrived at the fast-food restaurant at 9:45 PM, just before the start of his shift. He put his wallet, smartphone, and pistol in his employee locker. He continued to carry the gun in an ankle holster since its acquisition, not wanting to again be mugged, or worse, on the walk from his Tenderloin District hotel to his night job. Candido approached Steven.

"Steven, can you join me in my office?"

"Okay."

After Steven was again seated on the guest chair, comprised of a plastic crate, Candido advised, "The assistant manager just gave his two-week notice. His wife got a great job in the East Bay, so they're going to relocate. I've been impressed by how quickly you've picked up all of the aspects of running the restaurant. In fact, sales during your shift are up fifteen percent over the same period in 2019, before the pandemic."

"The night shift team has really come together well," said Steven, modestly.

"Would you be interested in moving up to the assistant manager position?"

"I've still got my day job, so I need to stay on the night shift," advised Steven.

"That can work. The additional duties are primarily managing inventory and scheduling the employee shifts. That can be done anytime. Have you performed inventory management before?"

"Not directly, but some of my prior work involved similar concepts. I'm certain I could learn quickly," opined Steven.

"The assistant manager job pays two dollars more per hour, plus, if you accept the position, we'll accelerate your ninety-day dollar per hour raise. All told, you'll gross about five hundred dollars more per month."

Steven's analytical mind quickly calculated that he'd net around $375 per month after payroll taxes and federal and state income tax withholding. He used to spend more than that each month on scotch alone! On the other hand, the promotion would look good to his probation officer and could be used to justify moving into an apartment from the low-end hotel. Anything Steven could do to become a low priority to his probation officer would be a good thing, especially since he was about to start working for cryptoman777.

"Sounds good. I accept. And thank you for the opportunity."

Candido extended his hand.

After a firm handshake, Candido added, "I'll have the current assistant manager work a couple of your night shifts next week so that he can show you the ropes. Let me know if you have any questions."

"Will do."

Chapter 89

Thursday July 29, 2021
San Francisco, California

The past several days had been a whirlwind for Steven. He had a good meeting with his probation officer on Monday. The probation officer congratulated Steven on his promotion to assistant manager and endorsed his plans to rent an apartment in the South of Market Street neighborhood. Steven had a quite successful streak trading stock options in his personal account thus far this week. Tuesday had been Steven's first day of trading for cryptoman777. Steven applied the algorithms he had developed for his own cryptocurrency trading, with those calculations proving even more effective given the enhanced range of positions possible due to the greater amount of capital supplied by cryptoman777. Last night had been the first shift shared with the departing assistant manager at the fast-food restaurant. Steven rapidly understood the inventory management and employee scheduling responsibilities, as they were in essence mathematical problems requiring far less advanced calculations than Steven employed in his trading.

Steven was cleaning the dining room area of the restaurant at 11:30 PM when a police officer entered. Steven recognized him as a regular, officer Paul Anderson. Candido had long implemented a policy of providing free coffee to people in uniform. This approach provided more security for the restaurant and also led to a notable volume of food item purchases. All-in-all an astute business practice, surmised Steven. The man in blue sat down at one of the tables to drink his coffee and eat a small order of French fries.

"How's it going tonight?" asked Steven.

"About the usual for the neighborhood," replied Paul. "Trying to keep the peace between the drunks, drug addicts, gangs, and homeless."

"All of the money spent by the city government, and nothing seems to get better," opined Steven.

"Got that right. These people needed intervention years ago. When they get to this point, there's not much we can do other than to try to keep the level of violence down."

Steven thought back to Veronica's passion for providing better educational opportunities to the urban poor and minorities. She was right. The various levels of government were running in circles to treat the symptoms of inadequate education, without ever addressing the root issues. Steven's thoughts were interrupted when one of the restaurant's customers vomited. This was unfortunately a regular occurrence. Each shift kept a mop, filled water bucket, cleaning supplies, and latex gloves ready to be used in a closet off the dining room. By the time Steven finished cleaning up the vomit, Paul had departed. Steven was just about done collecting the last of the trash from the dining room when he heard a loud voice from the front of the restaurant.

"Everyone put their hands where I can see them. Open the drawers and put the cash in a bag."

A man wearing a ski mask was in front of the ordering stations, brandishing a large gauge, sawed-off, pump-action shotgun. As Steven's mind raced to take in the scene, he noticed movement from the back door of the restaurant. Another man, also wearing a ski mask, was standing in the dining room directly behind him, this one holding some type of rifle that looked like the AK-47 models Steven had seen in the movies.

The second man called out, "Everyone in the dining room stay still. Do not touch your phones. Keep your hands where I can see them."

Steven observed that the second man had the weapon pointed directly at him.

His gaze was broken when the man at the front of the restaurant yelled, "Who's the manager on duty?"

Steven calmly replied, "I am."

"Come up here."

Steven complied, walking slowly and keeping his hands visible.

"Is there any more cash?"

"No. Excess cash from each shift is deposited to a bank night depository. Everything we have is in the drawers."

"Tell your employees to not hold anything back when filling the bag."

Steven looked into the eyes of each of the cashiers on duty and said, "Put all of the cash in the bag. Do exactly what the man tells you. We don't need any heroes here."

The night shift team followed Steven's directions. Each cashier passed the bag, typically used for large 'to-go' orders, down the line of registers to the next employee. Just as the last cashier was about done emptying his drawer into the bag, one of the cooks moved slightly, out of the clear line of sight of the thief. The robber noticed this and responded by firing a round from his shotgun into the ceiling.

"I told you to keep your hands visible and not move."

The cook stepped back to his original location, holding his hands up while trembling.

The last cashier placed the bag of currency on the counter.

The thief yelled loudly, so that he could be clearly heard in the dining room, "We're going to take a hostage. If we see anyone leave this restaurant while we're in eyesight, we will shoot the hostage. Have no doubt about what I have just said."

He fired a second round from his shotgun into the ceiling to emphasize his point.

The robber at the front of the restaurant then looked at Steven and said, "You, manager, you carry the bag of cash and stay in front of me as we walk out the front door."

Steven realized that this approach allowed the thief to keep both hands on the shotgun while also converting Steven into a human shield.

"We walk out in three, two, one."

Both masked men departed the restaurant through the same doors they used to enter. They met a block away, with Steven still carrying the bag of cash and being positioned as a shield.

After walking quickly for three more blocks and then turning down a dark alley in the Tenderloin District, the second thief grabbed the bag from Steven while the first one asked, "Do you have a cell phone?"

"No," replied Steven. "It's in my locker back at the restaurant."

"Good."

While Steven was facing the one robber, the other one hit him over the head, knocking him to the concrete sidewalk. The fall cut a gash into his forehead. One of the thieves then followed up with three swift kicks to Steven's midsection, each one harder that the last. Steven blacked out.

As he came to, Steven heard a familiar voice.

"Just focus on breathing and keep your head up."

Paul wiped the blood from Steven's eyes, and eventually helped him stand, providing support with a firm arm around his back. Steven reached up and gingerly felt the swollen lump above his temple.

"How did you find me?" whispered Steven, still groggy.

"I was only about two blocks away when I heard the first shotgun blast. I walked toward the sound, with my direction confirmed by the second discharge of the weapon. I saw you being held hostage and followed at a safe distance until the thieves abandoned you."

With Paul's assistance, Steven dizzily walked back to the restaurant. When he arrived, police cars with flashing lights were positioned at the front and rear of the building. A team of paramedics from the local fire station were also on site.

"Bring him over here," commanded one of the paramedics.

Paul helped Steven sit at the rear of the paramedic truck. The paramedics examined Steven and provided first aid.

One advised, "I've cleaned and bandaged the gash. I don't think it will need stitches. No sign of a concussion, but that lump's going to hurt for a while. Keep it iced and take some NSAID medication."

Steven nodded.

After he was finished with the paramedic, Paul returned and said, "Can you run us a copy of the video surveillance file?"

"Yes, no problem. I'll load that onto a flash drive for you."

Steven returned with the loaded flash drive in less than ten minutes. Candido had kept the security system for the restaurant up to date with the latest technology. Paul loaded the video file onto the laptop in one of the patrol cars and reviewed the subject five minutes or so of recording. Steven checked on the shift team in the restaurant at the same time. None of the employees was harmed, although two cashiers were visibly shaken from having stared down the barrel of the shotgun. Steven called and updated Candido.

Paul gathered the other police officers and explained, "The video shows that the thieves wore masks and gloves and did not touch anything other than the doors. The detective team should arrive soon. We'll have the employees close the restaurant to preserve any evidence, but that doesn't look likely."

Paul walked over to Steven and explained that the restaurant was to be closed. Steven understood and agreed. He noted to himself that the employees could use some time to calm down and that Candido would need to bring in some cash for the drawers once the bank opened in the morning.

As the police activity at the restaurant was wrapping up, Paul again approached Steven and said, "Watching the video, you sure kept your cool tonight. That was the right thing to do."

"Our parent company trains us to stay calm, comply with any robbers, and do everything we can to get them to leave the restaurant as quickly as possible. With all of the electronic transactions these days, we never have that much cash in the first place. It's never worth risking personal injury," responded Steven.

After saying these words, Steven realized that they were verbatim from one of the online training videos he had watched in preparation for his first day on the job.

"We'll follow up with you as the investigation progresses. Did you ever get a look at their faces?"

"No. They kept the masks on."

"That's typical," replied Paul. "If you remember anything else or if there's something we can do for you, here's my card."

"Now that you mention it, it wouldn't hurt to put in a good word for me with my parole officer," responded Steven.

Chapter 90

Monday August 2, 2021
Lake Como, Italy

Bruce, Kathi, Sofia, and Joseph were relaxing over morning coffee on the veranda of the grand villa they had rented for the entire month of August. The estate was located on the northern leg of Lake Como, the most scenic of the northern Italian lakes. The villa boasted a view down the lake toward the picturesque town of Bellagio and up the lake to the Alps. They had spent the month of July on a grand tour of Italy, from Sicily in the south to Umbria in the central 'green heart' of the country to Rome and most recently five days in Milan. They were all a bit weary after the trip from Milan yesterday via train and then ferry.

"This has to be the most beautiful place I've ever been," said Kathi.

"I could never get tired of this view," added Bruce. "This terrace is amazing. It's larger than the first apartment I rented after undergraduate school."

"Glad you like it," said Sofia. "I did a fair amount of research, including on websites that were only in Italian."

"Yet another fringe benefit of being with you, my love," smiled Joseph.

"Our timing was good. International travel opened up for us just at the right time, now that immunization for the coronavirus has become prevalent. This place had only recently been listed as available for rent," added Sofia.

It had taken almost a year to finalize the sale of Blazing Capital LLC. There was a delay in receiving the patents, multiple potential bidders who each conducted due diligence, the negotiation of the purchase and sale agreement, and finally the closing. Ken White had been a great resource to the team, directly offering advice and also referring them to outside specialists such as an attorney who focused on intellectual property transactions. During this process, they all agreed to quit their jobs following the closing to take some time off, and to also live a fuller life now finally free of COVID restrictions. The fact that they each had $15 million in their bank accounts facilitated that decision. The sale of Blazing Capital LLC had been highly lucrative.

As Kathi was finishing her coffee, supplemented with a *cornetto* covered in crushed almonds, she asked, "What are we up for today?"

"I've reserved a private launch to take us down to Bellagio. There's a tour this morning, in English, of the town and peninsula, including the ancient fortifications," replied Bruce. "I also researched local restaurants and selected one for lunch."

"That sounds wonderful. It looks like we'll have great weather all day," said Kathi. "Sofia and I can bring our swimsuits and a couple of towels in a day pack in case we have the opportunity for an afternoon swim."

"I'm afraid it will just be you and Bruce on that trip," interrupted Joseph. "I also booked a private launch, but made reservations for a grand tour of the Villa Del Balbianello. That's the estate on the lake that was used in one of the *James Bond* movies. The most famous scene is on one of the terraces overlooking the water, when 007 is recuperating from injuries."

"It's quite unlike you two to not be coordinated!" exclaimed Sofia.

"You're right. We should have talked about it. I guess we each had a great idea and got a bit carried away," said Joseph.

"Yeah, my enthusiasm apparently got the better of me," noted Bruce.

He stood up from the table, walked over to the edge of the veranda, and peered out over the lake.

"Look at that gorgeous yacht! I heard that George Clooney has a villa on the lake. I wonder if that boat is his?"

As Kathi and Sofia leaned over the low wall to get a possible look at Mr. Clooney, Bruce stepped back and nodded twice toward Joseph. Joseph returned the same action.

....

The walking tour of Bellagio, the surrounding peninsula, and the ancient fortifications was outstanding. The tour guide was an American woman who had married an Italian man from the surrounding region. She explained the history, architecture, and natural environment of the area with energy and a sense of humor. The views throughout the morning were breathtaking - the lake, the mountains, the natural horticulture, and the Renaissance gardens.

After the conclusion of the tour, Bruce and Kathi made the short walk to the point of the peninsula. Lake Como is shaped similar to an inverted 'Y", with the confluence of the three arms of the lake being an open and scenic point populated with a small beach and a restaurant. Following the written instructions from Sofia, Bruce spoke to the hostess in the best Italian accent he could muster.

"*Abbiamo una prenotazione di pranzare. Cognome Chu.* (We have a lunch reservation, last name of Chu)."

The hostess acknowledged and seated them at a table with

a view down all three legs of the lake. Educated by countless Italian meals prepared by Sofia, Bruce and Kathi had no trouble selecting and ordering their dishes, along with bottles of *Prosecco* and mineral water. As they enjoyed the freshly made *pasta*, a light breeze flowed down the lake from the Alps to the north, moderating the summer heat.

At the conclusion of their meal, while still seated at the table, Bruce glanced at his smartphone and noted the time.

He then looked intently into Kathi's eyes and said, "Love, I couldn't imagine a more memorable place to ask you a question."

Kathi inhaled deeply, her eyes opening wide.

Bruce stood up, positioned himself between Kathi and the view of the lake, and knelt down on one knee. He removed a small jewelry box from his pocket and opened it to display an emerald cut diamond engagement ring.

"Will you make me the happiest man on the planet and marry me?"

"I've been wondering what was taking you so long!" exclaimed Kathi. "Yes! Yes!"

As Kathi commenced a deep, lingering kiss, the entire restaurant, guests and employees, broke into a thunderous applause. Shouts of *'auguri'* (best wishes) filled the air.

After pausing their kiss to take a breath, Kathi looked around the restaurant, laughed, and said, "I guess certain things transcend all cultures."

She was barely able to complete the sentence when people began to approach the couple to give them hugs and kisses on their cheeks. It was a moment that neither Bruce or Kathi would ever forget.

....

The wood-hulled launch dropped Sofia and Joseph at the small dock at the bottom of the peninsula which comprises the Villa Del Balbianello estate. The location is as if out of a story book. The peninsula juts out about one-quarter of the width of the south-west branch of the lake. The land rises steeply from the lake, populated with gorgeous terraced gardens. The estate buildings present beautiful architecture, with components dating to a 13th century Franciscan monastery. The interiors of the buildings are decorated with antique furniture from various countries and eras, tapestries, and Oriental carpets.

Sofia and Joseph toured the Villa, led by a local Italian gentleman who claimed to be in the hereditary line of the Visconti family, which owned the estate during the 1800's. While the tour was in Italian, Sofia translated whenever Joseph indicated a lack of understanding. At the conclusion of the tour, the guide led them to an upper balcony containing a table set for two with white linens, elaborately-designed ceramic plates from Deruta, and crystal glasses. The gentleman gestured for them to be seated in the two chairs.

"This doesn't seem to be part of a typical tour," stated Sofia quizzically.

"It's not. Something special that I arranged with the linguistic assistance of a certain *nonna*."

Sofia smiled. This was just like her *nonna*. A zest for life continuing into her nineties.

A waiter appeared and asked them in Italian what they would like to drink. He explained that the meal had been pre-ordered, and that he would be bringing out the first plates in just a moment. Joseph suggested bottles of *Prosecco* and mineral water. Sofia concurred.

They enjoyed a delicious lunch of assorted *bruschetta* and a *pasta* dish with a rich sauce whose ingredients included black truffles from the province of Umbria. The views from the balcony were unforgettable. A light breeze flowed down the lake from the Alps to the north, moderating the summer heat.

After the waiter was removing their now empty plates, Joseph glanced at his smartphone and noted the time. He then stood up, knelt on one knee in front of Sofia, looked lovingly into her eyes, and removed a small jewelry box from his pocket. Sofia's heart rate jumped. She deeply inhaled the fresh mountain air. Joseph opened the jewelry box to display a round cut, diamond engagement ring.

He asked, "*Mia amore, vuoi sposarmi* (my love, will you marry me)?"

"*Certo* (of course)!"

Sofia reached down and embraced Joseph, pulling him off the ground and onto his feet. They shared a lingering kiss. A tour group of Italians from the Veneto region was walking by below the balcony at the same time, overheard the question and answer, and broke into a loud applause. Yells of '*bravi*' and '*auguri*' filled the air, followed by a spontaneous chant of '*bacio, bacio, bacio*' (kiss). Sofia and Joseph complied.

....

By 5:00 PM, the four friends were reunited on the veranda of their rented estate overlooking the lake. As the sun started to descend in the western sky, Sofia opened a bottle of *Brunello di Montalcino* red wine and poured four glasses.

"Wasn't it amazing that we texted each other this afternoon at exactly the same time?" asked Kathi of Sofia.

"I don't think it was amazing. Few coincidences are. Rather, I believe this afternoon's events were as carefully orchestrated as a moon landing."

Sofia and Kathi both turned and stared at their fiancés.

Joseph and Bruce looked at each other and paused.

Joseph eventually replied, "Guilty as charged."

"And how much did my *nonna* know?"

"While I didn't directly advise her about the proposal, I have no doubt she figured out what was going on. I distinctly remember hearing the word '*fidanzato*' (betrothed) during her long-distance call to Italy to arrange the lunch."

Sofia smiled broadly, "Not much escapes my *nonna*!"

The two couples raised their glasses in a toast, expressing their happiness at becoming engaged. Each of them had pleasant dreams that night, imagining what their weddings would be like.

Chapter 91

Things were finally all looking up for Steven. His trading for cryptoman777 based upon his algorithms was quite successful. So much so, that the trading account he accessed had been recently increased from $250,000 to $1,000,000. True to his word, cryptoman777 deposited twenty percent of Steven's trading profits to his personal cryptocurrency account each month. Steven also continued to profit from his equity and stock option trading in his online brokerage account. Candido provided Steven with the promised $3.00 per hour raise, plus a $1,000 bonus for his performance during the robbery. Perhaps best of all, officer Paul Anderson's good word to his overworked probation officer had resulted in Steven's now being required to check in only quarterly. This evening, he had an appointment to tour an apartment for rent in the South of Market Street neighborhood. That would be a huge upgrade from living in the Tenderloin hotel, although only about seven city blocks away.

Steven hadn't much time for a personal life since being released from prison, particularly once he began working for cryptoman777. Tonight, he planned to spend a few hours at one of the new hot spots in the South of Market Street neighborhood. He missed having a social life, and had not been with a woman in a very long time.

Steven entered the almost full pub at 8:30 PM. Despite this being a Monday night, the residents of the city were out in force, making up for the many months of quarantine during the pandemic. Steven took a seat at the bar and ordered an IPA. About half way through his glass of beer, a woman with flowing black hair who appeared to be in her early forties sat down next to him and ordered a cosmopolitan, the drink preferred by Veronica. That coincidence, plus the fact that she was attractive, spurred Steven to try to start a conversation.

"This is my first time here. I didn't think it would be so crowded on a Monday night."

"The pub's only been open for about a month. All of the new places draw a crowd eager to check them out," replied the woman.

"The beer and ale selections are outstanding. I think I saw ten countries represented on the drink board."

"I've heard that the pub food is really good. Would you care to share a couple of plates?"

Steven was pleasantly surprised at the directness of the woman.

"That sounds good. By the way, my name is Steven."

"I'm Marlena."

They clinked their glasses in a toast.

Over a second round of beverages and the pub food, which lived up to its reputation, Steven learned that Marlena was a certified financial planner, divorced a year ago after catching her husband in bed with one of the office assistants, and well educated, with an undergraduate degree from USC and an MBA from Pepperdine. Steven perceived that she apparently did quite well, financially speaking, through the divorce process and via her career. What Steven was already certain about was that Marlena had a brightness in her eyes and an engaging smile that he found quite compelling.

"I've spoken so much about myself, I've hardly given you a chance to talk," said Marlena.

"I've also had a career primarily centered in the financial business, initially in private capital, but more recently in equity, stock option, and cryptocurrency trading."

Steven thought it best not to mention his restaurant job at this point.

"I've studied the cryptocurrency markets, primarily in response to requests from my clients to allocate parts of their portfolios to Bitcoin or other cryptocurrencies. That said, I hardly feel proficient in that space. Would you mind terribly if I asked you some questions?"

"No, not at all."

Steven was happy for the conversation to shift from his personal background.

At 10:00 PM, Marlena noticed the time on her smartphone and said, "I've got client meetings in the morning. I'd like to see you again. Would you mind sharing contact information?"

"That would be great."

Steven was again impressed with the directness and confidence of Marlena. He made a mental note to allow her to next contact him.

Chapter 92

Tuesday December 7, 2021
San Francisco, California

Upon awakening, Steven felt the soft hands of Marlena wrapped over his shoulders as she spooned behind him in her king-sized bed. The past two months had been a whirlwind. Steven relocated to the much more respectable apartment in the South of Market Street neighborhood before the new relationship progressed very far. The move was facilitated by his considerably improved financial profile, including the dollars received in exchange for his cryptocurrency trading. By the first time Marlena entered the apartment, it was suitably furnished. Steven had also upgraded his wardrobe. Without the nervous tick developed at Blue Planet, Steven once again had a mostly full head of hair, one that was now professionally barbered.

The first week of November, his encrypted VPN access into the trading account for cryptoman777 suddenly ceased working, without any follow-up communication from his sponsor. Steven speculated regarding what might have occurred, and unsuccessfully monitored various cryptocurrency related online forums for clues. Surprisingly, a final payment in cryptocurrency did arrive in his personal account as per the normal schedule.

Steven never figured out that cryptoman777 had accumulated enough information from the cryptocurrency accounts and the specific transactions executed each day by Steven to reverse engineer his trading algorithms. Once cryptoman777 possessed this knowledge, Steven was no longer needed.

Freed from his obligations to cryptoman777, Steven requested that Candido move him to the morning shift, so that his work hours would correspond with Marlena's. Candido was happy to do so, particularly after recognizing that Steven's new inventory management formulas had increased the restaurant's profitability by ten percent.

Steven's intuition regarding Marlena's financial status was correct. While not approaching the wealth of Veronica's trust fund, Marlena did have a net worth in the tens of millions of dollars. They were not only intellectually compatible, but also sexually complementary, with Marlena often taking the initiative. On top of everything else, Marlena had arranged for Steven to have a job interview this afternoon with a contact of hers who ran a hedge fund out of London. That would allow Steven to return to the financial industry in an official capacity while complying with his restriction against working for any U.S. regulated financial firm.

Steven lightly kissed Marlena and gently climbed out of bed. He walked to the kitchen, where a professional Italian coffee machine filled one entire wall. As he commenced making them both a fresh *cappuccino*, he reflected on his life. He had made many mistakes, and had paid dearly for those errors. Prison. Being beaten in a mugging and while serving as a hostage. Living in a fleabag hotel. Even developing expertise in cleaning up vomit. Yes, he had suffered extensive retribution for his sins.

Now blessed with a second chance, he would live more meaningfully, putting greater value in relationships and engendering good character. Any future efforts to improve society would focus on seeking to lift up those from the bottom, rather than trying to command down from the top. His role models would no longer be politicians, celebrities, or captains of industry. Instead, he would never forget a beat cop named

Paul and fast-food manager named Candido.

Epilogue

Quinton Jackson relocated under the witness protection program to Roanoke, Virginia. After a transition period, he began coaching high school football. QJ's imposing physical presence immediately drew respect from the youth he coached. In addition to teaching the boys the value of teamwork, he effectively communicated the importance of obtaining a good education and applying oneself. Many of his players eventually went on to college football, with three being drafted by National Football League teams.

Through the connections of the Hopkins family, Billy landed another financial analyst position with a boutique investment firm. With the exposure and skills learned at Blue Planet, Billy enjoyed a moderately successful career, often using electronic communications to compensate for the social limitations associated with his autism. The special needs trust established by Maureen meant that Billy would be looked after by responsible individuals after Maureen's passing, for his entire life.

After a couple of years overseas, Samantha resurfaced in the investment business, this time in New York City. The wealth, variety of people, and pace of the New York City environment were well suited to her. Samantha enjoyed a notable amount of success, facilitated by her motivation and willingness to go the extra mile.

Veronica Hopkins Shaw never remarried, hurt to the core by Steven's betrayal. She changed her legal name back to Veronica Hopkins following the completion of her divorce. She did, however, enjoy meaningful relationships with several men over the years who shared her passion for helping disadvantaged children. The support of her non-profit led to over three dozen charter schools being opened in seven states during her lifetime. The non-profit was named as the sole beneficiary of her trust upon her death.

Jennifer Franklin and Matthew Haddock dated sporadically for a while before deciding to pursue other partners. They both enjoyed successful careers. Jennifer always paid particular attention to ensuring that she treated subordinates fairly, never forgetting her rude and unjust termination by Steven Shaw.

Maxine Scott served in the California Public Defenders Office for thirty-five years. She mentored many new attorneys, while always being clear and frank with her clients. She was well-known for her spunk and positive energy. Upon her retirement, a new facility for the Office was named in her honor.

Steven Shaw's probationary period was cut short due to a combination of an overwhelming volume of prisoner releases by California and his being among the least of the worries of his probation officer. Steven married Marlena after two years of dating. He professionally flourished while working for the London-based hedge fund, leveraging all of the information and experience he had gained over the years. He never used cocaine again, and was careful to moderate his alcohol consumption. Steven was completely faithful to Marlena. They eventually established and funded a new non-profit entity with the primary service objective of integrating newly released prisoners back into society.

Bruce and Kathi Chu returned to their careers following their global travel and wedding. Their nuptials were an energetic affair. Kathi would have it no other way. They agreed that they were too young to retire, despite their combined wealth. They each took part-time jobs in their fields of specialty, using the available hours to raise three children, all of whom were fortunate enough to inherit Bruce's height and Kathi's looks. Bruce and Kathi remained close friends with Sofia and Joseph for the rest of their lives.

Sofia and Joseph Giordano also married following their return from Italy. Their wedding was a wild and loud Italian-themed affair, with seven courses of food, a wide variety of Italian wines, and dancing into the wee hours of the night. Sofia wore a beautiful white lace wedding dress, along with flat shoes. After a passionate honeymoon, they each began accepting consulting assignments in their fields of expertise. This allowed them to control their schedules so that they could spend one summer month each year in Italy, always including at least one week on Lake Como. Joseph eventually became reasonably proficient in the Italian language, spurred by Sofia's ensuring that their four children, Maria, Nina, Franco, and Marco, were bilingual. Joseph and Sofia enjoyed a long and happy marriage, always enlivened by time shared with Bruce and Kathi.

Afterword

I hope you enjoyed *Financial Retribution*. If so, I'd recommend reading my other two books, *Financial Execution* and *Financial Initiation*. Both are historical fiction and financial thrillers. *Financial Execution* commences before World War Two and concludes in the mid-1980s. *Financial Initiation* covers over one hundred years of timeframe, although concentrated in the late 1990's and early 2000's. Each novel addresses various components of the financial and capital markets in presenting an interesting story populated with a diverse cast of characters. As with *Financial Retribution*, the other two books also indirectly incorporate social commentary and some light philosophical discourse. Individuals who enjoy financial and technical thrillers, mysteries, and stories that operate on several levels simultaneously will find *Financial Execution and Financial Initiation* engaging and thought-provoking reads.

Printed in Great Britain
by Amazon

81690754R00212